MIRACLES

A FATHER JAKE AUSTIN MYSTERY

MIRACLES

JOHN A. VANEK

THORNDIKE PRESS
A part of Gale, a Cengage Company

GALE
A Cengage Company

Copyright © 2019 by John Vanek.
Thorndike Press, a part of Gale, a Cengage Company.

Thorndike Press® Large Print Clean Reads.
The text of this Large Print edition is unabridged.
Other aspects of the book may vary from the original edition.
Set in 16 pt. Plantin.

LIBRARY OF CONGRESS CIP DATA ON FILE.
CATALOGUING IN PUBLICATION FOR THIS BOOK
IS AVAILABLE FROM THE LIBRARY OF CONGRESS

ISBN-13: 978-1-4328-7581-7 (hardcover alk. paper)

Published in 2020 by arrangement with Coffeetown Press, an imprint of Epicenter Press, Inc.

Printed in Mexico
Print Number: 01   Print Year: 2020

ACKNOWLEDGMENTS

I am extremely grateful to my wife, Geni, for her advice and patience, and to Jessica & Randy Dublikar, Jen & Matt Vanek, Father Thomas Winkel, Sterling Watson, Michael Koryta, Laura Lippman, Dennis Lehane, Les Standiford, and the Eckerd College Writers in Paradise family for all of their help and encouragement. Special thanks to Abe Spevack, Susan Adgar, Barbara Schrefer, Ann O'Farrell, Lee Summerall, Jeanne Hirth, and Richard Erlanger for their brutally honest critiques over the years. I am grateful for input and support from: Patti & Ron Poporad, JoAnn & Jim Gavacs, Leonor & Mario Macchi, Mary Winter, Kathy & Emil Poporad, the Pinellas Writers, and the Oberlin Heritage Center. I wish to thank the tireless team at Coffeetown Press for guiding me through the morass of the publishing world: Jennifer McCord, Phil Garrett, and Aubrey White. I also want to express my gratitude to all of the readers who supported my debut novel, *DEROS,* by recommending it to friends and posting kind reviews online.

Short segments of three poems appear in *Miracles:* one from my poem, "Bordeaux Simple," revised to fit the novel (originally published in the *LLI Review* and in my book of poetry, *Heart Murmurs: Poems,* and used with permission from Bird Dog Publishing); the second from "Oh, what a happy child I am," written at age eight by Frances Jane Crosby (poet and lyricist, 1820–1915); the third, part of the poem "Lo, Now, My Guest" by Robert Louis Stevenson (1850–1894).

The characters, settings, and all of the events in *Miracles* are fictional and entirely the product of the author's imagination. If you enjoy the Father Jake Austin Mystery Series, please tell your friends. Word of mouth is the lifeblood of independent presses and their authors.

CHAPTER ONE

Monday, July 24, 2002, 9:30 a.m.
Why do you test me so, Lord? You've already shaken my world like a snow globe. Please don't let my sister die! Wasn't my time in the fiery hell of war enough? True, that forged me into who I am today, and led me to You and the priesthood. I do all that you ask of me at the hospital and the church, and do it gladly. You have my entire life and my heart. Isn't that enough? Sweet Jesus, don't take Justine from me and orphan my nephew. I beg you! He's only four. Please don't crush his tiny spirit the way mine was ground to pulp as a child. Have mercy on our makeshift family! I ask this in your name. Amen.

In the wistful stillness of an empty Sacred Heart Catholic Church, a plaintive meowing aroused me from my prayer and meditation. Without looking, I knew it was Martin Luther, the tabby that kept the church free of mice. I'd named him that partly because

7

his stripes formed a perfect "M" on his forehead but mostly because, like his namesake, he loved the Church even though he detested her rules. My furry Martin particularly hated the rule that required him to stay in the basement with his water bowl, food, and litter box.

Having once again pulled a Houdini and escaped from what I called the cellar *catacombs,* my resident heretic sauntered over and deposited a dead mole at my feet, peered up at me, and purred. I should have named him Rascal.

My cellphone rang, displaying the number of the hospital.

I pushed up from the padded kneeler and dropped onto the oak pew. Except for Martin Luther, I was alone in the church nave. The few faithful who'd joined me as I offered morning Mass had scattered like seeds in the wind.

I accepted the call, morphing from a mender of souls to a healer of bodies.

"Austin."

"Marcus Taylor here. Hope I'm not disturbing you, Jake."

I'd been praying that he would call me today. Hope mingled with the faint scent of incense in the air. I gazed at the crucifix above the altar and crossed myself, my heart upshifting and pounding in my chest. Dr. Taylor was the Chief of Staff at St. Joseph's Hospital, and I desperately needed his help.

My turbulent past had swept me from a bloody overseas war, where I'd served as an Army medic, into medical school as I searched for inner peace. When I failed to find serenity healing the sick, I'd returned to my Catholic roots and entered a seminary. I was an anomaly. Although some Protestant ministers served both as physicians and clergymen, only the Camillian Order of the Catholic Church had welcomed my dual role. When I wasn't managing Sacred Heart Church, the small parish in the town of Oberlin, Ohio, I'd been assigned to work part-time at St. Joseph's, a nearby inner city hospital that cared for many of the indigent in Lorain County.

"I'm glad you called, Marcus. Please tell me you have good news about my sister's bone marrow transplant. Justine and her son have been staying with me at the rectory and I'm watching her slip away more every day. She can't hang on much longer."

"Sadly, no. I've contacted some colleagues at the Cleveland Clinic and I'm waiting to hear back, hopefully today." He cleared his throat. "I know you're not officially back to work at the hospital yet, Jake, but I have a

9

situation on my hands and could use your help."

A recent encounter with a serial killer had left me recuperating from broken ribs and a shattered collarbone. I'd just completed a three week leave of absence from the parish, however I was still on sick leave at the hospital. Nevertheless, I was not about to say "no" to a friend and coworker who was trying to save my sister's life.

"Sure. Whatever you need."

"EMS brought in a comatose one-year-old boy this morning, Jake. Might be a SIDS case averted by an alert parent."

Sudden Infant Death Syndrome. I'd practiced internal medicine for years before entering the priesthood, but had absolutely no expertise in dealing with crib deaths or children in comas. I had no idea why Taylor, the chairman of Neurology, had called me instead of a pediatrician or another neurologist.

"Okay, Marcus. How can I help?"

"It's touch and go. The child's teetering on the brink and his parents are coming unglued. They're Catholic, and I was hoping you could sit with them for a while and offer some spiritual support and guidance."

"Of course. I'll be there as soon as I can."

As I hung up, something touched my

thigh. Martin Luther hopped onto my lap and nuzzled my arm, covering my black cassock with cat hair. He was an affectionate little critter. No wonder my nephew kept begging me to move Martin into the rectory with us.

I stood and slid the dead mole under the pew with the toe of my shoe, intending to remove it later. Cradling Martin with one arm, I genuflected, returned him to the cellar, and headed to the rectory.

CHAPTER TWO

Monday, July 24, 9:45 a.m.

Outside of the church, the eastern sky was the color of claret and birdsong filled the air like a distant children's choir. Heat-devils, however, swirled across the asphalt parking lot and Ohio was already as hot as a blast furnace. Fortunately, a strong northwest breeze kept the treetops dancing and flags snapping, making the swelter bearable.

Entering through the backdoor of the rectory, I explained to Colleen that I had to run an errand and hoped to be back in time for lunch. She was the part-time housekeeper and my Girl Friday at Sacred Heart Church. Colleen told me that my sister felt better this morning and had taken her son to the playground for an hour, so I brushed the cat hair from my cassock, jumped in the parish's old Toyota, and drove to the Emergency Room at St. Joseph's Hospital in Lorain.

12

Like most inner city ERs, the place was jam-packed and chaotic. The triage nurse directed me to a small waiting room reserved for families in crisis.

I knocked softly and opened the door.

A uniformed police officer whipped around in his chair and pointed a finger at me.

"Get out!" he growled. When he noticed my clerical collar and cassock he added, "Ah, give me a few minutes, Father. Be done as soon as I can."

I closed the door and leaned against a wall in the corridor where I remained for almost half an hour, wondering what the heck was going on. When the officer finally emerged, I knocked again and entered the room.

A woman in her late teens or early twenties sobbed softly as she teetered on the edge of a couch, her elbows on her knees, head down, eyes fixed on the floor. She wore a tight pink halter top above a bare midriff and low-riding shorts tight enough to stop the circulation to her long, tan legs. Unaware of my presence, she ran her fingers through jet black hair, highlighted by a pink streak on the left. Her fingernails were painted in neon colors. Large gold loops dangled from both ears, flanking full, cupid-bow lips.

A man with bronze skin reclined against the couch cushions, his head cantilevered onto the sofa back, his eyes glued to the ceiling. Below a barrel chest, his beer belly was wedged into a wife-beater T-shirt stained with sweat. Red boxer shorts peeked out above filthy cutoffs. His heavily tattooed arms were thick but flabby. His left hand gently massaged the back of the young woman's neck.

They struck me as the odd couple — a scantily clad Snow White oozing pheromones, comforted by Dumpy, the eighth dwarf.

The door clicked closed behind me and their heads snapped to attention. They both sat up.

I approached them and said, "Dr. Taylor told me that a terrible thing has happened. May we talk for a while?" Two nods. "I'm Father Jake Austin from Sacred Heart Church."

The man extended a callused, moist hand. He was also young, though his face had lost the angles of youth. One glance told me that his life had been hard.

"Gracias, Padre. I am Miguel Hernandez." He wore the wrinkled forehead of a worried man. "I go to Mass at Sacred Heart sometimes."

14

The young woman tried for a smile without success. "I'm Martina, but everyone calls me Tina."

I'd seen Miguel at church. Never Tina. She was a striking woman and I would have remembered. Unlike Miguel, she had no accent and did not appear Hispanic. Her complexion and facial features suggested a European heritage, maybe German. She had a mole on her left cheek and except for her hair color, she reminded me of the actress who played Ginger on the old sitcom *Gilligan's Island*.

I pulled up a chair and sat. Miguel's body odor assaulted me, but didn't mask the smell of alcohol on his breath.

"Please, tell me what happened."

A long silence. Tina broke it.

"It's like a nightmare, Father." She fixed me with enormous ebony eyes made darker by copious eye shadow. "I had the day off from work, first time in forever, and we were watching some tube while our baby slept." Makeup followed tears down both cheeks like black jet contrails. "We got no air conditioning and the apartment's a damn oven, so I moved the fan from our bedroom into little Pablo's . . . ."

When she said the child's name, she choked on the word. More tears. Her eyes grew puffy, as though she was allergic to the memory, and she rubbed them so hard I feared she might gouge them out.

Tina rested her head on Miguel's shoulder until she finally composed herself.

"I plugged the fan in, fed him, and he conked out, you know, sound asleep on his belly, snuggled up with his teddy bear. When I came back to check on him, he was real quiet . . . too quiet."

Her upper teeth slid over her lower lip, and it blanched when she bit down.

"I didn't want to wake him, so I bent over the crib rail," she said. Her voice was strangled and so soft that I had to lean forward to hear her. "I couldn't see his chest moving, so I picked him up. He was floppy . . . like a rag doll."

Tina became formless, dissolving into the couch.

Visions of my nephew building sand castles on Huntington Beach and chasing a Slinky down the rectory steps flashed through my mind. He was the closest I would ever have to a child of my own. The thought of seeing him gray and lifeless on a stainless steel morgue table chilled me to the core. I ached for this young couple.

Miguel said, "I called 911. Took 'em forever to get there." Miguel swallowed

16

hard. "I tried the CPR stuff you see on TV but didn't know what the hell I was doing. I mean, Pablo was blue! And he's so tiny, I was afraid to push too hard on his chest." He cradled his head in his hands. "Diós mío. Ay! What a dumbass I am."

He moaned, then suddenly raised his head and stared at me.

"Where the hell was Jesus when my baby couldn't breathe? Huh? Tell me that, Padre! How can God let this happen?"

I had no answer. I'd asked the very same question when my mother died in a house fire and when my friends were killed in the war. Although I'd learned to accept the Almighty's passive silences over the years, I wasn't happy with the arrangement.

Reverting to my seminary training, I pontificated about faith and the Lord's incomprehensible plan, expounding with enough conviction to almost convince myself. The words sounded hollow and tasted bitter. I gave them the best that I could muster, wilting a bit with every time-worn phrase.

When I'd run out of platitudes, Tina said, "Help us, Father. The nurse sent us in here. They're working on him, keeping him alive, but . . . we need to be with our baby. Soon."

"I'll see if they're ready for you."

"Push 'em hard. We been here a long damn time," Miguel added. He stood, his face still flushed with anger. "And you can tell me why that cop treated us like *basura,* like garbage, like this nightmare is our fault. What the hell was that about?"

"I have no idea, but I'll try to find out." I felt I'd helped them so little that I added, "Do you want to speak with a hospital grief counselor?"

Tina shook her head.

Miguel looked down and took a deep breath. "Sorry I went off. It's not your fault. We'd rather stick with you, Padre, if that's okay."

"Of course." I wrote down my phone numbers and gave them to Miguel. He extended his hand again and thanked me *for all I'd done.*

Some days I hated my job.

CHAPTER THREE

Monday, July 24, 12:15 p.m.

Dying babies, grieving parents, and hostile cops? I'd walked headlong into a hornet's nest.

After I convinced a nurse to escort Tina and Miguel into the pediatric intensive care unit to be with their child, I needed some time alone to decompress. The inside of my head sounded like a bass drum. I downed three aspirin, called the rectory to say I'd be home by dinnertime, grabbed a quick lunch in the cafeteria, and then walked to the small hospital chapel.

Sunlight draped a rainbow of colors across the altar, yet there was no one else in the room to appreciate it. Crossing myself with holy water from a marble font near the door, I genuflected and pulled down a padded kneeler. Ever since the chaos and brutality of the battlefield, time alone with the Lord had become my refuge and source of comfort, and after my morning encounter with grief-stricken parents, I was in need of both.

I prayed the Liturgy of the Hours, a collection of psalms, hymns, and prayers required daily of all priests to maintain our spiritual focus. I finished with prayers for my sister and for baby Pablo's recovery. After a few moments of quiet meditation, I rose and wandered into the sacristy.

I slumped onto the desk chair and swiveled back and forth, trying to make sense of what I had witnessed. The serenity I'd regained in the chapel quickly evaporated and I became angrier with every swing of the chair. Finally, I dialed the Chief of Police, Tree Macon, at the station house. He and I had remained close friends since high school.

"So, Tremont, I have a question." The only people who called him *Tremont* were his wife, complete strangers, and me when I was pissed off. "Tell me all-powerful, Grand Imperial Poobah of Justice, why are your boys harassing Miguel and Tina Hernandez? My God, the poor couple's suffering as it is! Sudden Infant Death Syndrome is the most horrendous thing that can happen to parents. It's a miracle their child's still alive. Can't they be allowed to grieve in peace?"

"You done ranting, Saint Jacob?"

"Not even close. What happened here was damn near police brutality. What the hell was that, Tree?"

"My job. And unfortunately, they're about to be more upset. I just dispatched a detective and two CSI guys to their apartment."

"What? Why would you do that?"

"Because it's a possible crime scene."

"You're joking!"

"Do I sound as though I'm kidding? And we are not *harassing,* Jake. We're *investigating.* It's what we're supposed to do. Look, I don't like making life harder on them, but things aren't always what they seem. They live here in town and their child was initially taken to Oberlin Hospital before being transferred to St. Joe's pediatric ICU, so this case is in my jurisdiction. I can't talk specifics."

I heard a ruckus in the background and someone yelled, "Chief, I need you."

"Give me a minute, Jake." When he returned to the phone, Tree said, "Okay, Doctor, you tell me. How do you make the diagnosis of Sudden Infant Death Syndrome?"

"It's the unexpected death of a baby with no apparent cause. It's completely unpredictable and a diagnosis of exclusion. There

21

are no x-ray findings, abnormal lab values, or medical tests to prove it. We have to rule out other possibilities, like asthma, viral infection, or botulism."

"My point exactly. That's why the government *requires* a thorough crime scene investigation — to also rule out child abuse, neglect, or infanticide. Listen Jake, in my line of work, SIDS is considered the *perfect crime.* No evidence, no proof, no witnesses. About ten percent of crib deaths are actually homicides."

"What?"

"That's right. Either this is a case where the parents were lucky enough to realize their child had stopped breathing before he died, or it's a failed attempt at murder."

"Dear Lord!"

"I wouldn't mind some help from the Almighty, because most of you doctors don't even consider foul play when an ambulance brings in an infant who is DOA. The ugly flip-side of the coin is that the parents are sometimes *falsely accused* of murder. That's a mistake I sure as hell don't want to make, and the reason I'm going to their apartment tomorrow, after my lab rats finish CSI-ing. Problem is, I've dealt with only one crib death before, and I'm in over my head with this case."

He paused so long that I thought Tree had hung up until he said, "Glad you called, Jake. When I told them I needed to stop by their place in the morning, Miguel asked that you be present." Another silence. "They want you there as a priest; I want you 'cause you're a doctor. Got any experience with SIDS?"

"Zero."

"Well then, read up on it. Put your medical training to good use. If the good Lord doesn't assist me on this, I was hoping maybe you would."

"What do I have to offer?"

"Your eyes and your brain. We're a small department and inexperienced with this kind of thing. See if my guys missed anything. Check for signs of neglect, abuse, or living conditions that might cause SIDS. Heck, I don't know. I'm wandering in the wilderness here, buddy, and could use your help."

My day was rapidly going downhill. "Let me get this straight, Tree. You want me to go into their home as a priest and confidant, and *spy* on these poor folks?"

"I only want the truth. Nothing more."

It's always hard to say *no* to your best friend — and mine had saved my life a few weeks earlier.

"Okay, Tree, I'll come because Miguel and Tina asked for me, but I'm Switzerland — completely neutral."

"Switzerland, huh?" He uncorked a cavernous, James-Earl-Jones laugh. "When your hair was a lot longer back in school, you did kinda remind me of the little blond girl from that movie — what was her name? Heidi?"

"Very funny. I have to make some phone calls tomorrow morning after Mass to arrange for my sister's hospitalization, then I'm free."

"Perfect. I'll pick you up at the rectory around eleven. Wear your priest duds, and bring your eagle eye. Thanks, Jake. Mañana."

A click, and Tree was gone.

I had never been involved in a case of SIDS and didn't know much about the syndrome, so I walked to the hospital's medical library and researched the literature for two hours, feeling like a lowly medical student again — and a bit like a police informant.

Soldier, Doctor, Cleric, Snitch. My résumé had become a damn novel title.

CHAPTER FOUR

Monday, July 24, 4:00 p.m.

On the drive back to the rectory, Dr. Taylor called again.

"Jake, I spoke with my brother at the Cleveland Clinic and he pulled some strings with an oncology friend. Your sister will be admitted to their isolation unit at the end of next week in preparation for her bone marrow transplant."

"Thank you so much." *And dear Lord, thank you!* "Watching Justine's leukemia devour her a little each day has been torture. I'm in your debt."

"Nonsense, my boy. You're a valued colleague. In fact, I'd like you to join the Ethics Committee that I chair. Who better than someone with both medical and spiritual training?"

Damn, another commitment! My life had become one of tasks and obligations. No one ever hesitated to request help from a priest or a doctor. Between the church, medicine, and my family, I was struggling to manage all of my responsibilities.

But I owed Taylor.

"I'd be honored to join your committee, Marcus." Hoping he would forget that he'd asked, I changed the subject. "How in the world did you find a decent donor match? With Justine's rare blood type, it was such a long shot."

"Didn't my nurse call you? Sorry, Jake. There was just one match — you. Not perfect, but you're the best chance she's got. If we wait for a better candidate, we'll probably lose her. Let me know if you locate your father and we'll test him. Until then, you're it. Are you still okay with donating your marrow?"

"Okay? I'm raring and ready to go. You couldn't stop me if you tried."

"Great, I'll set it up and call you with the details. Take care."

Given Justine's deteriorating condition, nearly two weeks was a long time to wait for her admission, and I fretted about the threat that each passing day posed to her on the drive back to Oberlin. After I parked the car at the rectory and stepped out, my cellphone played the theme song from the old police drama, *Dragnet.* Chief Tremont

26

Macon's image appeared on the screen, looking a lot like Michael Jordan's older brother.

"Calling me back so soon, Tree? Did you miss the sound of my voice?"

"Don't be a smartass, Jake. You asked me to track down your father, and I wanted to give you an update. We finally got a hit. I was beginning to think he was a ghost. Your dad was arrested a year ago on a drunk and disorderly in Louisiana. There's an outstanding warrant out on him, but the Shreveport P.D. tells me they got no idea where he is. Your father's a minnow in the legal system, and the cops there have bigger fish to fry, so we're on our own. At least we have a place to start the hunt."

Exactly what I'd expected. Nevertheless, I was disappointed. I was not having second thoughts about donating my bone marrow to Justine. But she was my *half*-sister. Justine's mother was dead and statistically *dear old Dad* would be a much closer match for her transplant, giving her a better chance of survival.

Not that I ever wanted to see the dirt-bag who had deserted my mother and me when I was a child. *Never* would be soon enough. My mentor in seminary had pointed out that I was too quick to judge and too slow

27

to forgive. Although I now dispensed absolution for a living and had worked hard on my character flaws, no matter how I tried I'd never been able to forgive my old man for what he had done. To me, he would always be the Devil but with a lot less charm.

"Jake? You still there?"

"I'm here." I banished my father's image from my mind and told Tree about my sister's pending admission. "I appreciate all the effort, Tree, but don't give up yet. He is Justine's best chance, so please keep searching for him. Sorry to add to your workload, buddy."

"No sweat. Just another day in the life of a public servant." He chuckled. "Hell, that's what friends do. After your help stopping that crazy bastard, Burke, I owe you big time."

I had recently played Dr. Watson to Tree's Sherlock Holmes. Even hearing the killer's name made the healing fractures of my right ribs and collarbone ache. I'd completed my leave of absence from the parish while recovering and was scheduled to return to work at the hospital in a week.

"Anyway, that's it. Gotta go, Jake. I'll keep you posted."

I hung up and sidestepped a pothole in

the rectory driveway. My emotions were jumbled. Dr. Taylor's call had filled me with the lightness of possibility and lifted my spirits; Tree Macon's had popped my balloon and sent me plummeting back to earth. Barring a miraculous reappearance of my old man, I was my sister's only hope. And by the look of her, she definitely needed a miracle.

CHAPTER FIVE

Monday, July 24, 5:00 p.m.

Entering the rectory through the back door, I was greeted by the smell of freshly brewed coffee and the sizzle of bacon. The aroma uncorked my salivary glands and made my stomach grumble.

Colleen Brady, the rectory's part-time housekeeper, laid the bacon on top of a meatloaf large enough to feed half of the town. She wore a short white helmet of hair and a shamrock-green dress. Colleen was as Irish as Paddy's pig on St. Patrick's Day, with an accent as thick as Christmas pudding. Without glancing back she said, "Is it yourself at last, Father? I thought maybe you were on a starvation diet. Just in time. Supper is almost ready."

Being older than I was and a devout Catholic, propriety kept Colleen at a distance but never prevented her from speaking her mind or meddling in my business. With her

30

around, the rectory was like living in a fish bowl. If I failed to swim through life in a way that conformed to her idea of a proper priest, she was quick to rap on my little glass house. Colleen was definitely an acquired taste, but I was slowly getting used to her tang.

"I hope you're hungry, Father."

"I'd never say no to one of your meals." Not even if I wanted to. Colleen was the linchpin holding my fragile family together in our time of crisis, and I had no desire to upset her or suffer another blistering Irish rebuke.

"Your sister has no problem saying no. Thin as a post rail she is, God love her. On the other hand, your nephew is like a flock of gannets. He found the pantry, and hasn't he eaten everything he could lay his hands on? I'll go to the store today and stock up before the lad commences nibbling on the furniture."

The woman was a pistol — no, a rocket-propelled grenade launcher was more accurate.

Veiling her true feelings was not one of Colleen's virtues. Although she complained about the added work of caring for my newly-arrived family, she doted on my nephew. Colleen was like one of those candies with the hard-shell coating concealing the sweet, soft center. *Crusty* best described her demeanor.

"Please give me a few minutes before we eat, Colleen. I need to speak with Justine."

She grumbled and slid her cholesterol-laden concoction into the oven to warm. I knew her meals were clogging my coronary arteries but I'd fallen under the spell of her cooking, as my expanding waistline could attest. The ancient Latin phrase — Mens sana in corpore sano, healthy mind in a healthy body — reminded me that I'd been idle too long since my injury. Time to resume jogging.

Colleen turned toward me and tilted her head to one side. "You were up before the sun, Father. When I arrived, you were already in the church. Was it a bad night you had then?"

Ah, life in the fish bowl.

I had become comfortable in my new environment and hadn't had a nightmare in a couple weeks when a twisted vision of my former life as a medic in the war had pitched me from a sound sleep at four a.m. It had been too close to morning to take a sleeping pill, and herbal tea hadn't gotten the job done.

I carried a lot of baggage from my youth

— more like a steamer trunk with sharp, rusty edges. As a teen, I'd been reckless, unafraid to die for a noble cause. Now, I merely hoped to live humbly for one.

"No, I just needed to finish my homily before Mass this morning." Which was partly true. "I return to work at the hospital soon, and I wanted to get a jump on my next few sermons."

Colleen frowned. She found my "doctoring," as she called it, unseemly for a clergyman. Fortunately, my Camillian Order considered my dual roles at the hospital and church an asset in the same way that the Jesuit Order valued priests who were also teachers. In addition to poverty, chastity, and obedience, Camillians take a fourth vow to care for the sick. When I entered the seminary, they encouraged me to keep up my medical license and skills.

In truth, St. Camillus's life story was one of the reasons that I had entered the seminary. Though he lived in the sixteenth century, our journeys had been very similar. Not that I was a saint, far from it. Camillus had been a hot-tempered youth, fond of the ladies, and a soldier before he found the Lord and became a hospital worker and priest — which described my past perfectly. Given my tempestuous youth and time as an army medic, we were kindred spirits.

Centuries before the founding of the modern Red Cross, St. Camillus had worn a large crimson cross on his cassock as he cared for victims of the Bubonic Plague and wounded soldiers on the battlefield. All members of the Camillian Order now proudly did the same.

"Starting back at the hospital so soon, Father? Are you sure you're up to that after your recent . . . trouble and all?"

I nodded. The motion elicited a twinge of pain from my healing collarbone.

She shook her head in disapproval. "Very well, if you think it best to put your own health at risk, so be it. Why don't you go sit at table then? I'll be in shortly with food for you and your clan."

The answering machine in the kitchen winked at me, and I pressed the play button. Miguel Hernandez had left a message asking me in a shaky voice to be present at his apartment tomorrow when the police came. For better or worse, I was entangled in their family tragedy.

I peered into the dining room where my four year old nephew, RJ, had covered the table in green plastic soldiers. Justine, as thin and fragile as a spun glass figurine, sat nearby flipping the pages of a magazine. Her leukemia had left her gaunt and pale. Angular cheek bones threatened to poke through taut skin, and even her freckles appeared to be fading. I didn't need a microscope to envision her crazed white blood cells rampaging through her bone marrow.

She had shown me photographs taken with her mother when she was a child. Both had luxurious, flaming-red hair. Justine's was now rust-colored with several patches of scalp peeking through, and her eyebrows were painted on.

When her chemotherapy in Louisiana failed, she'd packed up her child and tracked me down in early July, hoping for a transplant match and my help. I'd offered them the spare bedrooms at the rectory and my connections at the hospital. Having been raised by different mothers hundreds of miles apart, however, we were genetically-linked strangers just beginning to get to know each other.

High-pitched explosions filled the room, and a plastic paratrooper leaped from the salt shaker. Justine set down her magazine.

"Randall James! I asked you to put your toys away ten minutes ago! It's almost dinnertime. Do it now, please."

"Aw, Mom!" RJ replied, pouting as he gathered his toy soldiers.

35

I strolled in and said, "Evening, y'all." I enjoyed teasing Justine about her molasses-thick, Louisiana drawl. "Goll-y, Sis, what's-a-matter? You look like the gravy done slid off your biscuit."

She returned my grin and added some butter to her Southern-fried accent.

"Well bless your pea-pickin' heart. Ain't you full of sweet tea and sassafras today, shugah? Or should I say . . . *old geezer?*"

My sister took great pleasure in reminding me that I was a decade and half older — although with the cancer, she appeared to be twice my age.

As I helped General RJ retreat his troops into a shoebox, I said, "I have some good news. The Cleveland Clinic will admit you next week."

Justine jumped to her feet and hugged me. She felt like a bundle of twigs in my arms. Strange how the most important things in life are often the most fragile.

"They found me a match?"

"Yup." I tapped my chest. "I'm your guy."

I didn't tell her that I was a less than perfect match or mention the long, difficult road that she had ahead. Instead, I said, "Have faith. We'll get you through this."

Her smile flickered and died.

"Good Lord, what am I gonna do with

RJ?" The last remaining hint of color in her complexion drained away. "Can you take care of him while I'm in the hospital, Jake? I got no one else."

That meant weeks, maybe months. I could barely juggle the two jobs that I had. Sacred Heart was a small parish, but when combined with treating patients at St. Joseph's Hospital there was little time left in my day. No way could I throw a third ball into the air.

Besides, what did I know about caring for a child? And Bishop Lucci had already made it clear that my medical practice could not divert my focus from the Church. Now, childcare provider? His Excellency would unleash the wrath of God on me.

Wringing her emaciated hands, Justine continued to stare, waiting for my answer.

And if she died? What the hell would I do then? Although a couple Catholic priests had adopted children with permission from the Church, no way would Lucci allow me to do that! Did I even want to? I had given up so much to my vows of poverty, chastity, and obedience, yet I'd finally reached a level of contentment in midlife that I hadn't had since my early childhood. Was it selfish to cling to that small comfort?

"Jake, please! RJ and I *need* your help."

RJ looked up at me expectantly, a mixture of fear and confusion on his tiny face. I must have looked exactly that way on the day my old man packed his suitcase and walked out the front door for the last time. I knew what came next. Could I do that to RJ? Was I my father's son? No way in hell! Or was I? I hoped not.

Uncertain how to respond, I faltered. Justine's expression registered disappointment.

Colleen stepped into the room and cleared her throat.

"If it's all right with yourself, Father, I'd be happy to be of assistance. I'm rather fond of the lad." She walked in, tousled RJ's fiery locks, then said to Justine, "Pay me what you can. Since my hours at the rectory were cut back, I've had . . . a bit of trouble making ends meet."

Justine's brow furrowed. "Thanks for the offer, but I'm flat broke. My illness has wiped me out."

I had completed a review of the budget, and Sacred Heart had slipped into the red. It would be closed if the ink didn't turn black soon. The Vatican had made it clear that every parish needed to get its fiscal house in order, and it had issued the eleventh commandment: *Thou shalt not use church funds for personal needs.*

All of my medical income went to the Camillian Order. I received only a small monthly stipend and had less than a hundred dollars in my personal savings account. But because Bishop Lucci didn't want me distracted from my parish duties, I thought I might be able to play the compassion card and convince him to reinstate Colleen's hours during my family emergency.

Besides, I had two aces up my sleeve. The Superior General of my Camillian Order had powerful connections in Rome. Bishop Lucci was his close friend and hoped to ride my boss's coattails all the way to Archbishop or Cardinal. My Superior General had loaned me to the Cleveland diocese during the illness of Sacred Heart's pastor, and Lucci didn't want to be seen as ungrateful — *friendship,* the ace of hearts. More importantly, I had recently played a role in saving the bishop's life from a deranged killer. *Obligation* was the ace of clubs and the big stick that I carried. At least for the time being, I owned His Excellency like a debt.

Colleen had gone silent and Justine was staring at the floor. I placed a hand on my sister's shoulder.

"I'll ask the bishop to cover the cost for Colleen's additional hours and delay my return to the hospital so I can help. With my vow of poverty, it's not as though they pay me much. Really, I'd love to, Sis."

Justine gazed from me to my nephew and back again, gave me another hug, then knelt next to RJ and explained our plan. He nodded gravely, then asked, "Can I play soldier now?"

The tension in the room evaporated, and we laughed. "Grand. That's settled then. Sit and I'll fetch the food, Father," Colleen said as smoke wafted in from the kitchen. "Good Lord, the meatloaf!" she shouted and bolted from the room to rescue her burnt offerings.

CHAPTER SIX

Tuesday, July 25, 9:30 a.m.

After morning Mass, I tracked down the oncologist at the Cleveland Clinic who would be performing Justine's transplant and spent fifteen minutes on the telephone with him discussing her condition and treatment. Then I shuffled some parish paperwork in the study, booted up my computer, and read more medical literature about sudden infant deaths.

As I finished, RJ entered the room and gave me his artistic rendition of me flying a spaceship, soaring over a forest of happy green trees. I thanked him and gave him a hug, and he skipped from my study intent on filling the world with more crayon masterworks.

I tried to name the feeling RJ's visit had aroused in me, but couldn't. It was an uncanny combination of joy, sadness, love, and dread. I spent the next twenty minutes

41

researching how to counsel young children with sick or dying parents. By the time Tree Macon wheeled his police cruiser into the rectory driveway at precisely eleven in the morning, I was emotionally drained.

Tree was wearing his uniform and a scowl. As we drove to Tina and Miguel's apartment, his head swiveled back and forth like a searchlight, radar-scanning his town for signs of trouble. He was all business as he sipped black coffee two shades darker than his skin color, and nearly as dark as his mood.

Ever since we first met years ago, Tree usually wore a grin, and I wanted to readjust his current attitude. Although it is unwise to poke a bear, I said, "Is it okay with you if I run the lights and siren?"

"No. And don't run your mouth either."

The big guy had been a lot more fun back in high school. "You okay, Tree?"

"Peachy."

"Well you look more like a prune. What's up?"

He glanced at me. "Some damn tagger spray-painted the F-word on the station house last night. First thing I saw this morning. If I get my hands on this clown, the First Amendment won't save his behind. I swear, this generation is going to hell in a handbasket."

"That's what happens when the Ten Commandments are downgraded to recommendations."

"My religion's based on justice, not faith." He gulped some coffee and sighed. "Guess it's nothing a coat of paint won't fix, so —"

The furrow between Tree's dark eyes suddenly deepened, and he swerved into the berm, crunching gravel and spewing dust as the cruiser came to a stop.

"Stay put, Jake."

Tree was a giant oak of a man. Six feet, six inches of muscle, and two hundred and fifty pounds of determination. He had been a first-team defensive lineman in college and an NFL prospect, but when he stepped from the car his stature dwarfed even his size. He was a man with a gun, a badge, and a mission. His shaved scalp glistened in the morning light as he sauntered toward a young couple.

A skinny black man with a cornrow hairstyle had a teenaged girl pinned against a telephone pole. She squirmed nervously. He was working his way through a long list of profanities. The girl saw Tree coming; the man did not.

Tree stopped short of the pair, placed a hand on his nightstick, and said something in a low voice. The man spun around and took a step toward Tree, his face full of rage, a grill of gold teeth gleaming in the sun. The girl slid to her left and disappeared through the door of a nearby bungalow.

Tree slipped the nightstick out of his belt and tapped it against the palm of his hand. The young man examined his sneakers briefly, then slinked away around the corner of a building.

When he returned to the cruiser, Tree was humming the old hit single "Every Breath You Take" by The Police. He opened the car door, saw the young man peek around the building, and shouted, "I'll be watching your every move, asshole. Don't even think about it!"

"Friend of yours?" I asked.

"We're acquainted. His name's Willy Warner. Nickname's Willy Wonka, *The Candy Man.* He's a low-level punk." Tree fired up the black and white and eased back on the road. "I busted him as a juvie for possession with intent to sell. His record was sealed and he was back on the corner peddling weed before I got home for dinner. Rumor has it he's graduated from grass to more mind-bending products. I reminded him that he's old enough now to do serious time."

44

"You just, what, stop out of the blue and . . . hassle the guy? Is that legal? Was he selling?"

Tree put on his turn signal and waited for traffic to pass.

"You remember my sister, Jake, right? That girl Willy was hassling had the same expression that my baby sis would get when she was cornered at a party by some jackass. I didn't like it then, and I don't like it now." He tapped his nightstick and chuckled. "And I never laid a glove on him. Old Willy eyeballed my *Silly Stick,* decided he didn't want to get slapped silly, and moved on. Warning delivered, problem solved. No blood, no foul."

We pulled into Miguel and Tina's small complex at the west end of town. Weather-beaten, beige cedar siding formed cubes of single floor apartments. Winter had pitted the asphalt parking lot like the skin of an adolescent ravaged by acne, and we bounced our way to a parking space near their door. A rusted air conditioner painted in pigeon poop sagged from a window in a neighbor's apartment, groaning and grinding vainly against the merciless summer heat.

We walked to the door, knocked at unit number six, and Miguel answered. He wore the same sweat-stained T-shirt I'd seen the

45

day before. A cigarette hung from his lips, and the neck of a brown bottle poked out above his meaty right hand.

I was met with a nod. "Thanks for coming, Padre."

Tree and his uniform drew a look of disgust.

"What the hell do ya want now, man? We already told the other cops everything we know. Can't you leave us alone?"

Tree had no search warrant, so he offered an apology and a slow, easy smile.

"I'm sorry to bother you, sir. I just have a couple questions. Can we come in?"

Miguel's nostrils flared, and he bared his teeth like a pit bull. "This is *mierda*!" He tried to stare Tree down, failed, and swung the door open into a small, dingy living room. "Fine. You got five minutes."

"Would you ask Tina to join us, please?"

"She's back at the hospital, and I'll be damned if I let you put her through any more of this crap. Our boy's in a coma, and she's been through enough!"

As Tree asked his questions, I scrutinized the apartment.

On an end table, a newspaper partially covered a pack of Zig-Zag rolling papers. The distant memory of a joint lingered in the air, but I was certain that Tree was not

46

interested in a misdemeanor possession bust. Three empty beer cans formed a pyramid on the coffee table, and a crushed can rested on the couch. Binge drinking? Numbing the pain? Not an unreasonable response to the near death of your child — or was this a lifestyle? Either Miguel had gotten so wasted that he'd forgotten to clean up before the police arrived, or he didn't give a damn.

A fine layer of dust coated yard-sale furniture. A few framed photos of Miguel and Tina in happier times decorated the walls. I saw none of their child. A fan whirred in the corner, but without air conditioning the room was a sauna.

Tree dropped his keys, bent over, and touched a small, red-brown stain shaped like Africa on the green shag carpet. He picked up his keychain and stood. "Can I see the baby's room?"

"Pablo. My son's name is *Pablo.*" Miguel snuffed out his cigarette in an overflowing ashtray and started walking. "This way."

We passed a small kitchen strewn with unwashed pots and dishes. The yellowed linoleum hadn't seen a mop in months. An empty pizza box lay open on the kitchen table, next to a bottle of two-buck-Chuck chardonnay.

An early-American rocking chair, small dresser, and an old-fashioned hand-me-down crib filled most of Pablo's tiny room. A frayed baby blanket draped wooden slats that were too far apart to meet current safety codes. Bumper pads with pictures of sheep leaping fences rimmed the periphery of the crib. A large, fluffy teddy bear napped at one end, a pillow with Big Bird's likeness at the other.

While Tree confronted Miguel with more questions, I reached down and touched the mattress. Soft, stained, and well-worn where the gray fitted sheet had slipped free at one corner, it had definitely cradled numerous babies before Pablo.

A single photograph on the chest of drawers showed Tina holding her baby. There were no nursery rhyme characters, mobiles, or other decorations present to amuse Pablo or celebrate his existence. The air was hot, sticky, and still, and its odor consisted of a strange blend of tobacco, baby powder, and mildew.

The entire apartment was a *how-not-to* guide for parents. Despite the swelter in the room, what I had seen so far chilled me.

Tree walked over, surveyed the room, and asked if Pablo's grandparents ever babysat.

Miguel glanced at me, probably hoping

that I'd run interference for him. I said nothing. He advanced toward us, his body odor mingled with the pungent aroma of garlic and alcohol on his breath.

"Tina's folks are dead, and mine live in Mexico — and they sure-as-hell wouldn't hurt their little nieto." He shoved a finger in Tree's face. "That's enough questions. We're done here. Tina'll be home soon, and I want you gone."

Miguel led us to the front door, and Tree thanked him for his cooperation. We left the apartment and walked silently back to the cruiser, both lost in our thoughts. As we climbed in, Tree said, "Let's talk over lunch. I owe you."

We entered Presti's Restaurant across the street. Our visit with Miguel had left me weary and depressed. We passed two old men at the bar who were working diligently on their next hangovers, and I desperately wanted to join them. The neon Saint Pauli Girl on the wall tempted me with a wry smile and a frosted mug of beer. I resisted, barely.

CHAPTER SEVEN

Tuesday, July 25, Noon

We settled into a booth, scanned the menu, and ordered sandwiches and coffee. Two young women were seated at the next table. The one in an Oberlin College polo shirt was complaining loudly about recent tuition increases.

Tree sighed and whispered, "How can kids afford to go to college these days? My baby just graduated from Kent State. Thank God she was on a scholarship! Hell, tuition at private schools now is damn close to my yearly salary."

He took a sip of coffee and focused on me, bright eyes flashing from his darkly clouded face. "Okay Dick Tracy, use your scientific knowledge and logic to dazzle me with your insights. What do your highly-tuned, medical senses tell you? Time to earn your lunch."

"I'm glad to see you're broadening your

literary interests, Tree. But if I'm not mistaken, it's you cops who are usually called *Dicks* — and whenever you give me a hard time, I always think of *you* as one." I chuckled, squeezed a wedge of lemon into my ice water, and got down to business. "Obviously, Miguel's drinking in the morning is a red flag. There's no question he's way too fond of alcohol, though I see no indication that he's mentally unstable."

"It's not morning for him, Jake. He's a nightshift janitor at a factory in Elyria. That beer may be his usual nightcap before bed. I doubt that he worked last night, but he probably didn't sleep much either with his son in ICU." Tree added enough sugar to his coffee to launch an entire kindergarten into a manic frenzy. "Their place was pretty filthy. Could that cause Pablo to stop breathing?"

"Dust, mold, and bacteria can predispose to SIDS. In fact, the entire apartment is a setup for it. A teenage mother who may have drugged and drank her way through pregnancy, and a house full of second-hand toxins are right out of the textbook. The soft mattress, stuffed animals, and even the bumper padding could be factors. The lack of AC in this weather can produce hyperthermia in an infant and that can be deadly.

Can't the town help poor folks get air conditioning in the heat of summer?"

"Not in my job description, Jake. Talk with social services. I got enough on my plate." Tree shrugged. "Sounds like the perfect project for your church."

"Not till I get the parish finances back in the black."

As I worked on my turkey club sandwich, I watch four twenty-somethings in a corner booth. Both of the men were hypnotized by the ESPN sports replays and the scores scrolling across the bottom of a muted television on the wall. The two young women were texting or emailing on their mobile phones. No one at the table had spoken a word since Tree and I had arrived. Justine was right. I *am* a geezer — and a dinosaur. Sometimes I no longer recognized the world I lived in.

Tree slathered a glob of mayonnaise on his prime rib sandwich, took a huge bite, chewed, and then said, "Man, I hate this. Every time I have a case involving a kid, I see my girls when they were young." Another bite. "Did you notice anything that *doesn't* suggest an accidental crib death prevented by alert parents?"

"Well, boys are more commonly affected, but their son's a year old and that's somewhat late for SIDS. And even if Tina didn't know it's unwise to place her baby on his belly, which she told me yesterday that she did, by twelve months the child should be able to easily roll over on his own."

"Anything else?"

"Rolling papers and the smell of grass."

Tree nodded. "And."

"That stain on the living room rug. I saw you drop your keychain and check it out."

"It was dry, most likely red wine, but Miguel has a temper. When you met the two of them, did you catch a whiff of any marital strife, or see bruising or anything that might indicate he's a wife beater?"

"No. Just the opposite. Miguel was very protective of Tina."

"Yeah, that's what my detective said. Besides, it'd be really stupid not to remove or hide that much evidence on the living room carpet. I did scrape a key across it when I bent down and I'll test it with Luminol, but I doubt that it'll be positive for blood."

I finished the last of my sandwich. "Sorry, Tree. That's all I saw."

"That's okay." He grabbed the bill. "Not to worry, you still get lunch. I'll pick up the check, given your vow of poverty and all."

We walked outside to his cruiser. Tree

loosened his collar, revealing a nasty-looking scar below his ear shaped like an exclamation point and darker than his skin. It ballooned into an irregular growth at the bottom about the size of a pencil eraser.

"What's that on your neck, Tree?"

He slid a hand over it. "Oh, this? I got slashed by barb wire when I was on the SWAT team. Long time ago. No big deal."

"Let me see it." I stepped closer and ran a finger across the lesion, which was raised with ill-defined margins and a crusty feel. "You should see a dermatologist and make sure that's not skin cancer."

"Cut it out, doc, and stop touching me in public. I got a bad-ass image to maintain." He stepped away. "Besides, if you haven't noticed, I'm a black dude. We don't get sunburned. The only time I get burned is when you piss me off, like you're doing now. It's nothing. Get in the damn car, Jake."

I snapped on my seatbelt and said, "That's the problem. Everyone thinks that, even some doctors. It's not true. African Americans *do* get skin cancer, not as frequently as Caucasians, but because of that misconception it's often caught too late to cure. Heck, Bob Marley died young from melanoma. Don't screw around with this, Tree."

"Let it go, man. I don't have time for this

54

crap. Hell, they give a guy a white coat and stethoscope, and he thinks he's Albert Frickin' Schweitzer." He slipped the car into gear and eased onto West Lorain. "Enough already. Time to take you back to the home for unwed fathers — *Father.*"

CHAPTER EIGHT

Tuesday, July 25, 3:30 p.m.

While Justine shopped for a few last minute items before her hospital admission, I spent a pleasant afternoon at the rectory with my nephew.

He promoted me to first lieutenant and placed me in charge of a squadron of plastic army men. Under General RJ's command, we made a relentless assault up the front stairs against overwhelming odds and finally liberated his bedroom just in time for his afternoon nap. Remarkably, our troops did not suffer one casualty.

I hadn't had much one-on-one contact with children in my life, and I was amazed to see how freely RJ could drift between fantasy and reality. Watching his expression of grim determination erupt into a happy dance at our decisive victory lifted my spirits, but left a hollow aching at my core.

Although everyone called me *Father,* I

would never be one biologically. I would, however, get a taste of fatherhood for several weeks when Justine had her bone marrow transplant, and I wondered if I would be relieved or disappointed to return the reins to her when she was released. *If* she was released. I couldn't even force myself to imagine what RJ's world and mine would be like if she didn't make it home from the hospital.

Justine returned around five o'clock, and we devoured a delicious meal of beef stew that Colleen had prepared. Well, RJ and I did. Justine merely pushed it around her plate. Afterward, she and I chatted into the early evening, swapping stories from our separate childhoods. She kept using the same nickname that I used for our philandering father — *Dirt-bag.* Concise and accurate. Having both been abandoned by him at a young age, we flaunted our anger with no remorse.

After he deserted us, my mother referred to my old man as a *tomcat.* As I grew older and learned what the term implied, I detested him even more. Now, with Justine sitting across from me, I grasped that the tomcat had fathered a kitten in Louisiana and inadvertently provided me with a family again. Having been without one for decades, it was an incredible blessing and an unexpected miracle — yet her illness raised the stakes enormously. If she died, RJ would be orphaned and I would be alone again.

Over a second cup of tea, Justine expressed fears about her upcoming procedure and our conversation returned to the present and grew serious. I tried to allay her concerns, and a few of my own, without flatout lying. Unless Tree Macon located our father and the dirt-bag consented to donate his bone marrow, I didn't like her chances, but kept my dark thoughts to myself.

When RJ became cranky, Justine put him to bed and retired early. Crawling around the floor with my nephew must have tweaked my healing fractures, because they were none too happy with me. I found the bottle of OxyContin that my physician had prescribed after my injury, took one, then put on the baseball game in the living room.

The Tribe and White Sox were in a slugfest with the score tied at nine. As they completed the eleventh inning, the opiate wrapped its arms around me and I slept until the mantle clock over the fireplace chimed seven, clanging me back to consciousness and into Wednesday morning.

My back felt fused to the sofa, and my

mouth tasted like used gym socks. The TV was still on and sun poured in through the front window, flooding the room with sweet dawn light and painting a bright yellow-orange rectangle across the rug.

Justine had been raised by an atheist mother, and my sister had made it clear that she and RJ had no interest in attending services of any denomination, so I didn't wake them. After a quick shower and shave, I scrambled to the church and dressed in my vestments.

Surprisingly, Wednesday morning Mass had a large turnout. I cleared my mind of all distractions, found my rhythm, and celebrated our Lord with joy and enthusiasm. Everything went well. The parishioners were attentive, the homily mesmerizing, and my timing spot-on. I felt like a great athlete who was "in the zone."

I was savoring the sublime simplicity of the Eucharist and feeling blessed that my strange journey through life had somehow led me to this wonderful vocation and this perfect moment — until I noticed Martin Luther asleep behind the statue of St. Joseph. The furry rascal had a lot in common with his namesake. No matter how many times the Catholic Church had thrown Martin Luther out, he inevitably found his way back to his flock, and every time I banished the cat to the church basement, he always found a way upstairs. At least this time, he didn't have a dead rodent in his mouth.

Martin remained motionless except for the occasional swish of his tail and I decided to let sleeping cats lie. As I recited the Lord's Prayer, I began to relax, but the moment I said, "deliver us from evil," the tabby made his move. He rose, nuzzled the statue, and strolled passed me into the sacristy.

Either no one else saw him or they chose not to react — or the congregation was simply interested to see what I would do. What I *wanted to do* was throttle the unrepentant reprobate. But I'd just said, "forgive us our trespasses as we forgive those who trespass against us," so I quietly asked my altar girl, Kristin, to evict him before he snuggled up to my black cassocks or left a hairball in my dress shoes. God only knew what mischief Martin would get into if left alone in the sacristy.

Kristin handled the crisis deftly and we finished Mass without further incident. I was changing out of my vestments when my cellphone rang.

"Jake, Marcus Taylor here. Sorry to bother you again. Could you come into the hospital ASAP?"

"What's going on?"

"I spent the last twenty nine hours working on the SIDS baby. The child may have been in cardiopulmonary arrest too long before EMS got there. The damage is probably irreversible and I doubt that he'll come out of his coma. I'll have to run a battery of tests first, but . . . I hope to hell I'm wrong. The idea of discussing brain death with parents always turns my stomach. When I broke the news that things aren't looking good, they asked if you could come and counsel them today. Miguel forgot to bring your telephone number and asked me to call. Please come. They're in the room across from pediatric intensive care."

"I'll be there in thirty minutes."

Traffic was light, my foot heavy on the accelerator, and I arrived in twenty. Tina and Miguel were huddled in the waiting room, his arms draped around her, their foreheads touching like conjoint twins telepathically exchanging their fear and sorrow. He wore cutoff jeans and a Browns jersey that barely concealed his beer belly. She amply filled out a tight blouse above a short skirt displaying miles of suntanned legs. Although she may not have written the book on sensuality, she'd definitely read the CliffsNotes.

Both heads lifted when I entered.

61

"Thank God you're here, Father," Tina said. "Help us, please!"

Sadly, I had very little relief in either my Bible or my medical bag for this kind of catastrophe. I walked over and sat next to Tina.

"Your physician filled me in." I placed a hand on her wrist. It was ice-cold and trembling. "I'm so terribly sorry."

Miguel whispered, "Doc Taylor said we might have to pull the plug on our baby." Tina glared at him, and he fixed his eyes on his shoes. "Diós mío! How we supposed to do that?"

"It may not seem possible, but you will get through this with God's help." The words sounded hackneyed and empty. "Would you like to pray?"

Tina said, "No, not now. We, ah, never . . . ." Her voice trailed off, and she stared at her long, manicured fingernails. "We never baptized Pablo. Could you? Now. Please?"

"Of course. Do you want to come in with me?"

"The nurse told us to stay here till they call us," Miguel answered, "but don't wait. Do it now, please." He kissed Tina's cheek and added softly, "What about Last Rites, Padre? Just in case."

"Pablo's not yet reached the age of reason and is too young to have sinned, so that's not necessary."

Tina stood, tears streaming down her cheek. "And pray that Pablo lives, Father. Please!"

"Certainly. I'll come back as soon as I'm done and we'll pray together."

I usually loved being a priest. Not that Wednesday morning.

Trudging slowly across the hall, I entered the pediatric intensive care unit, which always reminded me of a young girl who had died of meningitis under my care when I was an intern. The child's face was etched in my memory. I'd been a bumbling rookie then, and I've always wondered if I could have saved her had I been smarter, quicker, and more aggressive.

A PICU nurse recognized me. I explained my task and she led me to Pablo's crib.

He was much smaller than I'd expected for a one year old. An endotracheal tube protruded from his mouth. His chest rose with each whoosh of oxygenated air from the ventilator. His tiny arms had more needle-stick holes than a sieve. A central venous catheter peeked from the right side of his neck and an IV was taped to a vein in his scalp.

The nurse opened a bottle of sterile water, handed it to me, and said, "The child's in bad shape, Father. Make it as quick as you can."

Holy water from the church or tap water were not options given the risk of infection. I sprinkled a few drops of sterile water on the only available exposed portion of the baby's scalp and said, "I baptize you, Pablo, in the name of the Father, and of the Son, and of the Holy Spirit." He did not stir.

The nurse took the bottle and ushered me away from the crib. I stepped out of her way and whispered a prayer for all of the sick and dying, then added, "Lord, Pablo is so young and helpless. Please return him to his parents so that he may lead a normal, healthy life. Allow him to experience this wonderful world you've created." I wiped moist eyes. "This I ask in Jesus's name. Amen."

I gathered my composure and was walking back to pray with Pablo's parents when Dr. Taylor stepped from the elevator. He was the grand old man of St. Joseph's Hospital, a fixture for decades and the undisputed leader of the medical staff. I, however, thought of him as the grand old *snowman,* because of his pale complexion, coal-black eyes, and snow-white hair. Between Taylor's roly-poly, Frosty-the Snow-man physique and the oven-like heat out-side, I worried that he might melt into a giant puddle before he reached his car in the parking garage.

I remembered Tree Macon's question about whether there was any evidence *against* an accidental crib death interrupted by an alert parent.

"Marcus, I just saw the baby in PICU. He's somewhat old for a SIDS episode, isn't he?"

"It's not common at that age, but not impossible. SIDS usually occurs between two and six months, although it can happen later on."

"He's small for his age. Shouldn't a one year old be able to roll himself off his belly if he has trouble breathing?"

"That's true in general, but may not apply to Pablo. He was born prematurely and had a difficult delivery resulting in birth trauma. After a short stay in neonatal intensive care, however, he seemed okay and we discharged him home. He continued to gain weight and was on no medication, so everyone relaxed. Things appeared to be fine. But over the last few months Pablo's pediatrician noticed developmental delays indicative of underly-ing cerebral palsy from brain damage. Low birth weight premies are at higher risk for many things, including SIDS." He paused and looked down. "In some ways, that may make things easier."

"Easier? How?"

"The parents understand that Pablo was . . . damaged at birth. They're young and can have more children. That may make letting go a little easier if we have to withdraw life support. I won't know for certain for a few days, but I'll have to broach the subject of possible organ donation soon." He managed a weak smile. "That's the kind of discussion that turned my hair white. Never gets any easier."

Dr. Taylor patted me on the back and entered the intensive care unit.

Miguel and Tina were alone in the waiting room when I walked in. They set down their Styrofoam coffee cups, and we prayed the rosary together.

They thanked me and I got up to leave.

Tina stood and said, "One more question, Father."

"Yes."

"Would it be a sin if we . . . let the doctors take Pablo's organs . . . if he passes? That could save other babies, right?"

Miguel appeared as stunned as I was. He stiffened, signaling resistance. This was not

66

a question I expected at this stage from a parent. Usually families of dying patients initially oppose the idea of organ recovery. Some see it as a desecration of their loved one. With my sister's impending bone marrow transplant, however, I wished that all families would be more open to the possibility.

The question made me wonder. As a premie, Pablo had spent time in the Neonatal Intensive Care Unit. The NICU can be a terrifying place for parents, and it was possible that Tina had never developed the normal maternal bond with her son. I could understand how the mother of a baby who was brain damaged might eventually suggest donating his organs, but still couldn't imagine broaching the subject so soon after the child's hospital admission.

"The Church has no problem with organ donation, Tina. I carry a donor card myself. And yes, that kind of selfless act could save the lives of several children."

"Thank you. That's what I needed to hear. If we . . . lose Pablo, I hope we can save some other parents from this living hell."

"That's a noble plan, but it's too soon to talk about that, Tina. All we can do now is pray."

They both nodded and I left, feeling helpless. Their baby was in God's hands, and I hoped He would have mercy on this family in their hour of need.

I paged Dr. Taylor and told him that Tina was receptive to the idea of organ donation if Pablo was declared brain-dead.

Taylor sounded relieved. Tina's premature, almost casual discussion of the possibility of harvesting her child's organs, however, left me unsettled.

CHAPTER NINE

Wednesday, July 26, 11:00 a.m.

I wandered into the hospital cafeteria and studied the uninspired menu. Although not really hungry, I hoped that the distraction of lunch and some solitude might provide a fresh perspective on how to counsel Tina and Miguel about their dying child.

Placing a chicken salad sandwich and coffee on my tray, I paid the cashier from my dwindling cash reserves and was heading to an unoccupied table in the corner when I saw her.

Emily sat alone wearing jeans, a flowered blouse, and sunglasses. She was engrossed in a book, her fingers waltzing nimbly over pages of Braille. The long, flowing, auburn hair that had hypnotized me in high school was now cropped short, framing her face. She'd maintained her youthful figure, added a few laugh lines, and time had somehow enhanced her beauty. Despite all the years

69

that had passed since our graduation, I still couldn't look away.

Seeing her, however, always stirred up a silt of memories and emotions. We were bonded by history. Being assigned to my hometown had thrust her back into my life, which was both a blessing and a curse.

We'd spent considerable time together since my return. Emily was witty, warm, and attractive, and our past drew me to her like the tide to the moon. In her presence, I again felt the magnificent lightness that I'd felt as a teenager. I still cared deeply about her and always had — which for a Catholic priest, of course, was a prescription for disaster.

Relationships are like bridges — some you cross, and some you burn. I was unable and unwilling to do either when it came to Emily. When I'd confessed my feelings for her to Bishop Lucci, he'd instructed me to torch this one, but I couldn't bring myself to strike the match.

The situation would have been much easier if we hadn't briefly been lovers in our youth. We'd had a painful breakup our senior year in high school and hadn't communicated after graduation. While I was overseas fighting an unwinnable war, she'd married one of our classmates, a guy I particularly loathed. At first, I marinated her memory in whiskey. As our paths seemed destined never to cross again, I gradually became accustomed to her absence.

After the war, I'd thought of her often as I built my new life around treating patients, reconnecting with the Lord, and honing my medical practice and ministry at the sprawling campus of the Camillian Order near Milwaukee. My raw emotions had nearly healed and I was reaching a sort of détente with my past when my Superior General assigned me to fill in for an ailing priest in town and to treat indigent patients at St. Joseph's Hospital — the same place where Emily worked.

I'd been taught in seminary to deal with temptation and unwanted emotions by avoiding "occasions of sin," but that was difficult to do when I saw her nearly every day at the hospital. She was a constant reminder of what had been, and what could never be. To make things worse, we had both recently acknowledged our continued affection for each other.

I suspected that our current relationship bewildered her, because it sure as hell confused me.

I decided to skirt past Emily into the

privacy of the doctors' dining room in the back of the cafeteria. *Lead us not into temptation.* Sneaking past a blind woman should have been easy. It wasn't.

"Jake, what a surprise!" She cocked her head and a sheet of auburn hair drifted past one eye. "Have a seat and keep me company."

"How in the world do you do that, Em? There must be fifty people in here. How could you possibly know it was me?"

"Mystical powers and a sixth sense." She laughed, a sound that always melted my resolve. "Well that, and I heard you speak with the cashier. And your aftershave is also as distinctive as a fingerprint. That's what your learned colleagues call olfactory acuity, doctor."

Nothing got past Emily — including me.

I sat across from her. Maybe it was my paranoia, but I suspected that the innocent act of having lunch together had probably added grist to the rumor mill. Hospitals, especially Catholic hospitals, were like drought-stricken forests — any hint of a scandal, particularly about a priest, spread like wildfire. God only knew what people here were saying about our relationship. This place wasn't a little fish bowl like the rectory, it was a public aquarium. Although

72

I loved spending time with Emily and my intentions were pure, for the sake of both of our reputations we needed to be more careful about being seen together in public.

"How are RJ and Justine?" she asked in a wind-soft voice as light as candle smoke, which made her every word sound like a prayer. And with my sister's illness, we needed every prayer I could find.

I filled her in on my nephew's latest antics and Justine's failing health. A lull in the conversation followed, but we had always been comfortable with silence when in each other's company.

I took a bite of my sandwich, surprised that it was half gone.

Finally ready to share my morning, and hoping that Emily might provide a new perspective, I told her about the tiny comatose baby pin-cushioned with needles and tubes, the suffering of his parents, and the bedside baptism in the PICU. I neglected to mention the part about snooping through the grieving parent's apartment with Tree Macon the day before.

A tear slowly trickled across the freckles on her cheek. I'd been the cause of too many of her tears in our distant past, so I switched gears and asked, "Is your dad working today?"

Emily had a rare form of hereditary blindness, which had destroyed her vision and upended her world in her twenties. Her father was also blind. Together they had rebuilt their lives. The hospital administrator, a man of great compassion, had hired them both and provided a supportive environment in which they could function safely. They ran the snack shop and lived in the hospital dormitory as advisors and mentors to young interns and residents training at St. Joseph's, many of whom were foreign, far from home, and in need of encouragement and guidance.

"No, Dad flew to Boston to visit his sister for a couple weeks. A friend of his has been covering his shifts."

"The way your father puts in hours around here, he certainly deserves some R. and R." I took a sip of coffee. "So, Em, how's Everett?"

It was a question born of obligation. Although I cared little about her ex-husband, Emily cared a great deal. He'd been shot in the head three weeks earlier by the rampaging lunatic who'd nearly killed Bishop Lucci and me.

Emily wiped her eyes with a napkin and wilted in the chair. From our many years together, I was fluent in her gestures and the nuances of her expression. Seeing her in pain was difficult for me.

She drew a deep breath and gathered herself. "Everett's slowly getting better and should be transferred out of ICU soon. He'll need a lot of physical therapy, but I'm hopeful."

Given the appalling way he had treated her, it was hard for me to understand why she still cared about the guy.

"Do me a favor, Jake. Say a prayer for him."

I gazed at the pale scar extending from her lip that the abusive bastard had left her as a memento. Clearly, she was a better practicing Christian than I.

"Sure, Em," I said. "Be happy to."

I'd asked Emily to marry me before Uncle Sam sent me off to war, and she'd turned me down. Not that I was a good prospect back then, between my boozing, drugging, and the chance that I would come home in a body bag. I had asked again in a letter from overseas; she'd never responded. The next thing I heard, she and Everett were engaged.

Emily removed her sunglasses, slowly lifted her tea bag from her cup, and stirred in sweetener. Then her hand wandered across the table and found mine. Mischief twinkled in her blue eyes like sunlight on lake water.

"How's that piece of junk you call a car, Jake? Does it still run?"

"Today, yes. Tomorrow, who knows?"

The parish's ancient Toyota Corolla creaked, groaned, and farted foul-smelling exhaust like an octogenarian after two bowls of three-bean chili. At least Emily couldn't see that the car's body was a quilt of dents and chipped paint. Time and UV rays had faded its once bright plum color to a patchy, anemic orchid that any red-blooded male would have been too embarrassed to drive. But I had no other options.

"Even though His Excellency had the air conditioner and leaking gas tank repaired, and replaced the bald tires after the incident, Em, it's still junk."

She knew about Bishop Lucci's near plunge from a fifth story window, which he always referred to as *the incident.* Helping to save him, however, had left me basking in his good graces, at least for the time being.

"Don't fret, Jake. Maybe someday you'll be allowed to drive a big-boy car."

"You have to admit, the holes in the muffler make it sound like a muscle car. So, why the sudden interest in my wheels, Em?"

"What do you know about the St. Wenceslaus parish southwest of Cleveland?"

"Not much."

She fingered a ginger-colored strand of hair. "Don't you read the papers?"

I shook my head and felt foolish. In my mind, we were both still high school seniors, and sometimes I forgot that she was now blind.

"No, I only read the sports page and comics. The rest is too darn depressing."

"Well, St. Wenceslaus has been all over the news. The Virgin Mary statue there reportedly weeps blood, and parishioners claim to have been healed by touching the tears."

"Unfortunately Em, the media is quick to confuse *mystery* with *miracle*. Headlines sell laundry detergent and toilet paper. As a man of faith, I do believe God makes all things possible." I understood the deep human need to believe in miracles, however I was also a scientist by training and inherently skeptical. "Why do you ask?"

"I'd really like to go. How about a road trip to St. Wenceslaus?"

"You?" I snickered. "A believer in supernatural phenomena?"

I watched her enthusiasm collapse. Emily usually wore a mask of courageous acceptance, but losing her vision had been a crushing blow. I prayed for her daily, though I'd learned that sometimes you make do with unanswered prayers.

"Hell Jake, I've been mauled by dozens of specialists with no improvement. What do I have to lose?"

"I just don't want you to get your hopes up." My inner skeptic was shouting that Emily's desire to regain her sight was like a wish tied to a helium balloon that would eventually explode in the atmosphere. "Every time someone waves a potato chip that vaguely resembles Jesus, the eleven o'clock news trucks come roaring into their driveway. The Church has debunked hundreds of so-called miracles."

"You always were the Sultan of Cynicism. What about the statue of Our Lady of Akita in Japan? It wept for over six years and bled from a wound on its hand for days. There were hundreds of witnesses and it was broadcast live on national television. Tests showed the tears and blood were not merely human, but of three different blood types." She banged her empty teacup down onto the tray. "How do you explain that, Jake?"

"Well I have to admit, you've done your homework. Listen, I'm not saying miracles don't occur, but *most* alleged miracles are fraudulent. The Vatican sets a very high bar and uses all the science available to disprove these claims. Our Lady of Akita is the only bleeding statue case recognized as miraculous by Rome, and that was after years of investigation."

"Come on, doctor, where's your scientific curiosity? Let's go investigate. Prove the claims bogus, if you can."

"Okay, let's check it out." I'd spent much of my day dealing with a dying baby and my sister's illness. A car ride on a beautiful summer's afternoon seemed like a great idea. "Let me call Justine and RJ first. If all is well at home, then I'm free for a few hours. Do you have time to leave right now?"

Emily nodded and slipped into an aristocratic British accent, one of many she'd acquired in high school drama class and perfected over time.

"Do fetch the limo, James. I shall meet you at the front door shortly for an outing in the country. Step to it, lad, and do not tarry."

CHAPTER TEN

Wednesday, July 26, 1:00 p.m.

When I called the rectory to check on Justine and RJ, Colleen answered.

"Everything's fine here, Father. Your sister and nephew went out for a walk, and I'm preparing a nice meal for this evening."

Thinking that Emily and I might have dinner after our visit to St. Wenceslaus, I said, "That's very kind of you. There's a chance I may be late, so please serve Justine and RJ if I don't arrive on time."

"Of course. But Father, your injuries! You're barely out of the hospital. It's home resting you should be, not tearing around like a dog on a hare. Isn't it hard enough for me to care for you now, let alone in a sick bed?"

Vintage Colleen. Was she concerned about my health or her workload? Life was never dull with her around. She was definitely one of a kind.

I thanked her, collected Emily at the entrance to the hospital, and rolled my dilapidated Toyota southeast along a two-lane country backroad flanked by cornfields, oily exhaust trailing behind us. A road trip with her after all these years brought back fond memories and reminded me just how much I'd missed her friendship over the years.

Emily inquired about the new Catechism classes at the church, and I asked her about the poetry therapy workshop that she taught at the hospital for grieving patients and families. She was a published poet and utilized writing as a technique to help others deal with the stress and fear associated with illness.

When our conversation lagged, I tuned the radio to a classic rock station and Emily sang along with golden oldies until we stopped for ice cream cones at a small Mom-and-Pop store in the middle of nowhere. As we placed our orders, her cellphone beckoned and she answered.

"Oh, hi Todd." A pause. "A concert? Absolutely! Sounds wonderful. It's a date."

Emily stepped a few paces away and lowered her voice.

"I'd love to go on a picnic, Todd, but I'm busy today. Thanks for thinking of me.

Another time, okay?" A smile. "You too. See you soon. Bye."

When I first returned to town, I'd been told that Emily was seeing someone. Once over coffee, she'd mentioned that she'd recently heard the Cleveland Orchestra perform at Severance Hall with *a close friend.* And why not? She was beautiful, smart, witty, and divorced. When I'd asked her if things were serious with her friend, she'd said no, she was still searching for Mr. Right. I wondered if *Todd* was trying hard to be Mr. Right.

I opened my mouth to enquire about him, but licked my ice cream cone instead. What right did I have to ask? What business was it of mine? None. No matter how I felt about her, *I was the one* who was unavailable.

We arrived at St. Wenceslaus parish twenty minutes later and parked in an empty asphalt lot peppered with potholes. The church was small, very old, and beautiful, constructed of blue granite with arched windows and a slate roof. Flowers lined both sides of the main entrance in a vibrant riot of colors.

Emily took my arm and we ascended stone steps that had been polished by the shoes of generations. I muscled open enormous oak doors, and we were welcomed by the faint scent of incense. Entering an empty church always felt mystical to me, like stepping into Heaven's foyer or God's waiting room.

Stained-glass light fell from a high window onto the crucifix, then tumbled down onto the altar. The Virgin Mary statue was elevated on a pedestal immediately to the left. We genuflected and walked over. Nearly every prayer candle at the foot of the statue was either burning or completely consumed. Their flickering light animated Mary's appearance as if she sensed our approach.

I stopped and said, "We're here, Em."

"What do you see?"

"The statue is life-sized and made of ceramic, with a few areas of chipped paint. The Holy Mother has a veil over her hair and appears to be gazing up at Heaven. She's wearing a white gown under an azure robe, which is open in the front, revealing the classic image of the Immaculate Heart. Her hands are folded in prayer position, and several rosaries have been hung from them."

"Is she weeping?"

I stepped closer.

"No sign of tears or blood. There's nothing unusual about the statue, but this is a very interesting church." I described the ornate stained glasswork, hand-hewn pews, sandstone floors, and enormous wooden crucifix over the altar. "It has a personality all its own and an early nineteenth-century quality."

I heard a voice from behind us say, "That it does, and you're close on the dates."

We turned to face a bandy-legged man in his mid-fifties, waif-thin, and barely five feet tall. A sprinkling of white stubble salted his chin, and pink scalp glistened through thinning ivory-colored hair. He wore round wire-rimmed glasses, blue jeans, and a red and black checkered lumberjack shirt with the sleeves rolled up. A carpenter's tool belt hung from his waist. He stepped forward and continued.

"It's the second oldest Catholic church in Ohio. Only the one in Somerset is older. And its personality is distinctly middle European. Czech, German, and Slovak immigrants who worked the local mills, stone quarries, and mines built it in 1820. Far from home, they wanted a parish where they could cherish their culture and speak their mother tongue without scorn."

He set a cardboard box on the front pew and extended a small, veined hand.

"I'm Father Marek, pastor and custodian of this little-known gem." He gestured proudly around the room. "I've been here thirty years keeping the doors open and guiding the faithful to the Promised Land. Excuse my duds. I'm in janitorial mode today."

"I'm Jacob Austin, and this is my friend, Ms. Beale," I replied, touching my Roman collar. "I'm filling in as pastor at Sacred Heart in Oberlin. And no apology is necessary. I live in my civvies whenever possible."

Emily released my arm, reached out a hand, and Marek shook it. "I'm Emily," she said. The gentle echo in the church made her name sound like a hymn. She gestured toward the statue. "We've heard a lot about what the Cleveland Plain Dealer called the *Miraculous Sorrows of Mary.* Curiosity got the best of me."

"Ah, the publicity. The press can't get enough. Well, I guess it's better than focusing on witchcraft or voodoo. Have to say, though, it fills the pews and the church coffers. Now I can finally afford to resurface the parking lot." He pointed to the cardboard carton and chuckled. "I have to replenish the Virgin's votive candles almost every day, and I may have to put in a bigger donation box."

Marek conjured up an impish grin.

"Listen" he said, cupping a hand behind one ear. "Listen to the glorious silence! It's rare these days that the church isn't chock-full of visitors. You just missed a busload of *pilgrims* from West Virginia."

Emily snapped her cane to full extension, tapped the floor, and stepped toward the statue.

"Father, what about all the stories we've heard concerning the Virgin?"

Marek sighed. "I hope you didn't come here expecting to feel the hand of God." He walked over to a movable stand above the statue, which held an emerald banner with gold letters reading PRAISE HER. He adjusted its position slightly so that the lone ceiling spotlight beam fell directly on the words. "Don't get me wrong. Something marvelous and extraordinary has been happening, but I've never personally witnessed the Virgin's . . . *Miraculous Sorrows*. And I certainly won't promise any miracles."

A telephone rang nearby.

"Excuse me, I've got to get that. I'm also the secretary here," he said, sauntering out of the church nave with a wide-based, somewhat unsteady gait.

Emily released a weighty sigh and leaned against me.

"I'm sorry I dragged you here, Jake. Thanks for humoring me and driving all this way. I don't know why I'm disappointed. *Marvelous and extraordinary* is actually more than I expected."

"It was no problem. I really enjoyed the pleasant drive and interesting diversion. Give me a second, Em, I want to light a prayer candle."

Whenever I saw a statue of Mary, I thought of my mother and said a prayer for her. She had not been a saint, but she'd done the best that she could raising me as a single parent. The crucifix above the altar always reminded me that although my biological father had deserted us when I was a child, at least I had a heavenly father who hadn't abandoned me. My mother's untimely death, however, had left me wandering without a compass until I found my way back to the Church.

I deposited two dollars in the collection box, lit one of the few remaining candles in my mother's memory, looked up at the Holy Virgin, and whispered, "Hail Mary, full of grace, the Lord is with thee. Blessed art thou —"

It was then that a thick red substance appeared on Mary's cheek.

CHAPTER ELEVEN

Wednesday, July 26, 3:00 p.m.
My heart was racing and my mind blank. I felt no sense of awe, skepticism, or anything else. I was totally numb and dumbfounded.

I must have gasped because Emily asked, "What is it, Jake? What's wrong?"

She swept her cane across the sandstone floor until she reached me and took my arm. I snapped out of my trance but didn't know what to say.

"Em, there's . . . a drop of blood. It appeared on Mary's cheek."

"Appeared? What do you mean by *appeared*?"

"Just that. It wasn't there and . . . then it was."

"How is that possible?"

Emily squeezed my arm, but I didn't look away from the Holy Mother. I couldn't. My attention was fixed on the crimson drop slowly rolling toward her lips.

"Jake, talk to me. Is this real? Did you witness . . . a miracle?"

"I'm not sure. There *has to be* a logical explanation." I studied the ceiling. It was quite high and earth-brown in color, supported by thick roughhewn beams. I saw no evidence of moisture or red staining. "Stay here, Em."

I scanned the empty church, skirted around the votive candles, and climbed up onto the low pedestal supporting the statue.

The substance was oozing down the Virgin's cheek too slowly to be colored water. I touched it. It felt lukewarm and sticky like blood. I brought my finger close to my nose but couldn't smell anything distinctive.

Although the statue was nearly my height and quite old, Mary's face was unmarked and intact. Her dark eyes seemed to follow me as I examined her. I saw no evidence of cracks, crevasses, or pits through which the material might have seeped.

"What are you doing up there? Get down this minute!" Father Marek lumbered up the main aisle toward us, clutching adjacent pews for balance. He stopped, fury reddening his face. "You of all people, Father, should know better!"

I climbed down from the pedestal, walked

over, and showed him my red-stained finger-tip, then pointed at the statue.

Marek's expression transformed from anger to confusion, then to recognition. "Praise God!" he exclaimed, crossing himself. "I'd begun to think Mary had forsaken us."

He suddenly slumped into a pew. His eyes drifted down and he whispered, "Lord, why today? I don't understand. Why now?"

It wasn't clear if he was talking to himself, me, or God.

"Father Marek, are you okay?"

He nodded. "Sorry. It's silly and . . . self-ish of me."

"What is?"

"It's just that . . . . Why you? Why now? You walk in, a complete stranger, yet I've been here all these years and she . . . I don't understand." He raised his gaze to mine, his eyelids puffy. Marek threw his hands up in frustration "I've given my life to the Lord and this parish. But the Holy Mother has never shown herself to me." He cradled his head in trembling hands for a moment, then stood. "Sorry. Forget it. I'm a foolish old man."

"Father Marek, have you reported this to Bishop Lucci?"

"Of course, several times. His Excellency,

however, is skeptical and too busy to be bothered with . . . my problem."

"Problem? Whatever I witnessed, *problem* is not the word I'd choose to describe it." I shook my head. "I was praying to Mary, looking directly at the statue when the blood simply . . . materialized."

"I know, I know." The flush had faded from Marek's complexion, but his eyes retained their sad, basset-hound appearance. "Exactly like the other times."

I heard the cane tapping behind me before Emily spoke. She had removed her sunglasses and her eyes were wide.

"Jake, is it really blood?"

"Good question. I'm not sure. Father Marek, have you had this substance analyzed?"

"Bishop Lucci did. It's definitely blood. Ask him. His people crawled all over the Virgin's statue, probing her, tearing my church apart for days. They were . . . downright sacrilegious." Marek's cheeks flared red again. "Believe me, this is no hoax. It's a sign from God!"

"What did the bishop tell you?"

"He said he'd get back to me, but never did. That's the way our fearless leader operates: say nothing, delay as long as possible, hope the hoopla will die down, and if need be, issue a vague statement. It worked. And Mary stopped revealing herself . . . until today. Truth be told, I don't think His Excellency believes a word I say, even though his own investigation confirmed that it was human blood. He loathes the publicity and isn't interested at all in my tiny church. Could you speak with him?"

"I may not be the right person to ask. My involvement could backfire, Father Marek." Lucci considered my medical practice a distraction from the priesthood, and the risk of a malpractice suit a threat to his treasury. He was also nervous about my troubled youth and background as a soldier. His Excellency detested waves of any kind, and I was a potential tsunami that might upend his ecclesiastical cruise to becoming a Cardinal. Only saving his life had removed me from the diocesan doghouse. "The bishop and I have . . . a love-hate relationship."

Marek popped a stick of gum in his mouth and stepped forward. I smelled alcohol on his breath before I caught the scent of peppermint.

"But you actually *witnessed* an occurrence," he said. "You're not some hysterical parishioner or publicity seeker. Lucci's *got to listen* to a priest. Please, tell him exactly what you saw."

As shaken as I was, there was no question that I had to report this to Church authorities.

"All right, Father Marek, I'll contact His Excellency."

"Thank you. I'd appreciate that. Bishop Lucci wants to close several churches, including St. Wenceslaus. It's all about money with him. He lives in a world of red and black ink. The possibility of a genuine miracle here, however, might delay his plan to shut us down."

Emily stepped between Marek and me.

"Jake, could you bless me . . . using the blood?"

Father Marek pretended not to hear her, walked to the front pew, opened the cardboard box, and began filling the candleholders.

I stared at my fingertip and my mind flashed back to the war. This wasn't the first time that I literally had blood on my hands. And as a physician, I worried about placing Emily at risk for hepatitis, HIV, or blood-borne toxins.

"I'm not sure that's a good idea, Em. We don't know for certain what this substance is, let alone whether it's dangerous or infectious. I don't want —"

"I'm begging you!" she said, her lips

93

trembling. Her soft blue eyes wandered over my shoulder as her desperation washed over me. "Please, Jake, anoint me with the blood. I have nothing left to lose."

She was wrong. Although she was blind, she'd built a thriving, productive life with a family, friends, and plenty at stake. And the recent rebirth of our relationship meant I also had something to lose.

When I didn't respond, anger scudded across her face like a storm cloud, and she stamped a foot. "Damn it, Jake. For the love of God, do it for me!"

While the substance didn't burn my skin and I didn't feel ill, the last thing I wanted to do was endanger her in any way.

A tear rolled down her check and my resolve melted.

"Okay, Em. For you."

I touched her forehead and anointed a tiny cross below her hairline as I recited, "In the name of the Father, and of the Son, and of the Holy Spirit." I considered daubing her eyelids or near her lips, but they were open portals to infection so I stopped, hoping I hadn't already crossed too many medical and religious lines.

This satisfied her, yet only added to my frustration and concerns.

Bleeding statues. Dying babies. My sister,

and what remained of my family, fading away with each passing day. The desperate need for miracles, both scientific and supernatural. Christ!

It was bad enough that Tina and Miguel were praying for a miracle for their baby, Dr. Taylor was searching for a medical one, and my sister desperately needed both. Now with no medical options available, my dearest friend had staked all her hope on the longest of long shots — divine intervention. How in the world had I been sucked into the vortex of all these storms? And what would be left standing when these tempests had passed?

CHAPTER TWELVE

Wednesday, July 26, 4:00 p.m.
I carefully wiped the blood-red substance from my thumb and forefinger onto the corner of my handkerchief and placed it in my pocket for further examination. As we walked from the subdued stained-glass luster of St. Wenceslaus Church into glaring sunlight, Emily slipped on her sunglasses. Mine were in the car, which felt like an oven when we got inside. The steering wheel was hot enough to cauterize flesh, searing the palms of my hands. I cranked up the air conditioner, threw the car into gear, and bounced us across potholes as we left the parking lot.

Needing to process what I'd seen, I did not speak. Emily eyes were closed, lips moving as she prayed silently. When we were children, she and I had attended Parish School of Religion classes together, what people call Sunday school. I'd been the PSR class reprobate, taunting the nuns with questions and wisecracks, and telling dirty jokes in the boy's room on breaks. Emily had been the teacher's pet and much more devout than I.

My head told me that I'd seen some sort of scam, but my heart yearned for a miraculous cure for Emily's blindness. Hopefully, the Lord would hear her prayers in either case.

I should have called the bishop immediately and reported what I'd witnessed, but I needed to assess what I'd seen and organize my thoughts first. Approaching Lucci was like walking through a minefield. It didn't take much to detonate His Excellency. I also wanted time to research weeping statues and fraudulent miracles.

As we approached Lorain County on Rt. 90, rush hour traffic became a hot-tempered boil that thickened and curdled, and orange construction barrels turned the road into a labyrinth. The deadly combination of senior citizens dawdling in the left lane combined with impatient teenaged drivers and exhausted employees weaving their way home from work converted the drive into a Dodge-Em amusement park ride. My fingers ached from clenching the wheel, and my neck muscles cramped and went into spasm. Not wanting to be one of the bumper cars, I exited the interstate and took what I hoped would be a shortcut on a two lane country road.

Finally, Emily removed her sunglasses and spoke.

"Could this be real, Jake?" Her voice was distant and as vacant as her sightless eyes. There was a plaintive edge to her question and a yearning that cut like a razor. "Was the Virgin's statue actually bleeding?"

Faith could leap wide chasms and hope was a powerful panacea. We all possessed a deep human hunger for mystery and miracles. I had no doubt what she wanted my answer to be, but the Jesuits at Xavier University had taught me to be a critical thinker, and I couldn't lie to her.

"You have to understand that most of these cases have logical explanations, Em, or are frauds perpetrated by desperate or devious people."

Back in school, she had always been a glass-half-full optimist, while my glass had been half-empty, cracked, and leaking. I didn't want to hurt her, but I did want to gently dispel the mist from her mysticism — so her disappointment would be less if this *miracle* was proven to be a hoax.

She parried with, "What about Our Lady

of Akita?"

"That's the rare exception. Simple condensation trapped in the microscopic cracks of old ceramic figurines cause most cases of apparent weeping."

"Those tears aren't sticky or red, Jake."

"True, although in one scam, a Madonna icon's so-called *blood* was an exact match to Glidden's candy-apple red paint. In others, religious zealots put their own blood on statues or paintings. That couldn't have happened today with me watching, but it's unlikely we witnessed a true miracle. That said, I'm going to push Bishop Lucci for a thorough investigation."

This was clearly not what Emily had wanted to hear. She ran a finger along the earpiece of her sunglasses, then nibbled the arm. I'd seen her do this whenever she was upset. It was her *tell.* She would have made a lousy poker player.

Hope slowly faded from her face, and I felt like a bully who'd taken a little girl's lunch money.

I switched topics. "Did you notice anything unusual in the church, Em?"

Since her loss of vision, her other senses had become heightened. She could hear whispered conversations across crowded rooms, perceive the world through her fingertips, and deduce the origin of wine by taste and smell alone.

"Unusual? What do you mean?"

"Aromas, sounds, anything out of the ordinary."

"Not really. Just the scent of incense, some creaking roof rafters, and the burbling of a coffeemaker somewhere nearby. Why, Jake?"

"Some witnesses have reported the fragrance of roses associated with miracles."

Emily touched the tiny crimson cross I'd anointed on her forehead and brought her finger to her nose.

"Definitely not roses. It smells metallic to me, faintly of copper or iron. Similar to a butcher shop. I think it's blood."

I wasn't sure if her conclusion reflected her highly-refined sense of smell or the desperate desire for the return of her vision.

"That's exactly the *problem,* Em. We were at the church a long time and we've been driving for an hour, and it still hasn't clotted. That doesn't sound like blood to me, but I'll have it tested."

Emily grew mute. I was afraid that I'd dumped her hope in a coffin constructed of logic and driven in the final nail. Feeling like hell, I transferred my self-loathing to the grayheaded geezer doing twenty miles per hour ahead of me in his huge battleship of a car, converting my shortcut into a near roadblock. I thought about crossing the double yellow lines and passing illegally. Instead, we crept past soy and corn fields, farm ponds, and the occasional stop sign peppered with .22 caliber holes until he finally turned into a driveway and I gunned the engine. When we arrived at the hospital, Emily and I said our goodbyes, and I headed back to rectory, my mind filled with more questions than answers.

CHAPTER THIRTEEN

Wednesday, July 26, 5:30 p.m.

On the drive back to the rectory, I called Tree Macon's mobile phone, explained what I'd witnessed at St. Wenceslaus, and asked for his help.

"Blood? Heck, that's easy, buddy. I'm wrapping things up here at the station house. Stop by and we'll test it."

Five minutes later, I pulled into the police department parking lot. When I entered, Tree directed me into a small room with a Ridgid Tool Company calendar hanging on the wall. Miss July was very well equipped with her power drill, hard hat, and string bikini.

As Tree prepared the Luminol, I stared at the angry, raised growth on his neck, hoping he'd made an appointment to see a dermatologist.

When he was done, Tree flipped off the room light and sprayed the soluton on part of the red stain. The corner of my hankie glowed blue.

"Consistent with blood, Jake, but it doesn't rule out other possibilities like an animal source."

"Could you run it for DNA?"

He laughed. "Now I've heard everything."

"I doubt it, Tree. The century's still young."

"Sorry, buddy. You just wandered completely off the reservation into la-la land. The crime lab's understaffed, underfunded, and under pressure to solve major crimes. Unless there's a rape or a dead body involved, no cop is going to give you the time of day."

I sighed and changed the subject.

"Any luck finding my old man? Justine's fading fast, and I'm not a great match for her transplant. Dear old dad might give her a much better chance of survival."

"Nope, not yet, but the scuttlebutt around New Orleans is your daddy's very friendly with some mob guys there. That upgrades him to a person of interest, so I assigned my best I.T. officer, Shirley Kadu, to search for him. If he has a paper trail, she'll find it."

Tree handed me my handkerchief and draped a big arm over my shoulders.

"Keep the faith, Father, Shirley is one persistent lady. Her folks moved here from Mumbai and run the Seven-Eleven in town, but she's way too smart to be working as a counterjockey. Kadu's the best I've ever seen with a computer. Hell, when we busted a local bookie, the guy blew a hole through the motherboard of his P.C. with his Thirty Eight, but she reconstructed enough data to put him away. Shirley will probably be my boss in a few months. Here at the cop shop we call her *Sure Can-do.*"

"Thanks, Tree. I appreciate all your help. You're a prince."

"Funny, my wife thinks I'm a frog."

We shook hands and I returned to the rectory, hoping that Officer Kadu would live up to her nickname.

At supper, RJ entertained us with a lengthy description of a cartoon show he'd seen on TV, replete with talking dogs, magic, and ghosts. I enjoyed his enthusiasm but Justine barely cracked a smile. She appeared haggard and sported a large, angry plum-colored bruise on her left arm that I'd never seen before. It scared the hell out of me. When she complained about pain in her knee and thigh, I feared ongoing bone marrow destruction and wasn't sure that she would even make it to next week's hospital admission.

I had played the good-natured, long-suffering priest long enough. Time to track down Dr. Taylor, get pushy, and call in favors. He had leaned on me for help in the SIDS case; now it was payback time.

After Justine tucked RJ into bed, she made a cup of tea and joined me in the living room for a chat. I hadn't known that she and her son existed until a few weeks earlier, and we were still getting acquainted.

I'd been without family for so long that their presence in my life was a joy, though a fragile one. Everyone's deck contained a couple of cards that read Game Over, capable of clearing all the chips from life's table. Because Justine had drawn the leukemia card, my time with her was bittersweet. Family was a gift, and like Emily's vision, it could be lost — in the blink of an eye.

Justine related an amusing tale about her first day in kindergarten, and then it was my turn. She had been raised as a devout agnostic and I hesitated to reveal what I'd witnessed at St. Wenceslaus. I remembered the glimmer of hope on Emily's face when I blessed her with the blood, however, and relented.

"Bleeding statues? Are you kidding me, Jake? And I don't even begin to understand the whole Virgin-Mary-worship thing. Shoot, no wonder they fed you people to the lions. I'll take my chances with quack doctors who only *think* that they are god."

Justine leaned back, then added, "What if there is no God? Maybe this world is as close to heaven as we get. What then, Father?"

"Well, for starters, there will be a lot of very disappointed priests. But the real question, Sis, is . . . *what if there is*?"

Having barely managed a stalemate, I retreated from theology and told her stories of my teenaged rebellion, my brief stint in the Army, and my reconciliation with God, trying to bridge our thirty year separation. I focused on humorous memories, saving my darker tales for brighter days.

She entertained me with a funny story about dating, then segued to her own wild-child youth. Her tone turned somber when she described her fling with a married man that resulted in RJ. The guy wanted nothing to do with her or a child. Instead, he gave her money for an abortion and shut her out of his life.

Justine trembled as she described her struggles as a single mother. She produced the scented hankie embroidered with lavender flowers that she always carried and dabbed away her tears. I took her hand and held it. She didn't pull away. Finally, out of words and energy, she finished her tea, kissed me on the cheek, and retired to her room.

After she'd gone, I listened to the unnerving stillness of the rectory and pondered the long odds of Justine's survival if Tree Macon couldn't locate my old man. Worries and doubts engulfed me, and I began to slip into one of those lunar eclipses of the soul that everyone has, including clergy. Although priests spend the day trying to spread the light, every now and then we search for it in the solitude of the night.

Before the quicksand of melancholy could suck me under, I scurried to my study, booted up the computer, and busied myself researching miracles involving statues. I confirmed Emily's account about Our Lady of Akita. In addition to blood on the statue, a painful laceration in the shape of a cross developed on the hand of a nun, Sister Agnes, a Buddhist convert. Agnes claimed that the Virgin Mary appeared to her in 1973 and made two predictions: that the Almighty's anger over earthly evils could only be appeased by prayer and penance, and that Agnes's complete deafness would be cured. The documentation was extensive and compelling. After eight years of investigation, the Holy Office finally gave its ecumenical approval to the miracle. Agnes unexpectedly regained her hearing in 1982.

The number of cases that the Church had *disproven,* however, was staggering. The myriad ways of faking tears and the ingenuity of the perpetrators made my head ache. Do-it-yourself weeping statue kits were even for sale on the internet.

I gave up, swallowed two aspirins, prayed The Liturgy of the Hours from my breviary, and fell into a restless sleep.

CHAPTER FOURTEEN

Thursday, July 27, 10:15 a.m.

I was brewing a pot of coffee after morning Mass when RJ flew a green-plastic jet into the kitchen. He landed his plane on the table with a loud *varoom* and said, "Whatcha doing, Uncle Jake?"

I'd never thought that I would ever be an *uncle* but had already come to love the sound of the word — and my nephew.

"Making coffee."

"How?"

"Well, first you chop the beans into tiny pieces." I showed him a handful, put them in the grinder, and turned it on. "Then you put them in the coffee maker and it pours hot water over them and poof, coffee comes out here." I took a sip from my cup. "And like magic, the coffee makes me wide awake and ready for action."

RJ tilted his head to the side, pondered my explanation with a puzzled expression, then grinned.

"Oh, I get it, Uncle Jake. They're . . . *magic* beans. You know, like Jack and the Beanstalk. Cool."

I laughed, but before I could delve further into the wonders of the four year old mind, he flew his jet into the living room to join his mother, filling the rectory with explosions and machine gun fire. Clearly, the little general needed some more constructive and less violent toys and games.

I went up to my study to finish my research on fraudulent miracles, closed the door, and spent a few minutes staring out of the window, wondering what I would do if I were in Father Marek's shoes.

The fact that the bishop had resisted Marek's claims of a miracle was no surprise. Organized religion was not unlike the medical establishment; both produced red tape and bureaucrats much faster than results. Lucci may have weighed the risks to his career verses the benefits. He was a rung-climber who desired to rule over his fiefdom in peace until a bigger and better empire came along. Cleveland was a mere pit stop on his journey.

I knew that St. Joseph's Hospital was strapped for cash and the lab wouldn't run expensive tests on the material I'd collected on my handkerchief, so I needed Lucci's help. I dialed his office and did a song and dance to get past his secretary.

"Jacob, my son. How nice of you to call. I was just thinking of you."

Saving Lucci's life had temporarily transformed me from an S.O.B. to a favorite *son*. While I still had his approval and his ear, I described what I'd witnessed at St. Wenceslaus Church.

His voice took on an icy edge. "Father Marek and his holy-roller circus! Exactly what I don't need . . . another distraction. I should have shut that parish down years ago for lack of parishioners and funds. With the recent publicity, now I can't. Marek's a cagey old fox, Jacob. He probably put the blood on the statue as a ploy to keep the church doors open. Please don't spread more rumors of *miracles* in my diocese."

"Your Excellency, you don't understand. I was looking directly at the Virgin Mary when a red substance appeared below her left eye. He couldn't have put it there. Marek wasn't anywhere near the altar. He'd left the room to answer a phone call."

Lucci was quiet for so long that I thought my cellphone had dropped the call.

"So, you believe this might really be a miracle, Jacob?"

"No, I believe this occurrence needs to be evaluated. The substance is consistent with blood, but it needs further analysis to determine if it's human . . . and to exclude Father Marek as the source."

"Oh, it's human blood, and definitely not Marek's. I had it analyzed. Two of my priests spent a week examining every inch of the church. They even x-rayed the statue and found no explanation. No hidden compartments or tampering of any kind."

"Doesn't that suggest that this might be a true miracle? Why are you so skeptical, Your Excellency?"

"I'm not, I'm . . . reluctant. The Church has always underplayed these events publicly, because the vast majority prove to be either fraudulent or due to natural causes, like old pipes dripping rust-colored water. I would prefer that Catholics base their faith on Jesus Christ, rather than . . . extraordinary occurrences." Lucci released a weary sigh. "I've prayed on the situation a great deal. No one wants this to be an authentic miracle more than I do, but I'm also practical, realistic, and very suspicious. The Cardinal knows Father Marek to be a heavy drinker, and *His Eminence* is skeptical. We . . . consider him unreliable.

Ah, the royal "we." The Cardinal was

112

Lucci's boss. Enter the church pecking order and politics.

The bishop took a slurp of something. "Anyway, how are you feeling, Jacob. Are your injuries any better?"

"I'm fine, thanks," I said, massaging my right ribs.

"And how's your sister? I've been praying for you both."

"Thank you for your prayers and for asking. Justine's barely hanging on. They're admitting her to the hospital next week. I didn't want to interfere with my duties at Sacred Heart, so I've arranged for the rectory housekeeper to help care for my nephew until Justine recovers. But the cost may devastate the parish finances." I swallowed hard. "She'll need to be paid, and I don't have much money of my own. Is there anyway the Diocese could subsidize Sacred Heart during my family crisis?"

Spending money, Lucci's least favorite subject. His usual officious tone replaced the empathy in his voice.

"The diocese already provides you with room and board, my boy. Can't your Camillian Order cover the cost?"

"I've made the request, but they didn't sound encouraging. Being as you are friends with my Superior General, I'd appreciate it

113

if you'd ask on my behalf."

The Very Reverend Father Stefano Demarco ran my Camillian Order. He was on the Vatican fast-track and a rising star in the Church, with access to the Pope's ear and maybe God's. He and Lucci had earned their doctorates together as seminarians at the Gregorian in Rome. The bishop had hitched his ecclesiastical ascent to Demarco's coattails, and I was sure that the last thing he wanted to do was to bother the Superior General over petty cash.

Another slurp.

"I don't know. My budget is tight as it is. Here's an idea. The priests who investigated Marek's so-called miracle didn't have your scientific background. Tell you what, Jacob. Use your training to prove Marek to be the fraud that I believe him to be, and the diocese will cover the cost of your housekeeper's overtime during your sister's illness. I will also finance any ancillary services you require, like X-ray and lab testing."

Lucci paused and cleared his throat.

"Come to think of it, Jacob, you're a perfect choice for the job. The priests I sent were bullied by Marek, which may have limited their investigation. Given your effort to save my life during *the incident,* I doubt that his intimidation will work on you."

"Intimidation? Marek? Did he threaten them?"

"Not in so many words. He obstructed their efforts, and every time they drove there, they had . . . car trouble. A tire punctured by a nail, engine problems, a shattered windshield. Some of their equipment mysteriously vanished. Marek's doing, no doubt, but we couldn't prove it."

My turn to hesitate.

"Do we have a deal, Jacob? You help with Marek and the diocese will cover the additional cost while your sister recovers."

I needed Lucci's help and was drop-to-my-knees grateful to get it, but it sounded like His Deviousness was pressuring me into undermining St. Wenceslaus parish in exchange for helping my family.

Two, however, could play the manipulation game.

"Yes, we have a deal. Thank you."

"Wonderful. Keep me posted on your progress. And remember, Jacob, the outcome of your inquiry is very important to me."

"I can assure you, Your Excellency, that I will conduct a thorough investigation on your behalf."

And an unbiased one.

CHAPTER FIFTEEN

Thursday, July 27, 12:30 p.m.

After my conversation with Bishop Lucci, I enjoyed a pleasant lunch with Justine and RJ, then checked the parish mail, which consisted mostly of bills. I signed a marriage certificate and other sacramental records, tweaked my Sunday sermon, then met briefly with Mrs. Burton about her wayward husband, who preferred to donate his money to the racetrack instead of his family. As I escorted her out of the front door, a raspy barking noise startled me. I poked my head into the living room where Colleen was cleaning just as she was seized by another coughing fit.

I steeped a cup of Earl Gray for her in the kitchen and considered how best to handle the situation. Justine's leukemia made her extremely susceptible to contagion. If she developed a fever or the flu, her bone marrow transplant would be postponed, which itself might be a death sentence given her rapidly failing health. And in her condition, any infection, no matter how minor, could kill her.

Placing a lemon wedge and sugar packet on the saucer, I reentered the living room, offered Colleen the tea, and said, "Poor thing, you sound awful. Allergies?"

"Thank you. That's very kind of you, Father." She took the cup. "No, no. Not allergies. It's a little cold, that's all. Nothing to worry about."

My mind filled with worries.

"Colleen, you appear exhausted. We've been working you too hard. You should get some rest."

She released a phlegmy cough, deep and damp. "No need to fret. I'll be fit as a fiddle in a day or two."

A little cold or Bubonic plague — the outcome was the same for my sister, and in a day or two Justine could be dead. I conjured up my concerned physician expression.

"That sounds more like early pneumonia than a cold. Let me get my stethoscope and have a listen to your chest."

She looked at me as if I had suggested stripping her stark naked in front of the entire parish.

"That won't be necessary. Thank you all the same, Father. I'll be fine. Just let me be."

"Okay, but allow me to write you a prescription for an antibiotic. And I want you to take a week off."

Her cheeks reddened and she scowled. "I'll not be shirking my duties!"

"I *insist*, Colleen," I said, then explained the danger that infection posed to Justine as tactfully as I could.

"But Father —"

"No buts. Think of it as a vacation, with pay of course. We'll manage here till you come back. Besides, when Justine is in the hospital, I'll need your assistance a lot more."

She thought about it, then brightened. "Well, 'tis true I've not had a holiday in ages."

"I spoke with Bishop Lucci, and he's agreed to pay you for helping to care for RJ."

She smiled, an occurrence as rare as a blue moon. "Well now, isn't that grand!" She produced a handkerchief from her apron pocket, blew her nose, and peeked at its contents. Apparently finding nothing of interest, she placed it back in her pocket. "My sister's husband passed away three months ago, and I've been sending her money to help out. My purse is now as empty as a dullard's mind, and I do need the income. And it would be delightful to visit her for a few days. Okay, Father. I'll see you in a week then. Call me if you need anything."

Scribbling a prescription for her, I hustled Colleen out of the front door. No doubt her coughing had already scattered bacteria throughout the rectory, and I wanted to wipe the entire place down with disinfectant and fill the air with Lysol spray. But the dice had already left the cup. I prayed that they wouldn't come up snake eyes for my sister.

Losing Colleen's help, however, meant that Justine and I would have to shoulder the burden of riding herd over a four year old with the energy of a young colt. My time was already stretched very thin, and I wasn't sure my sister could handle the added strain. I began calling parishioners, enquiring about local childcare options and babysitters. If I couldn't find an acceptable solution soon, I'd somehow have to make time in my day to take the load off of my sister.

I played with RJ until it was time for his nap, then took the opportunity to drive to the St. Joseph's Hospital laboratory. Handing my handkerchief to the head lab tech, I told her what tests I required and exactly what I needed to know, including whether the source of the blood was human and what blood type. She grumbled about the added workload but didn't resist. Bishop Lucci's command to cooperate had already come down from on high, and at a Catholic hospital it carried considerable clout.

Dr. Taylor was unlocking the door of a sleek, black Mercedes as I reentered the parking garage. At a distance, his Pillsbury Doughboy physique was easy to spot. Seizing the opportunity, I called, "Marcus, a moment please."

I described Justine's worsening symptoms, emphasizing her weight loss, night sweats, intermittent fever, bruising, and fatigue.

"I'm sorry to have to ask this. Please urge your brother to use his influence at the Cleveland Clinic to get her admitted sooner than the end of next week. She's dying before my eyes and . . . I feel completely helpless." I dropped my gaze. "Please, Marcus. I have nowhere else to turn."

He went quiet for a moment, then said, "I'll see what I can do, Jake. No promises."

I wanted to say, *Come on, you owe me for the SIDS case,* but instead I said, "Thank you. I understand. How's baby Pablo?"

"Vegetative. I've tried everything I can

think of, yet I can't find a single damn rabbit in my hat." His shoulders slumped. "I'm failing the boy."

"No, Marcus, you're doing all that you can do. You knew it was a long shot when EMS brought him in."

"It's just that . . . I *hate* losing children." He sighed. "And those parents! They're unbelievable."

"Why? What happened?"

"When I spoke with them and raised the possibility that Pablo's lack of response to therapy may indicate irreparable brain damage, all hell broke loose. The mother jumped up and suggested that it might be time to shut off the respirator and donate her baby's organs." Taylor leaned against his car and shook his head. "Then the boy's father went ballistic and started screaming at her about mercy killing being an abomination against God. Out of nowhere, Pablo's dad whirled, shoved his finger in my face, and threatened to sue me! The guy was growling like an animal, and smelled like a brewery."

Taylor opened the door to his car and continued. "Hell, it's only mid-afternoon and *I'm the one* who needs a stiff drink. I know the child had cerebral palsy before this happened and that both parents are under a terrible strain, but damn! I tried to calm them down and explain that I still had to do further testing before any decisions could be made. They didn't hear a single word. I may have to get the Psych Department and hospital lawyer involved. Would you speak with them about their religious concerns?"

"Of course, Marcus."

Taylor eased his enormous bulk into his car, slammed the door, and rolled down the window. "And not to worry, Jake. I'll call my brother at the Clinic and see if he can get your sister admitted sooner."

I sagged against a concrete pillar as his Mercedes purred down the parking garage ramp, leaving me alone with my thoughts.

CHAPTER SIXTEEN

Thursday, July 27, 3:30 p.m.
With Colleen on mandatory vacation because of her cold, all household chores fell to me. Justine could barely get through the day caring for RJ, and I couldn't ask her for help. I didn't mind though, because my temporary leave of absence from the hospital gave me more free time than I'd had in years.

On my way back to the rectory, I stopped at a grocery store and grabbed bread, sandwich meat, a few microwavable meals, milk, and Lucky Charms cereal for RJ. I tossed a six-pack of Molson's Ale into the shopping cart and proceeded to checkout.

I don't enjoy cooking and I'm not good at it, so I picked up a large pepperoni pizza and antipasto salad for dinner at a local restaurant. After lighting the candles on the dining room table, I loaded my CD player with Simon and Garfunkel's Greatest Hits as background music, and enjoyed a quiet dinner with my new family. For most of my adult life, the idea of *family* had been an abstract concept, but I had quickly grown quite fond of the notion.

My sister again ate very little, complaining of stomach pain and nausea. I wanted to examine her abdomen to be certain her liver and spleen were not enlarging, but the poor woman was already frightened out of her mind. As Art Garfunkel sang about bridging troubled waters, I could almost hear her leukemia clock ticking to the beat.

After dinner, Justine said that she was exhausted and asked if I would mind giving RJ a bath and putting him to bed.

I gave her a thumbs up. She walked toward the stairs, then turned and said, "And tomorrow, I'll pick the music. Something from my generation. I'm not quite as ancient as you are, *Father Time.* How about some Melissa Manchester or Red Hot Chili Peppers?" She tilted her head to the side and grinned. "Maybe R.E.M.'s 'Losing My Religion.' That okay with you — Father?"

Anything Justine did was fine with me. I even enjoyed our verbal jousting.

"Now that I've gotten to know you better, I would have guessed that something by Twisted Sister was more your style."

She laughed for the first time that evening and disappeared slowly up the stairs.

I soon found that bathing a rambunctious four year old boy was surprisingly difficult. The uncle gig was much easier than babysitting. RJ's hands became submarines and seaplanes, soaking the bathroom floor and covering me in shampoo, and toweling him off was about as easy as drying a wet cat. I had to chase the naked, pint-sized cyclone around before I could wrangle him into his Sesame Street pajamas.

When I offered to read a bedtime story, RJ grabbed a dogeared copy of Dr. Seuss's *The Cat in the Hat.* Apparently, I wasn't the only doctor in his life. I caved repeatedly to his pleadings and read much later than I should have, finally managing to tuck the rascal into bed and get him to sleep.

I'm not sure which of us had more fun, although by the time I got downstairs I felt as if I'd just finished a night on-call at the hospital. Popping the top on a Molson's, I flopped onto the living room sofa and tuned in to the baseball game. The Indians' usual summer swoon was fast becoming a deep coma. The Tribe was hopelessly behind by the fifth inning and I turned off the television.

I was sipping on my beer and mindlessly

staring out the window at passing traffic when I heard tapping on the glass pane. I couldn't see anyone, so I got up and cautiously edged closer. The tapping came again and a crow hopped along the sill. His feathers were as shiny as black glass. As a child, my grandmother had told me in her Old World accent that a bird tapping at the window was a sign of death. I, of course, didn't believe that kind of superstitious nonsense, but the sight of the crow carried my thoughts back to Pablo's vegetative state.

The contrast between my nephew and Pablo was stark. While RJ was safely tucked away in his bed with his stuffed animals and ratty old blankie, baby Pablo was tethered to monitors and machines in the PICU. The similarities, however, were terrifying. Both of them and every one of us, including Justine, clung to this world by our fingernails. Only God's tender mercy could keep us safe from the irrational whims of fate.

I remembered Dr. Taylor's request that I speak with Tina and Miguel about organ donation and autopsies. As the crow pecked an urgent rhythm on the window pane, I began to dial their number, then decided that it was too late in the evening to phone them.

Miguel attended Mass regularly, so I

wasn't surprised that he might balk at terminating life support and organ donation on religious grounds. I had more trouble with Tina's easy acceptance of the idea. Usually it takes time and considerable persuasion for parents to face hard choices about their children. Maybe she was mentally and physically exhausted and unable to deal any longer with the crisis, or maybe she merely wanted part of her child to live on, but I didn't like the other possibilities floating around in my head. They were disturbing enough that I started to punch Tree Macon's phone number into my cell. I hesitated.

Did I really want to unleash the police hounds on this unfortunate couple? What evidence did I have? Did I owe them my confidentiality as a clergyman? As a physician?

I took another sip of beer and stared out the window. The crow stopped pecking and eye-balled me intently as if waiting to see what I would decide. Technically, Miguel and Tina were not my patients and they had confessed nothing to me as a priest. I dove through the small loophole and dialed.

"Hey, Tree. Are you watching the game?"

"That's no game. It's a massacre. Glad you called though. I spoke with a Louisiana vice cop who thinks your father may be tied to drug trafficking in The Big Sleazy. Not good. If we do locate him, he may end up in jail and be unable or unwilling to help your sister."

I was disappointed but not surprised. "I don't care if he's the spawn of Satan, drag his tail back here. Soon. Justine needs his bone marrow, and I'd be happy to personally suck out every drop!" I took a long draw of Molson's and refocused. "Anything new on the couple with the SIDS baby?"

"Funny you should ask, buddy. Guess what? They moved here not long ago from Pennsylvania and get this, they lost their first baby two years ago — wait for it — to a sudden infant death. A four month old girl."

I wondered why Dr. Taylor hadn't mentioned that. Perhaps it hadn't seemed relevant in the chaos of treating a dying infant, or maybe the admitting intern hadn't taken a family history. Or maybe the parents had chosen not to disclose that information.

"Jake, hello? You still with me?"

"Sorry, Tree. I'm listening."

"Anyway, two kids, same problem. Pretty damn suspicious if you ask me, but not *proof* of anything. The only past dirt I found on Mommy is a speeding ticket. Hell, my grandma has a longer rap sheet than that. Daddy, however, is not so clean. I like him as the doer. The guy's got a history of boozing, bar brawls, and DUIs."

"Heck Tree, so did I back in the day, before I finally got my shi . . . ah, poop in a group."

"Yeah well, there's no evidence that Miguel has gotten *his shit* together. Their apartment smelled like a beer hall and looked like a landfill. What I need is an excuse to drag his sorry ass to the station and read him his rights."

"Easy, big guy. Most of the time, sudden infant deaths occur with no indication of wrongdoing or known cause."

"Two dead kids in one family? I told you before, Jake, I don't believe in the tooth fairy, unicorns, or coincidences. Does their son show any medical evidence of child abuse?"

"I spoke with Dr. Taylor today and he didn't mention anything like that. He did say that Pablo initially appeared normal but developmental delays began appearing around nine months of age, which the pediatrician thought was probably due to cerebral palsy from birth trauma. I'll see what I can find out."

"Appreciate it. The doctors aren't likely to

talk to me, what with patient privacy rules and all." Tree paused. "So, why'd you call? What's up?"

"I wanted you to know that Tina brought up the possibility of pulling the plug on Pablo and donating his organs. That's very unusual."

"Brain damage, huh? So maybe Pablo's a burden on his parents? A little caring euthanasia to ease the boy's suffering and end the financial drain? That sure as hell casts a different light on things. I'll check the details of the first baby's death. Thanks, Jake. Call me if you hear anything else."

I considered opening another beer but headed upstairs instead. Sleep did not come easily.

CHAPTER SEVENTEEN

Friday, July 28, 9:45 a.m.

By the time I returned from morning Mass, Justine and RJ had already had breakfast and relocated to the living room. My sister was reading on the couch and my nephew sat on the floor in front of the television, mesmerized by colorful, talking cartoon fish.

I grabbed a coffee, said good morning, and kissed RJ on the top of his head. Although the rectory was warm, Justine shivered. I walked over and touched her forehead but she didn't feel feverish.

She pushed my hand away. "Stop it, Jake." Justine had made it clear that she was tired of my *hovering like a damn turkey vulture.*

There was also a new rash on her forearm that looked like a cluster of petechiae, tiny red spots caused by the rupture of capillaries in the skin. She needed to be admitted to the hospital soon, but I didn't think I could push Dr. Taylor any more without alienating him.

I retreated to my study, called Miguel and Tina's apartment, and got their answering machine. Tina was either working or at the hospital with Pablo, and Miguel was most likely sleeping after his night shift at the factory. I left a message asking to speak with them this weekend, along with the number of my mobile phone.

Shuffling through my snail-mail, I compared three quotes to repair a small leak in the church roof, decided to give the lowest bidder the contract, and downloaded my email. In addition to the usual medical conference notices, church-related correspondence, and spam, I received a nasty note from the hospital complaining about several charts that I'd failed to complete. There is no sin more grievous to administrators than unfinished paperwork, and an irritated pencil pusher can make a doctor's life hell. I checked my calendar and for once my schedule was wide open. Talk about miracles!

When I asked Justine if she was well enough to hold the fort until suppertime while I ran errands, she replied that she was fine, gave me *the look,* and again told me to stop hovering. I slipped on a pair of jeans and a Polo shirt, threw my camera and a few other things into my backpack, and trekked to St. Joe's record room.

Sign here, initial there, scribble a note, and voila — the hospital bureaucrats were back in compliance heaven. The practice of medicine was like going to the bathroom — the job wasn't done until you completed the paperwork.

As I finished the last chart, Dr. Taylor wandered in. We exchanged greetings.

"Marcus, I've been thinking about that couple you asked me to counsel. Does their son show any evidence of child abuse or Shaken Baby Syndrome?"

"Nope. The Silverman x-ray series was completely negative for fractures of differing ages. His CT brain scan showed no subdural hematomas or shear injuries. Why do you ask?"

Not wanting to reveal my involvement with the police, I said, "Guess I've had too much time off and my imagination's running wild. How's Pablo doing?"

"I just finished examining him and I'm not sure, but I think there were subtle signs of improvement today. It might be wishful thinking on my part. At least for the time being, I can postpone any further discussion of terminating his life support."

Although I wanted to bring up my sister's

deteriorating condition, I'd already pushed Taylor hard yesterday about an early admission, so I let it slide.

"I'm on my way to the hospital chapel," I said pointing heavenward. "I'll put in a good word with my boss."

"Thanks. Pablo and I could use a little help from above."

When I arrived, I knelt in the first pew and prayed for Justine, baby Pablo, and my departed mother, then retired to the privacy of the sacristy and phoned Tree Macon. I got his voicemail and left a message that Dr. Taylor had found no evidence of child abuse.

The sound of weeping drifted in from the chapel, and I peeked out. Rabbi Epstein was comforting an elderly couple. I couldn't hear his words, but their expressions made my heart ache. A distraught silver-haired woman trembled violently, and an elderly man wrapped his sport coat around her like a shawl and took her in his arms. She buried her face in his chest.

Our small chapel was a refuge for people of all faiths from the chaos and suffering that are a part of any hospital. A local Baptist minister performed his service here every Sunday immediately after Mass. No religious discord existed in this room. We might wear different jerseys, but we all played for the same team.

Stealing back into the sacristy, I worked on Sunday's homily until I could not delay my drive to St. Wenceslaus any longer.

I called Emily, told her about my assignment from Bishop Lucci, and asked if she would come to the church with me. "You'd be a real asset on my mission, Em."

"How very cloak and dagger! I'm in. I'll wear my shades, so no one recognizes me."

"Good idea. I'll slip on a pair of glasses with a rubber nose and bushy eyebrows. We can go as Mata Hari and Mata Hairy."

"Perfect." She chuckled. "I'll meet you in the lobby. Wear a carnation on your lapel so I can identify you."

I was grateful that she was willing to accompany me. I wanted her heightened senses and keen intellect along to aid in my investigation. And I suspected that she could charm information from Father Marek that he would never give to me.

We both hoped to confirm the authenticity of the bleeding statue. Any sign from God in this world of doubters would be a tremendous spiritual boost for the faithful, myself included. I worried, however, about involving her directly in the investigation. With no medical options left for regaining

135

her vision, a miracle represented her last hope. If the statue proved to be a fraud, the loss of that hope would undoubtedly crush her.

On our way to St. Wenceslaus, we stopped for a quick lunch at a diner in the country. Pickup trucks were parked out front like horses at a hitching post, indicating that the food was good and the price reasonable. Dutch treat, of course. Emily had made it clear that we were *just friends* and had laid down the ground rules of our relationship when I'd first returned to town.

For dessert, we purchased two milkshakes to go and slurped our way to St. Wenceslaus, arriving in the early afternoon. The church and sacristy were unoccupied. A sign on Father Marek's office door read BACK IN TWENTY MINUTES, which was ideal because I had hoped to avoid a confrontation.

I went about my examination as quickly as possible. The Virgin Mary's forehead had been wiped nearly clean, but a trace of red remained. I opened my backpack, removed the kit I'd borrowed from the lab, swabbed the substance, and was surprised to find it still moist. Blood should have coagulated long ago.

I'd also brought a small pair of binoculars

and I scanned the high ceiling for the red substance amid the roughhewn beams, but saw nothing. A lone ceiling spotlight lit the Virgin's face. The movable stand with the emerald banner reading PRAISE HER, which had hung above her head on my first visit, was nowhere in sight. I wondered if it had been present during other "miracles" and whether it could be the source of the blood.

I inspected every crack and crevice in the statue with the aid of a magnifying glass and small flashlight, swabbing any surface that may have been the source of the red substance. I labeled each in separate plastic bags but suspected that I was on a fool's errand.

Emily had extended her collapsible cane and was carefully wandering through the church. I hoped that she could smell or hear something that I couldn't.

"Anything, Em?"

"Zip, nothing, nada."

Frustrated, I pulled out my camera and took photographs from various angles. I returned the equipment to my backpack, genuflected, made the Sign of the Cross, and began to examine the altar area.

A throat cleared behind me.

"Can I be of *assistance,* Father Jake?"

Marek glared at me, then charged down the main aisle toward us like a scrawny munchkin high on meth. He wobbled as he advanced, grabbing on to nearby pews to steady himself.

Feeling like a kid caught chugging the altar wine, I played deaf and dumb, took two more steps, then turned.

"Ah, Father Marek! I was on my way to the vestry to see if you were in." A venial lie in service of Mother Church.

He stepped forward into my personal space and might have gone nose to nose with me if he hadn't been a foot shorter. His ruddy complexion, puffy eyelids, and the roadmap of capillaries around his bulbous nose screamed full-blown alcoholism. I nearly got a buzz from the booze on his breath. It appeared that the bishop's misgivings about Marek were correct.

"Checking for me in the vestry, is it? A likely story." Marek popped a stick of gum in his mouth and pocketed the pack without offering us any. His breath transformed from the tang of ethanol to peppermint schnapps. He poked my chest with a finger emphasizing every word. "What can I do for you two?"

I took a step backward. "May we speak

with you for a few minutes?"
He hesitated. "In my office. Follow me."

CHAPTER EIGHTEEN

Friday, July 28, 2:30 p.m.

The veneer of hospitality that Father Marek had displayed two days earlier had vanished. I grabbed the backpack with my equipment, Emily took my arm, and we followed him. He unlocked the door and ushered us into an office warmly furnished in Early American style. A small mantle clock ticked softly on a bookshelf along one wall.

Instead of offering us a seat on the maroon couch or matching armchairs that dominated the room, he grabbed two metal folding chairs from a closet and positioned them in front of his desk. His message was clear. We were not welcome. He wanted a short conversation and our quick departure.

Marek flipped a wall switch and a ceiling fan whirled above us without cooling the air. His soft leather desk chair sighed loudly as he plopped down on it.

"Snooping?" He drummed his fingers

140

impatiently on the desk. "Really Father, how *un*collegial."

I struggled to maintain a calm expression. Given their mutual animosity, I didn't want Marek to know that I was working for Bishop Lucci. It was too soon to lay my cards on the table. If this was a true miracle, I wanted Marek's cooperation in my investigation. If he was a fraud, I hoped to catch him in the act.

A drop of sweat rolled down the back of my neck, and I placed my hands in my lap to stop them from shaking. In contrast, Emily leaned back and casually swept hair behind one ear. She appeared completely relaxed and entirely innocent of any skullduggery. All her years in high school drama class had paid off. She was a much better actor than I.

While male-bonding with Tree Macon over baseball and beer, he had expounded on his philosophy of interviewing suspects. He had three rules: Always approach the person-of-interest initially as the *good cop*. Extract information without revealing any of your own. And don't interrupt the silences, because others often filled them with useful details.

I waited.

"So what's your game, Father Jake?" he

finally asked, his words slightly slurred.

"No game. Emily and I have been discussing what I witnessed in the church on Wednesday. We're intrigued and completely baffled. We hoped that you'd fill us in on the prior . . . occurrences."

"Uh huh. I was born at night, Father, but not last night." Marek lowered his head and stared at us over the top of his wire-rimmed eyeglasses. "Crawling all over the Virgin's statue and snooping around the altar? What you were doing was downright sacrilegious and an affront to me and all the faithful of this parish."

I certainly could understand a priest protecting his church. Marek, however, was positively hostile from the moment that he saw us. It looked as if the good padre might become a very nasty fellow when under the influence.

"Intrigued but baffled, is it? Well, join the club." He tapped his fingertips together. "Did you contact Bishop Lucci and describe what you saw here, as I asked?"

I nodded.

"What did His Excellency say? Did he believe *your* account?"

"He took the matter very seriously."

"Is he willing to keep St. Wenceslaus open until the miracle is confirmed?"

"Bishop Lucci is committed to learning the truth and has vowed to pursue the matter, so your church is safe for the time being."

Marek reclined his desk chair, crossed his arms over his chest, and gazed up at the finely crafted crown molding, which was probably as old as the church.

The mantle clock chimed softly. He refocused on us and cleared his throat.

"Okay, let's talk. About a year ago, Maude Dvorak was the first to witness the statue bleed. She's a very devout woman in her eighties who'd lost her husband to cancer. We all wondered if she'd become . . . unhinged by his death. She had a Band-Aid covering a cut on one finger, and frankly I suspected she'd put her own blood on Mary's face. No one took her seriously, so I didn't report it to Bishop Lucci."

Marek removed his eyeglasses, covered his mouth, and released a soft belch.

"While Maude was explaining to me what she'd witnessed, another parishioner overheard our conversation, climbed up on the statue, touched the blood, and rubbed it on her arthritic joints. That Sunday, she told everyone at Mass that her pain had miraculously disappeared. Personally, I didn't know whether to believe her, but word spread like a brushfire. Folks started pouring into the church. Sunday Mass went from nearly empty to standing room only." He polished his glasses with a cloth and put them back on. "I must admit, I was entirely thrilled — at first. Especially when Bishop Lucci balked at closing the parish. Though when the media got involved, St. Wenceslaus became a circus, with busloads of 'pilgrims' arriving daily, some who weren't even Catholic. Now, I'm not sure how I feel.

"A month later, Milan Cierny was praying to the Virgin when it happened again. He was looking directly at her when suddenly he saw the blood. Mr. Cierny is a pastoral council member and highly respected in the community. No one had reason to doubt his account — no one except Bishop Lucci, who merely pretended to investigate and then swept everything under the diocesan rug."

My suspicions drifted back to the banner as a possible source of the blood.

"Father Marek, I noticed that the PRAISE HER banner over Mary's statue has been removed. It was quite lovely. Where'd you find it?"

"One of my parishioners made it to my specifications and donated it."

"Pity. I was thinking of purchasing one for

our church. Could you show it to me so I can order something similar?"

He frowned, his patience wearing thin. "Sorry, it's in storage, and I don't have time to fetch it."

"Was the banner hanging there when the other bleeding episodes occurred?"

Marek tilted his head to one side and eyed me with misgiving.

"I don't remember." He stood abruptly. "That's the whole story. Now, if you'll excuse me, I have work to do."

CHAPTER NINETEEN

Friday, July 28, 3:15 p.m.

Father Marek escorted us from his office, slammed the door with a thud that echoed in the rafters, and locked it. He left us in the foyer and walked into the church nave.

As we exited St. Wenceslaus, Emily said, "Wow. Think we touched a nerve? I doubt that we'll be invited back for tea."

"Catching someone rummaging around the altar would set off any priest. Marek may simply have been protecting his turf."

"I have to admit, I'm praying that he told us the truth, for my own sake. I'd love to be able to throw my cane and sunglasses away and resume a normal life. His story sounded convincing to me."

"The story is either true, Em, or he's a darn good liar." I opened the passenger door for her. "But I don't think I found anything useful, and the swabs and photos I collected probably won't help. Guess I make a lousy Sherlock Holmes."

"Just a minute, you have the casting for this little drama all wrong." A smirk creased Emily's lips. "I'm the brains of this team, and *you* are Dr. Watson." She mimed puffing on a meerschaum pipe and added, "And the game is definitely afoot."

I laughed and climbed into the car. We had been at St. Wenceslaus longer than planned, so I called Justine and asked how things were going.

"Not to worry, bro. I may not look it, but I'm tougher than a two-dollar steak. See you soon."

I refocused on my partner in crime. "Well Em, we tried. Sorry I dragged you along."

"Oh, we weren't completely foiled, Watson. Marek gave us the names of two eyewitnesses that you can interview."

"Good point, Sherlock."

I drove back through the quaint downtown, which looked like a Chamber of Commerce brochure. There were no vacant buildings, the shops were well cared for, and some of the homes reminded me of cottages painted by Thomas Kinkade.

Near a convenience store at the north end of town, I spotted an old-fashioned payphone and pulled over. Unlike the few remaining phone booths in the city, this telephone directory hadn't been destroyed or stolen. Milan Cierny and Maude Dvorak were both listed. I wrote down their telephone numbers.

Wondering what my next move should be, I was completely lost in thought when Emily spoke.

"Why are you so glum? It's like riding in the car with a zombie, and a boring one at that. Buck up, Jake. We had a lovely day, and I always appreciate a chance to get away from my contracted world at the hospital. Thank you for asking me."

"You're welcome. And not to worry, I'm already back to my charming self."

I tuned the radio to some soft rock and the conversation flowed freely until we arrived at the hospital. I escorted Emily to the Women's Residence Hall and thanked her again for coming with me. She gave me a peck on the cheek and went inside. Then I walked to the lab. The head tech groaned and rolled her eyes when I handed her the swabs that I'd collected at St. Wenceslaus.

Ignoring her frustration, I asked, "Did you get any results back on my handkerchief yet?"

"It's definitely stained with human blood." She opened a nearby folder. "AB positive, which is rare. That's all so far."

I thanked her and called the bishop's office. Lucci checked Father Marek's file, which indicated that his blood type was O negative, confirming that the blood on the statue was not Marek's. I pondered this as I drove back to the rectory.

Much to my surprise, Justine was in the kitchen cooking a casserole. Although the room was warm, she wore a long sleeve blouse, probably to cover more bruises. When she noticed me, she gave me a bear-hug, pinning my arms at my side. A tear trickled down her cheek.

"What's wrong, Sis?"

She released me, took out her embroidered hankie, and dabbed her eyes.

"Nothing's wrong, Jake. Not a single thing." Justine beamed and did a pirouette — the most exuberance she had displayed since arriving in town. "The Cleveland Clinic called. They're going to admit me tomorrow morning!"

She performed another pirouette as RJ came into the room. He stared at her, spun himself around three times, wobbled, and began giggling. Soon, we all were.

"Dear Lord, Jake, I'm sooooo ready."

It was the best news I had heard in a long time. A bottle of wine and a prayer of gratitude were definitely in Dr. Taylor's future for expediting her admission. And not cheap altar wine, the good stuff.

After I'd set the table for supper, I went to put on some background music, but found a Melissa Manchester CD on the player.

Justine chuckled. "My choice today, old guy. She's one of my favorites."

I popped in the CD, hit "play," and sat down. When "Just Too Many People" came on, Manchester sang about changes coming, renewed strength, and sunnier days.

Justine grinned at me and said, "I'm feeling lucky, Jake."

"Me too, sis. Me too."

RJ and I devoured Justine's tuna casserole. She nibbled around the edges and pushed the rest away. I'd purchased an apple pie for dessert on the way back to the rectory, hoping to stimulate her appetite. She managed only a few small bites, while RJ ate enough to feed an entire pre-school class.

She had coughed and sniffled throughout dinner, which scared the hell out of me. Any sign of infection would postpone her admission, and she had no time left to lose. Any delay might be deadly.

I fetched a thermometer, ignored her protest, and took her temperature. Normal.

"See Jake. No problem. Now stop hovering."

I stopped but continued to worry while making decaf coffee for both of us. After dinner, we played the "I spy" game with RJ. He would stare directly at something in the room, say "I spy with my little eye" and name its color, then Justine and I would pretend to struggle to guess the object while he nearly vibrated with delight. RJ took great pleasure in proving us wrong, sometimes even when we were right.

Justine kept fidgeting. A sneeze caught her by surprise, and when she wiped her nose, I saw it. Blood. Her leukemia was rampaging.

We needed to have a serious talk about my nephew's care in case the bone marrow transplant failed, but she noticed me staring and without a word Justine kissed RJ and went upstairs to pack. I maneuvered my nephew into bed early, started a load of laundry, and called Colleen.

"How's your cold? Are you any better?"

"I'm right as rain, Father. Told you it was nothing. I've been lying around the apartment, watching the soaps on the telly, eating potato chips, and feeling entirely useless."

"Did you take the antibiotic I prescribed?"

"That I have, and if it's all right with yourself, I'd like to come back to work soon."

"How about tomorrow at ten? Justine's being admitted to the hospital, and I'll need your help with RJ."

"Grand! I'll see you in the morning then."

Next, I dialed Milan Cierny's number. He answered on the third ring and confirmed that he had been looking directly at the Virgin Mary when he saw the blood, exactly as Father Marek had said. The lone surprise was that it had appeared *in* Mary's eye, not below it on her cheek as I'd seen. He sounded like an intelligent and credible witness. When I asked if the emerald banner had been hanging above the statue that day, he replied that it had. I pumped him for more details but came up dry.

Maude Dvorak didn't answer. As a widow in her eighties, I suspected that she went to sleep early. I left my number and a message on her machine indicating that I was a priest and needed to speak with her. She must have been screening her calls because she phoned me a minute later.

"Yes Father, I was praying to the Virgin when the miracle occurred. Suddenly there was blood. No one believed me, but I *know* what I saw."

"On her left cheek?"

"No, Father, on her forehead, above her left eye."

From the quickness of her responses and the clarity of her thoughts, age apparently hadn't impaired her mentally.

"Ms. Dvorak, was there anyone else in the church when this happened?"

"No, I was alone."

"Was the PRAISE HER banner hanging above the statue?"

"I'm not sure, Father. It's been over a year."

I bombarded her with the same series of questions that I'd asked Milan Cierny. Had she seen, heard, or smelled anything unusual? How did Father Marek react? How long had she stayed in the church afterward? Did anyone else arrive?

"Hester Lonly came in while I was telling Father Marek what had happened. She listened in, walked to the statue, put a drop of blood on her fingertip, and rubbed it on her neck. Then before Father Marek could stop her, she dabbed the blood again and rubbed it on her arthritic knuckles. She claims all her pain completely vanished! I must warn you, Father, Hester is . . . somewhat of an odd duck."

I thanked her, hung up, tracked down Hester Lonly's phone number, and made the call.

She answered immediately. When I told

153

her that I was a priest, she went off on a diatribe about how Satan had lead the Church down a false path at the Second Vatican Council, and that she didn't believe a word of that "new poppycock."

I couldn't have disagreed more. The Council had allowed the Mass to be celebrated in English rather than Latin so that parishioners could better understand its meaning, and it encouraged priests to interact with their congregation. Pope John XXIII, one of the most compassionate and down-to-earth popes in history, had orchestrated the Second Vatican Council, but my reverence for him was more personal. He had served in World War I as a chaplain and a stretcher-bearer. We were brothers-in-arms as well as in the faith.

I needed information from Hester, however, so I bit my tongue as she reeled off a long list of complaints against Mother Church. Her speech pattern was frenetic, pressured, and erratic. She became defensive when I asked about her arthritis pain.

"Cured. Like I told you, it was a *miracle*. I won't have nobody say no different. My Mama was a missionary in Indonesia, where she met my Pa, and she told me about such goings-on. No, Father, it was a miracle, sure as I'm sittin' here. I went into the ladies' room and put some blood on my aching back as well, and now my lumbago's cured too. Ain't had a tetch of rheumatiz since that day. My sister, Betsy June, was visitin' and she seen the signs too. We been blessed, that's what it is."

"I'd like to speak with her. May I have her phone number?"

"Ain't got none. She don't trust modern gadgets, thinks the devil's hunkered down in the innards of such things. Betsy June lives back home near Spruce Knob, up in the Alleghenies. She loves to jaw and don't need no phone. Prob'ly told everyone on the mountain what we seen."

The mere suggestion of a miraculous healing was enough to get the snowball of desperation careening downhill until sick folks came from everywhere — including Emily. For her sake, I prayed to God my skepticism was unfounded.

Hester confirmed that the emerald banner had indeed been hanging over the statue that day. She rambled on about the lack of faith in the world hurling us into the End Times. After a great deal of probing and prodding, she admitted that her arthritis pain had resolved shortly after beginning whopping doses of Aleve, which she continued to take for her headaches. It sounded to me as if she was describing a *medicine-induced* miracle. When I asked who her physician was, she told me Dr. Sheila Steinberg in Strongsville, then quickly added that she had to go, and hung up.

I googled Dr. Steinberg. She was a psychiatrist, specializing in bipolar disease and paranoid schizophrenia.

Terrific. It looked as if Ms. Lonly might be a bit loony and not the most credible eyewitness.

I opened a bottle of Molson Canadian and sipped as I gazed out of the front window at passing cars, replaying everything that I'd been told. Then I called Milan Cierny back and continued my inquiry.

"That's correct," he replied. "Father Marek left the church about ten minutes before the blood appeared. Grocery shopping, as I remember."

"And when you spoke with Bishop Lucci about what you'd seen, Mr. Cierny, how were you received?"

"He asked a lot of questions but honestly, His Excellency seemed cold and distant, as though his mind was on other things." Cierny's phone beeped. "Sorry, I have another call and have to take this. Let me know if I can help in any way. Bye, Father."

Interesting. Father Marek had never personally witnessed anything. Both Cierny and Dvorak had been alone in the church, gazing at the statue when the blood materialized, and the banner had been hanging above Mary on both occasions. The less reliable Miss Lonly had actually seen nothing herself, but had stoked the miracle fire.

Tree Macon's skepticism about the existence of unicorns and coincidences came roaring back to me. I shifted the laundry to the dryer and listened to it spin as I finished my beer.

CHAPTER TWENTY

Saturday, July 29, 10:00 a.m.
It was a good thing that there were very few worshippers at morning Mass because my mind kept drifting to my sister's illness and her impending hospitalization. Father Vargas had kindly consented to drive over from Lorain to cover my six p.m. Saturday Vigil Mass so that I could spend more time with Justine if problems arose.

I hastily greeted my parishioners after the service, then hurried to my study, printed the photographs that I'd taken at St. Wenceslaus, and slipped them into an envelope. I didn't change out of my clerical shirt and pants as I normally did after Mass, in hopes that being clergy might somehow streamline my sister's hospital admission.

When Colleen arrived to care for my nephew, I asked her to stay in the kitchen until we left. Although she was no longer coughing, I wasn't willing to take the chance that Justine might catch her cold, delaying the transplant. Colleen was not pleased and mumbled something in Gaelic that didn't sound complimentary.

Justine and I had prepared RJ for this moment, but when my sister picked up her suitcase, he wrapped his arms around her leg, burst into tears, and refused to let go. We tried to calm him. Nothing worked until Colleen peeked through the doorway and promised my nephew an ice cream cone and an outing to the toy store. When she upped the ante to include a visit to the park, RJ relented, and Justine and I crept out to my car and made our escape.

St. Colleen, the patron saint of blarney and bribery.

Hope and fear filled my car, and Justine and I remained deathly quiet on the drive downtown. On weekend mornings, traffic on I-90 was light, and we breezed in to the massive Cleveland Clinic complex nestled between Carnegie and Euclid Avenue. We encountered a logjam, however, at the admissions desk.

While Justine filled out paperwork, I called the bishop's office. I had encountered Lucci's secretary before and anticipated resistance. She was the palace guard. Her primary responsibility was to protect him from unnecessary intrusions, and she was a master at her job.

"The bishop isn't available on Saturdays, Father. May I take a message?"

Donors often preferred to meet on weekends, and Lucci was the consummate fundraiser. I was certain he was in his office and only unavailable to folks without hefty checkbooks.

"Please tell him that I have information about St. Wenceslaus. I'm sure he'll take my call."

"Maybe I wasn't clear. The bishop isn't —"

"I'm on special assignment for His Excellency, and this is important."

"Oh. I'll see what I can do. Please hold."

A Gregorian chant filled my ear as I waited, its monotonous, hypnotic drone nearly lulling me to sleep by the time Bishop Lucci answered.

"Jacob, my son. You have news for me concerning . . . my problem down south?"

"I'd prefer to discuss this in person. I'm downtown and can be at your office in an hour."

"Very well. I'll see you then."

Bone marrow transplantation required preparation in the isolation unit, and I knew I couldn't accompany Justine upstairs.

160

When a transporter arrived with a wheel-chair, all I could do was promise to care for RJ and vow to keep God's inbox filled with my prayers. A new swelling was now visible on the right side of her neck, most likely an enlarging lymph node. I hugged her for a long time. She felt so frail that I feared she might shatter in my arms. When the trans-porter finally cleared his throat, we both dabbed moist eyes, and she disappeared into the elevator. I stood in the hallway for a minute before I could move again, my eyes locked on the elevator door.

Justine's physician required additional screening tests from me prior to donating my marrow, so I stopped at the lab where the vampires drained several tubes of my blood. I'd always believed that it was better to give than to receive, but best to stay away from needles wielded by phlebotomists in-training. By the time I left the hospital, my arm was an archipelago of jagged blue is-lands.

I arrived ten minutes late for my meeting with the bishop at the Diocese of Cleveland building on East 9th Street. Passing the four life-sized, ceramic saints guarding the lobby, I buttoned my clerical shirt, slid in a white Roman collar insert, took a wood-paneled elevator to the penthouse, and entered

161

Lucci's office suite.

The Most Reverend Antonio Lucci's antechamber was a study in elegance, with vaulted ceilings and hardwood floors. Plush oriental rugs dampened sound, the hushed silence conveying the aura of a holy site. Every time I entered this room, I caught the scent of money seasoned with power — and Lucci had a nose for both.

Unlike myself and other Order priests, Diocesan clergy like Lucci took no vow of poverty, but the extravagance of the room felt wasteful given the tremendous need of the poor in downtown Cleveland and throughout the world. I was more comfortable in the homes of the sick or the chaos of the hospital than in this monument to excess.

Oil paintings of pastoral scenes in gilded frames adorned one wall. Portraits of Cleveland bishops dating back to 1847 lined another. Lucci's image was solemn and forbidding.

On an adjacent wall, the likeness of Lucci's friend and political ally, the Superior General of my Camillian order, appraised the room wearing our traditional black cassock emblazoned with a large red cross.

As I waited for His Excellency to see me, I realized that I'd completely forgotten about my promise to speak with Tina and Miguel. They had not responded to the message I'd left yesterday, so I called their apartment, got their answering machine again, and asked permission to stop by and discuss Pablo's condition.

Lucci's secretary finally set a fashion magazine on her desk and whisked me through heavy oak doors decorated with hand carvings of the Stations of the Cross. The sweet aroma of pipe tobacco and leather-bound books filled the bishop's inner sanctum. Except for neutral cream-colored walls, scarlet accents dominated the room — the color reserved for Catholic Cardinals. Lucci made no attempt to hide his aspirations.

His Excellency was a large man, and his robes overflowed his chair. He wore a purple sash indicative of his rank, but not his violet zucchetto skull cap. What little of his hair that remained encircled his bald pate like a silver halo. A pectoral cross adorned with gemstones hung from a gold chain around his beefy neck.

Lucci was on the telephone and gestured for me to take a seat, which I did. He held up a finger in my direction and continued his conversation.

"No, Senator, I'm not after a donation."

He chuckled, then winked at me. "I was hoping you were free to play a round next Saturday. I do so enjoy embarrassing you on the links." A pause. "Excellent! I'll meet you at nine sharp."

He hung up, focused on me, and his smile faded. He crossed his massive arms and leaned back. The chair groaned loudly.

"I hope you're the bearer of good news, Jacob."

"The lab work isn't back yet, but my initial examination of the statue and altar revealed nothing significant, though Father Marek interrupted me before I could finish. I'll go back soon and complete the job. His story, however, sounded believable, and two eyewitnesses have confirmed it."

I re-counted my conversations with Maude Dvorak and Milan Cierny.

Lucci shook his head. His heavy jowls and wattle had lost the battle with gravity and swayed slowly side to side.

"Including you, three people have seen this . . . occurrence? And no evidence of fraud?" He swiveled his chair and gazed out of the window, then spun back. "That's not at all what I had hoped to hear."

"It's puzzling, I'll grant you. And the pictures I took didn't help."

I handed the envelope with the photographs to him. Lucci removed his tortoise-shell glasses, studied the prints, and rubbed his eyes. His round, pink face wasn't the least bit jolly.

"So, where do you suggest we go from here, my son?"

"I've given this a great deal of thought. Although I can't explain what I saw, the other witnesses said something that made me . . . suspicious."

The bishop cocked one bushy eyebrow and brightened. "Please elaborate."

"They both were alone looking directly at the statue when the blood materialized, just as I had been. Father Marek had left the church before each occurrence, and he claims he's never witnessed an episode him-self."

"So, you think Marek may have slipped out and somehow . . . fabricated this fraud?" He slid his glasses back on, the thick lenses magnifying the bags under his eyes. "But how does a drop of blood appear from nowhere?"

"I'm confident from my examination that the blood didn't come out of the statue, though I'd have to remove and inspect it carefully to be certain. I'd rather not do that, given the belief of his parishioners in a bona fide miracle." I shifted in my chair, searching for the right approach to take. Since my assignment to his diocese, the bishop had become a minor deity in my life. I wanted to guide him without being pushy or painting him into a corner with his superiors, so as not to incur his wrath. "I believe you said the key word yourself, Your Excellency. *Drop* of blood. If it didn't come from the statue, then it must have dropped from above."

"Above?" Lucci sounded confused. "You're not saying . . . from Heaven, are you?"

"I doubt that the Almighty is involved here." I told him about the emerald banner that had been positioned over the statue on all three occasions that miracles occurred. It had been removed before I returned to investigate. "I suspect that banner may be the source of these incidents."

"Okay, so how do you suggest we proceed?"

"Father Marek will resist any further investigation. I need you to contact him directly and request that he allow me free access to the entire church."

Lucci snorted. "I don't *request.* I'm done playing nice with that man. Do anything you need to do. Go through his underwear drawer, if that's what it takes."

"Your Excellency, I can't coerce the man." A line from the Mission Impossible movies came to mind. *Should you be captured or killed, we will disavow any knowledge of your actions.* In the event of a sinking ship, I was certain that Captain Lucci wouldn't go down with me. "What if Father Marek calls the police and I'm arrested?"

"You worry too much, Jacob." Lucci stared at me as if I had just denied Jesus for the third time. "Fine, fine. I'll make sure you're protected. Give me a second and I'll prepare a document authorizing your search of the church and rectory, including Marek's sleeping quarters."

"Wouldn't we need his permission to search his room?"

"St. Wenceslaus belongs to the Church. It's in my diocese, under my stewardship. Marek has no say in the matter. As to his quarters, he may be outraged and raise holy hell, but I don't think he'd dare challenge me. I've already spoken with the Cardinal, and His Eminence agrees that this is a top priority, requiring a thorough investigation to uncover the truth." Lucci picked up his desk phone. "I'll call the Diocesan Consultors and tell them how I see the situation. I'm sure they'll agree with my recommendation. Then it's full speed ahead."

Lucci was the quintessential politician, always enlisting allies and covering his own behind. He might easily manipulate his handpicked, sycophant Board of Diocesan Consultors, but what he may not have considered was the blowback from other priests when they heard of this invasion of privacy — or maybe he planned to strong-arm them too.

Before dialing the phone he added, "Well, well. St. Wenceslaus may be closing after all." He let a moment pass, probably while he mentally tallied the financial benefit of shuttering a small rural parish versus the cost of sending Marek to an alcohol rehab facility. Finally, he gestured toward the door. "Please take a seat in the waiting room. I'll get you the paperwork shortly."

When Lucci's secretary brought me the document, I read it carefully. Despite his bluster, it protected his Excellency's butt more than mine. What a surprise.

CHAPTER TWENTY-ONE

Saturday, July 29, 4:00 p.m.
Father Vargas's willingness to cover my Saturday Vigil Mass allowed me time to stop and place flowers on my mother's grave at Holy Trinity Cemetery in Avon before visiting sick parishioners at St. Joseph's Hospital on my way back to the rectory. My stomach growled as I entered the hospital lobby, reminding me that I had missed lunch. I phoned Emily and invited her to join me in the cafeteria for an early dinner. Since dropping my sister off at the hospital, dark thoughts had enveloped me. The priesthood could be isolating, and I hoped that Emily's company and some light conversation would dispel my impending gloom. More importantly, I'd concocted a plan and needed her help.

"The thing is, Jake, five o'clock is too early. I just completed my shift at the snack shop and was about to take a swim. After physical therapy finishes their last afternoon patients, they open the therapy pool to staff and residents. Can we have dinner around five thirty?"

"No problem."

"Terrific. I'll meet you in the cafeteria."

That allowed me plenty of time to visit my parishioners. I phoned Colleen and asked if she could feed RJ and stay with him a few more hours. I expected resistance, but got none.

"My pleasure, Father! And isn't he a grand lad to be minding? He loves the reading, and I think I might find him a story or two about St. Patrick, if that's all right with yourself."

Colleen was widowed and had no children. I had been concerned that she couldn't handle a four year old, but if RJ won her heart, my worries were over. When the woman committed to something, she was unstoppable.

As she rambled on about how they had spent the day, I heard joy in Colleen's voice, a rare occurrence since I'd moved into the rectory. Her good mood didn't last long.

"While I'm on the subject, won't the boy be making his First Holy Communion before you know it? And since you're so busy, Father, I thought I'd start teaching him his catechism. Wouldn't it be a terrible embarrassment altogether if he didn't have all the answers on the tip of his tongue when he's tested, with you being clergy and all?"

Was it my imagination or had she impugned my competence as an uncle and priest? Sometimes it was hard to tell with Colleen. She always cloaked her determination with deference.

"RJ's a bit young for that, Colleen."

"It's never too soon to place your foot on the path to salvation, Father."

Between Colleen's obsession with my nephew's religious schooling and Emily's easy acceptance of miracles, I was beginning to feel like a heathen.

I needed to apply the brakes to Colleen's frenzied, holy-roller freight train. Justine had made it clear that she had no interest in organized religion of any kind. I hoped that my influence might change that over time, but I had no intention of broaching the subject until she was well.

I chose not to explain my reasoning to Colleen and had no desire to debate with her about my nephew's immortal soul, so I said, "Let's hold off on catechism for now. I'd prefer to handle RJ's instruction myself when the time comes."

"As you wish, Father." After a long pause,

Colleen recovered and cleared her throat. "And might I suggest that the lad needs a diversion other than those toy soldiers. In my way of thinking, they're not the *turn the other cheek* and *love thy neighbor* message we should be sending the little goster. I've a few parish dollars left over from grocery shopping, so I plan to buy him some puzzles and such, and maybe a few bible stories, if you've no objection, that is, Father."

Bible stories. The woman was like a hound dog with a hambone, and she wasn't about to let go. I had too much on my plate to deal with her.

"Fine. Do what you think is best. I'll be back as soon as I can. Thanks for holding the fort until I get there, Colleen. Bye."

I went to visit sick parishioners, wondering if I would be eating ramen noodles or beans and franks until Colleen was satisfied with RJ's religious library and toy collection.

On the medical and surgical floors, I heard confessions, offered Holy Communion, anointed those in need, and listened to a series of fears and hopes, providing what comfort I could. I finished around five o'clock and began to walk to the cafeteria.

Instead, I took an elevator down to Physical Therapy in the basement, entered the chlorinated humidity of the pool, and waved

172

a greeting to one of the physical therapists.

Emily was swimming in the first lane. She had been an avid runner and tennis player before she lost her vision. A long-haired young man swam in lane two, but the other lanes were unoccupied. The pool was inviting and I decided to take advantage of the facility. Maybe I could even begin to teach RJ to swim.

My loafers echoed across the concrete as I walked to the edge of the pool. Emily's pink swim cap plowed the water like the prow of a speedboat. Her right side remained three feet from the sidewall as she streaked toward the far end. Her well-toned arms snaked through the water and her head rolled out on the beat for air. A yard from impact, she glided into a perfect underwater flip turn and resumed her effortless crawl. She churned five more laps, all straight as a laser beam, followed by the breast stroke for a dozen laps, and the backstroke for twelve more.

She stopped at my end of the pool, climbed up the ladder, cautiously located a nearby chair, and grabbed her towel from the seat. She wasn't even breathing hard. As she dried herself, Emily turned in my direction.

"Father Austin, I presume. Afternoon, Jake."

"Let me guess, Em. You heard my footsteps and smelled my aftershave?"

"Yup. Well that and my Wonder Woman superpowers."

"I don't think I'll ever get used to whatever the heck it is that allows you to do that. And tell me, Em. How do you not crash into the pool walls? Sonar?"

"I count my strokes, just like I count steps in the hospital. And the sound under water is different near a wall. The pitch shifts. Adapting to my disability is a matter of maximizing strengths, minimizing weaknesses — and keeping a sense of humor and prospective. Fanny Crosby, the famous blind hymn composer, said it best. Ever heard of her?"

"Nope."

Emily sang softly in a sweet soprano,

Oh, what a happy child I am,
although I cannot see!
I am resolved that in this world
contented I will be!

How many blessings I enjoy
that other people don't!
To weep or sigh because I'm blind,
I cannot and I won't.

"Words to live by, Jake — for everyone, not only the sightless." Emily slipped on flip-flops and finished toweling off.

The young man who'd been swimming in lane two heaved himself out of the pool as though he were weightless. Half my age, he was thin but muscular, with olive skin, Asian eyes, and a long blond mane, suggesting a pleasing blend of all the races that the American melting pot had to offer.

He marched over and gave Emily a quick hug. His eyes undressed her and he glanced at me to see if I was watching.

"That was wonderful, Emily, absolutely wonderful. We simply *must* do this again soon," he said with a hint of an East Coast accent and all the pretensions of an F. Scott Fitzgerald character. "May I assume we're still on for the Cleveland Orchestra concert Monday night?"

"Sure, Todd. Pick me up around seven?"

"Perfect. I'll give you a call the next time I'm free to swim."

"Oh, Todd, this is . . . my friend, Jake. Todd's an MRI tech here."

We shook hands. His grip was surprisingly strong. He combed back his thick blond mop with his fingers and sauntered toward the men's locker room with the grace and swagger of a jaguar.

"I hate to tell you this, Em. Good old Todd ogled you with a hungry eye."

She chuckled, placed one hand on her hip, and in her best Mae West impression said, "It's better to be looked over, darling, than to be overlooked."

"So, tell me about Todd."

The Mae West persona vanished. "Oh, Todd's a good friend, a lover of classical music, and a fellow poet." Emily threw the towel over her shoulder and headed for the women's dressing room. "Give me a minute to shower and change, Jake, and we'll go to dinner."

CHAPTER TWENTY-TWO

Saturday, July 29, 5:30 p.m.

A United Nations of interns and residents occupied much of the cafeteria, filling it with white coats, surgical scrubs in blues and greens, and a smattering of turbans and colorful saris.

Emily and I both selected an entrée that vaguely resembled fish and took seats at a corner table. I updated her on Justine's condition and hospital admission, then recounted my visit with Bishop Lucci.

Emily added Sweet'N Low to her tea, splashed in some milk, and said, "A diocesan search warrant that includes his bedroom? Sounds rather draconian. Poor Father Marek. He strikes me as a gentle and kind man merely trying to protect his parish."

True, he had been kind and gentle the day we first met and he was sober. The last time, however, he'd been three sheets to the wind and had charged up to the altar and poked me *not so gently* in the chest. I'd seen enough drunks in my time, my old man included, to know that the most affable person could become unpredictable, even violent, when mixed with enough booze. I wondered if a darker Mr. Hyde alter ego lurked somewhere inside Marek. Were we dealing with a Father Jekyll?

"It is a perfect plan, Em — for his Excellency. If Father Marek goes to war, as the messenger I'll take the arrows. But I won't resort to Lucci's nuclear option unless I have to. That's why I want your help. Will you come with me to St. Wenceslaus tomorrow? I examined the statue and altar area on our last visit. Now I want to explore his office and the rest of the church while he offers Mass. If I haven't finished by the end of the service, I'll need you to divert Marek and keep him from getting suspicious."

"How am I supposed to do that?"

"Hey, you were queen of the drama club. You'll think of something. Just keep him away from me while I investigate."

She nodded, grinned, and slipped on her sunglasses and a persona that I'd never heard her do before.

"Bond. Jane Bond. I taught my little brother, Jamie, about vodka martinis and everything else he knows." She lowered her voice. "I guess that makes you . . . Pussy Galore."

I laughed hard enough to swivel heads at nearby tables.

"Father Marek will be putty in your hands, Em."

After we finished dinner, I walked Emily back to the residence hall, called Father Vargas, and asked him to cover my Sunday morning Mass. He grumbled at first but consented after I played the bishop card. Then I called Colleen, asked if she could care for RJ on Sunday while I ran an errand for Bishop Lucci, and apologized for the added burden.

"Nonsense, Father. No burden at all. RJ and I get on like two peas in a pod. And as I told you, I need the overtime."

"I'm afraid you may get more overtime than you want in the next few months while Justine's in the hospital. Should I hire a part-time babysitter to help out when I can't be available?"

"That won't be necessary, but if I change my mind I'll let you know."

I hung up, took a moment to thank God for Colleen's steadfast support, then walked toward intensive care to bless baby Pablo. Despite many years in medicine, seeing sick children still cast a dark pall over me. And since Justine and RJ arrived in town, every time I entered the pediatric floor I thought of my nephew and trembled.

As I approached the PICU, I saw Pablo's mother through a window in the door. Tina appeared agitated as she hovered over her boy. She lowered a teddy bear into the crib, hesitated, then withdrew it. I stepped back and watched.

Pablo lay motionless on his back, still in a coma. Two IVs dripped, one into his arm and one into a scalp vein on his head. An endotracheal tube protruded from his mouth, connecting him to the respirator, and I could hear the whoosh of each mechanical breath.

Tina's focus shifted from her child to the array of color-coded valves in the wall near Pablo's crib that supplied oxygen, suction, and compressed air. Her eyes darted around the room, only occasionally landing briefly on Pablo. She studied the valves for a moment, then turned her attention to the nursing station.

She watched one of the nurses escort a wobbly young mother from her baby's bassinet to a rocking chair in the corner, took note of a second nurse unlocking the narcotic cabinet on the far side of the room, then Tina dropped the teddy bear and bent down. She looked from the bear to the ventilator plug in the wall. A third nurse trotted over to help her. Tina retrieved the stuffed animal, stood, produced a weak smile, and spoke briefly with the nurse.

What the hell was she up to? Certainly, a young mother with a baby in intensive care had every reason to be anxious and emotionally volatile. I tried to make sense of Tina's actions but didn't like the implication. Were my suspicions valid or was my imagination simply running wild? Unsure, I remained on guard near the door.

Tina's hands were shaking and she shifted the teddy bear nervously between them. She read the medication label on the IV bag, then stepped toward the ventilator control panel and gazed at it. Finally, she wandered to a side window and stared out onto the hospital courtyard below. Sunlight lit her face, her expression blank. No tears. No emotion. Occasionally she would glance around, then revisit the view out the window. After a few minutes that felt like hours, she headed toward the door.

I stepped backward so as not to be seen, but was a second too slow.

"What are you doing here, Father?"

"Oh, hi Tina. Making my hospital rounds.

I came to pray for Pablo."

"Funny, I saw you from the corner of my eye. Took you a long time to decide to come in, kinda like you were watching me. Silly, huh? Why would you do that?" She checked her watch. "Well, I better get home. Thanks for thinking of my son."

I waited until she got into the elevator before entering the Pediatric Intensive Care Unit. The nursing station, PICU's nerve center, was in the back of the room. Computers and telephones lined the desk, and cardiac monitors beeped softly on the wall behind it. Pediatric intensive care was an astounding combination of mind-boggling science and extraordinary human compassion, where love and determination kept a relentless 24 hour-a-day vigil.

A dozen adjustable cribs and bassinet baskets with overhead radiant warmers were arranged in a semi-circle in front of the nursing station. Pablo's crib was on the end near the wall.

The head nurse was scrubbing her hands at a wash basin. She noticed me and waved.

I returned the gesture and walked over. "A word please."

Jenifer Dublikar had run the intensive care unit for a decade. She was smart and tough-minded, and we had a solid professional relationship. I knew I could depend on her.

I described what I'd seen and suggested that Pablo's mother might pose a danger to him, stressing that I had no proof. I requested that nursing personnel keep a sharp eye on Tina whenever she was in the room.

"You got it. I'm usually here during visiting hours, but I'll give my team an inservice on patient safety and security." Her azure eyes narrowed to slits. "Not to worry. I can be a pit bull. Nobody hurts my babies! Nobody."

The problem was, I was beginning to think that someone already had.

"Thanks, Jen. I'll sleep better."

"Now that you mention it, Father, Tina acted strange a few days ago. When it appeared that Pablo might not make it through the night, I offered to let her hold him. I tried not to be obvious about how sick her son was, so I told her the standard lie: that we needed to clean the crib and put on fresh bed sheets. She refused. What mother doesn't want to hold her sick baby?

An excellent question.

I thanked Nurse Dublikar, blessed Pablo, and departed.

CHAPTER TWENTY-THREE

Saturday, July 29, 7:00 p.m.

On the drive home, my mind pinballed between Justine and little Pablo. For different reasons, both were defenseless and vulnerable.

I called Tree.

"My sister's been admitted for her transplant." That left me as her only chance for recovery, and the odds that my bone marrow was a decent match for her was a coin flip at best. "You have to find my old man soon, Tree! Any leads?"

"Sorry, buddy. The news ain't good. Vice cops stumbled on a surveillance video of your father with Angelo Giordano in Bogalusa. Big Angie's the drug kingpin in Louisiana. I pulled his rap-sheet. The guy's a real nasty sucker. Been in a bloody turf battle with the Russian mob. Problem is, if your dad's still alive, he's in the wind and off the grid. Like I told you, I put Shirley Kadu on the case. She's got mad tech skills. If anyone can find him, she can. I'll let you know if she comes up with anything."

"Thanks, Tree. Don't give up. Justine's almost out of time."

"I never inherited the quitter gene. Keep the faith."

As I rolled into town, I told Tree about Tina's antics in the PICU.

"Sounds . . . worrisome, Jake."

"That was my impression. With Pablo in a coma, pin-cushioned by needles and tubes, it's hard to say what a mother's *normal behavior* should be under those circumstances. Nerves are a given. Fear and grief might make it hard for some parents to even go near their babies."

"You, my friend, are much too softhearted and evenhanded. Lucky for you, *suspicious* and *judgmental* are part of my job description. Trust me, if you expect the worst from people, you rarely get disappointed." He sighed. "Would it be possible for Tina to harm her child without the nurses being aware?"

Tina had caught me watching and darn near accused me of spying on her. You would think that if she was plotting murder, she'd at least assume a low profile and try to stay under the radar, not confront me. I wondered if she could possibly be that dumb, or if she was simply that brazen. Some psychopaths considered themselves so clever that they felt invincible.

"Hurt Pablo without the nurses noticing? I doubt it, Tree. The nursing station has a clear view of all the cribs and bassinets, and Pablo is hooked to monitors with alarms. And when one nurse is on a break, others are always in the room."

I remembered the wobbly mother being helped to a rocking chair by a nurse and added, "I suppose if one of the other children had a crisis, or Tina somehow created a diversion, attention would be temporarily directed away from Pablo and she might be able to turn off the ventilator or oxygen. When all hell broke loose, however, it wouldn't take the nurses long to figure out what was wrong. Though, if the confusion lasted a couple minutes, it might be too late to revive Pablo."

"From what you described, the nurse who ran over to help when Tina dropped the stuffed animal near the ventilator plug may have saved Pablo's life. Or maybe Tina was just scouting the terrain, or this was a dry run. Hell, that settles it. I'll find out if intensive care has video surveillance and if not, I'll get a hidden camera placed in the room."

"If the staff gives you any trouble, use my name with the head nurse. We're friends. But cameras aren't enough, Tree. My concern is *preventing* a catastrophe, not catching a killer."

"My job is also to prevent scumbags from getting away scot-free." I heard a radio crackle in the background. Tree continued. "I made some calls to Pennsylvania and checked up on Pablo's parents. Miguel was a regular boarder in the town drunk tank and a graduate of anger management classes, apparently without honors. And it sounded like Tina couldn't hold down an entry-level job longer than six months." His radio squawked again. "I tried but couldn't get a warrant, so I got one of my troops snooping around their finances. Don't ask how. Their bank accounts are empty and their credit cards are maxed out. The last cash in their checking account went to a lawyer in town who, get this, specializes in divorce. Tina signed the check. I think the Love Boat is taking on water."

"Stir in the stress of a screaming baby, maybe brain damaged since birth, and any marriage would be tested."

"No doubt about it. Pablo should have

chosen his parents more carefully."

I thought about my philandering old man abandoning the children he spawned and cavorting with drug dealers. Talk about choosing the wrong parent.

"Listen, Jake, I need your help — as my consultant. I got the medical records of their first baby, the one that died in a small town near Sharon, PA. Our coroner said they did a half-ass job, but she thinks the findings are consistent with SIDS. I want a second opinion. I dropped copies off in a sealed envelope with Colleen Brady at the rectory and gave her strict orders not to open it. Let me know what you think."

"Sure, Tree."

"One question. What are the odds of having two SIDS babies in one family?"

"About one in four million. I looked it up. Possible but . . . ."

"Damn frickin' unlikely."

"It's also rare for parents to kill their babies, Tree. These folks, however, set off all my alarm bells."

"Mine, too. Thanks, buddy. Gotta go." Click.

When I arrived at the rectory, RJ was sullen, demanding to see his mother. After explaining again that she was in the isolation unit and couldn't have visitors yet, we

188

phoned Justine. She sounded exhausted. RJ recounted his day for her in great detail until a phlebotomist arrived to draw her blood, and she ended the call.

RJ immediately slid back into his funk. Since he'd moved into the rectory, all he did was watch cartoons and play with his toy soldiers. The boy was becoming a couch potato. A romp at the school playground sounded like a perfect remedy, but dusk was already blanketing the town.

Through the living room window, I glimpsed a twinkling near the maple tree. God provided better entertainment than mankind could ever invent.

"Come on, RJ. I have a special treat for you."

He followed me into the kitchen, where I rummaged through cabinets until I found a Mason jar and wax paper. We walked out into a darkening world freckled by twinkling fireflies, as God lit a billion candles in the heavens. My nephew and I set our cares aside and chased lightning bugs across the thick green lawn that stretched from the rectory to the church. RJ's giggles and the constant chirp of crickets became the soundtrack of a perfect summer's evening. I wasn't sure which of us had more fun.

By the time we'd gently corralled ten of

the critters in the glass jar, I secured a wax paper cover over it with a rubber band, poked in air holes, and declared that it was bedtime.

RJ protested. For a change I refused to buckle. I set the twinkling jar on his dresser and told him that we would release our overnight guests tomorrow so that they could join their friends. I slipped on his pajamas, however he was still wired and getting him under the covers was more difficult than herding an entire swarm of lightning bugs.

Finally, I cajoled him into bed with promises of more firefly safaris, read him a story, and flicked off the bedroom lights. The brave little bug hunter was asleep before I made it out of the room.

Taking care of RJ until Justine recovered would be exhausting, but as I watched his quiet breathing from the doorway, I felt . . . a strange contentment. Looking after my nephew was a mouthwatering taste of what it must feel like to be a parent. I considered what might have been with Emily until regret and sadness seeped in, then walked downstairs, found the sealed envelope that Tree had sent, and opened it.

Pablo's sister had been declared DOA at the hospital. The file was thin and didn't take long to review. I phoned Tree, left a message on his voicemail, and turned on the tube.

I stopped surfing channels at a rerun on AMC when I saw a face that I recognized — Dolores Hart, at least that was her stage name. She'd debuted as the romantic interest to Elvis Presley in *Loving You* and had acted in a dozen or so other major films and TV shows. She'd even garnered a Tony nomination for her work on Broadway. Hart once said that her fifteen second kiss with Elvis had lasted her forty years. With her great beauty and talent, she'd often been compared to Grace Kelly. I'd followed her career because she had unexpectedly walked away from show business in the 1960's at the age of twenty four — and became a Benedictine nun. And I thought *I'd made* a huge leap from physician to clergy.

As a priest alone in a rectory, it felt weird to watch her in a rerun of a bunch of hormone-driven teenagers cavorting on the beach, but I was lost in nostalgia when the phone rang. I muted the television.

"Say something insightful to me, Doctor."

"I wish I could, Tree. The CT scan of Pablo's sister showed no fractures or hemorrhage, and only mild swelling of the brain. That's not conclusive. It's virtually impossible to distinguish between SIDS and accidental or deliberate suffocation with a soft object like a pillow. Babies can't fight back. The coroner interviewed Miguel and Tina and decided against an autopsy based on their statement and the hospital chart. Is that legal? I thought an autopsy was mandatory in SIDS cases."

"That's true for Ohio, Jake. It's *optional* in Pennsylvania. There, the decision's up to the coroner. I checked."

"Well, I googled *this* coroner, and he's a local family doctor with no background in forensics. He wouldn't have been my choice for the job, but the locals elected him by a landslide. Sorry, that's not much help."

"It was worth a second look. Thanks anyway, Jake. Get some rest."

I unmuted the TV and watched the movie until the eleven o'clock news. The lead story concerned a baby in Cleveland dying of a congenital heart defect. The video showed an affluent couple from Pepper Pike outside the hospital asking the public for their prayers and begging for help securing a transplant for their child. Although they tried to sound upbeat, their body language read helpless and hopeless. A bubbly, blond newswoman milked the drama as long as possible, then jumped to a story about a lost dog located in Indiana.

That was the problem. These days, news and life were reduced to sound-bites. People were so busy and self-absorbed that few folks bothered to volunteer as organ donors when they got their driver's licenses — and people like this unfortunate family and Justine lived every day in medical purgatory awaiting a match. Lord, Lord. My next homily would focus on *charity,* with an emphasis on organ donation.

I pushed the power button on the remote and sent the television screen to a peaceful blackness. As I trudged my tired body toward the stairs, a red number "3" blinked at me from the answering machine.

The first message was from a Legion of Mary member about an upcoming potluck dinner, the second from a nun reporting a leaking faucet in the women's restroom at the church. The third was so muffled and distorted that I couldn't tell if the voice belonged to a man or a woman. The meaning, however, was crystal clear: MIND YOUR OWN DAMN BUSINESS, OR YOU'LL BE SORRY!

What the hell? Drunks could be unpredictable, so my first thought was that Father Marek was threatening me. Slowly, my mind drifted to other possibilities: a Pro-Life

193

sermon I'd given that had irritated two folks enough to write angry letters to Bishop Lucci; my involvement with Miguel and Tina; and finally to a patient who'd nearly assaulted me at the hospital when I refused to write a narcotics prescription for him.

I listened again but was too weary to make sense of it. I didn't want to bother Tree again late at night and decided to call him in the morning. I did not, however, erase the message.

CHAPTER TWENTY-FOUR

Sunday, July 30, 3:00 a.m.

I tossed and turned that night until my nephew charged into my bedroom sobbing, clutching his beloved blue blankie.

"Uncle Jake, Uncle Jake." He crawled into my bed. "I had a bad dream!"

Mine had been no picnic either, somehow combining the pediatric intensive care unit with a demon-possessed child from an old horror movie, drenching me in sweat.

I wrapped my arms around my nephew. His tattered blue security blanket smelled rank and was in desperate need of a washing machine.

"Shhhh. It's okay, RJ. It was only a dream."

The standard adult refrain had no effect. He buried his head in my chest.

"I want my mommy! I *want* her."

"I understand. I miss her too. We'll see her soon," I lied. A few days wasn't even close to *soon* for a scared little boy. "You know what would make me feel better, RJ? If you slept in here tonight. Would that be all right?"

He nodded and slid under the covers. We both dozed fitfully until five, when my human alarm clock declared that he was hungry.

RJ was still weepy and sulking. As a pathetic rookie without a clue how to deal with him, I filled a bowl with the sugary cereal that Justine had expressly forbidden, and we ate breakfast in the living room watching cartoons.

I'd just finished dressing him when Colleen charged in like the cavalry and saved the day. After a shower and shave, I put on a sport coat and tie so that I would blend in with the crowd at St. Wenceslaus. Then I called Tree and left a voicemail indicating that I was busy this afternoon but asking him to stop by when he had time to listen to a menacing message left on my answering machine.

As I was leaving the rectory to pick up Emily, Martin Luther scampered through the open kitchen door. Occasionally sneaking into the church from the basement apparently wasn't good enough for the scoundrel; now he was invading my home! The

196

cat, however, hadn't reckoned on Colleen and her broom. The last I saw of the tabby was his backside as he sprinted across the parking lot toward the church.

Emily was waiting outside for me when I arrived. In a lovely floral dress with a touch of makeup, she looked ready to mesmerize Father Marek if necessary.

I opened the car door, helped her in, and told her about the message on my answering machine.

"Who the heck threatens a parish priest, Em?"

"You took a pretty hardline stand against abortion not long ago. Could that have set off some crackpot?"

"I doubt it. It's not exactly breaking news that the Church is Pro-Life — although in today's world, who knows?"

"Have you had any disgruntled patients at the hospital? Didn't someone there assault you?"

"Only verbally. He did invade the heck out of my personal space. That was nearly a month ago. Why would he threaten me now, after all this time?"

Pablo's parents were a powder keg and I wondered if spying on Tina in the intensive care unit could have lit their fuse?

"There's no doubt Father Marek was

upset, Jake, yet I can't imagine . . . ."

Having hung around with drunks and druggies in my youth, I had less difficulty imagining.

"Have you told Tree?"

"I left him a message and I'll play it for him. One disaster at a time."

Actually, there were several ongoing disasters, and it was hard to stay focused on any one of them. Justine's condition weighed heavily on my mind, but I wanted to complete my task for Bishop Lucci before the bone marrow transplantation, in case things didn't go well.

As we drove in silence, I forced myself to ponder the task at hand. How do you search a church without getting caught when it is full of people attending Mass? And what about locked doors? I definitely didn't want breaking and entering on my resume. Visions of orange jumpsuits danced in my head.

"Hello, Jake? Are you okay? It's like I'm alone in the car."

"Sorry. I'm spooked about doing this. If I'd wanted intrigue, I would have joined the CIA."

"I don't understand why you're worried. You have *me* watching your back," she said, tapping her sunglasses and laughing. "Besides, I'm Catholic, you're Catholic, and God's Catholic . . . what could go wrong?" Her mood abruptly shifted to somber. "Just so you know, I sure hope that you *don't* find an explanation for the miracle. I'm praying that Marek told us the truth."

"Me too, Em. Me too."

Even though we arrived well before Mass, the church parking lot was already half full. Miracles were definitely good for business.

"We'll need to blend in with early arrivals, Em, so Marek doesn't notice us and stop me before I get started. Leave your cane folded up in your purse and we'll take a leisurely Sunday stroll inside."

She chuckled. "You mean, act like a normal couple?"

"Exactly. Hey, we're normal — only in a really odd way."

I silenced my cellphone and opened the passenger door. Emily took my arm and we joined a group of parishioners near the church entrance. Sunlight pierced the branches of a large oak tree shading the walkway, adding shimmering gold highlights to Emily's auburn hair. As we entered the foyer, it almost felt as if we *were* a normal couple — and I loved the feeling.

While Father Marek prepared for Mass in the sacristy, Emily removed her sunglasses and I seated her on the main aisle near the back of the church, directly behind a large man so that she wasn't easily recognizable in the crowd from the pulpit.

We had discussed her part of the plan during the drive. If I hadn't returned by the time Mass ended, Emily would explain to a nearby worshiper that she was blind and ask to be told when Marek approached. She would intercept and delay him as he headed from the altar to greet his parishioners. I hoped her help wouldn't be necessary, but if I hadn't completed my search by then, she was my Plan B. There was no Plan C.

I headed for Marek's office, wondering what in God's holy name I was doing. Undermining the integrity of a brother of the cloth, invading his life, rifling through his things? If the tables were turned and he rummaged through my few remaining personal possessions — photos of friends killed in the war, poems written by Emily in school, the promise ring I'd given her as a teenager — I probably would have rearranged his teeth.

Now here I was, cast in the role of a modern day Grand Inquisitor: *Thou shalt not deceive Mother Church! Your actions force us, Father Marek, to make an example of you. If only you would tell me what I need to know, this would go much easier for you. Don't force me to crank the thumb screws again.*

Bishop Lucci's document authorizing my search of the premises weighed heavily in my pocket. It was supposed to be my get-out-of-jail-free card, but if Marek called the police, would secular law trump a church decree? My freedom depended on Bishop Lucci coming to my aid. He was a ladder-climbing bureaucrat, however, who wanted no blemishes on his personal record. I wondered whether it would be my head tumbling into the executioner's basket if His Excellency required a scapegoat.

A pipe organ filled the church with the entrance hymn. It sounded more like a steam calliope, adding a circus atmosphere to the service. And what a circus St. Wenceslaus had become. *Come one, come all! See the sword swallower, the unicorn boy, and the bleeding statue!*

People poured into the church, filling all of the pews. Late-arrivals stood shoulder-to-shoulder in the back. Initial whispered exuberance had given way to a hushed reverence. Body heat replaced the cool of the morning, and the church felt uncomfortably stuffy.

Father Marek's office was located in a hallway off of the small church foyer. I felt like a traitor as I stood before his door. I suspected that the blood had been dropped onto the statue from above and that a search of Marek's office was unlikely to produce evidence, but the only safe time to examine it was when he was busy offering Mass.

The emerald banner that had been hanging above the statue each time the blood appeared was again missing this morning. Had it been removed for a reason? Was it the source of the blood? I hoped that Marek had stashed it in his private office. Time to find out.

Alone in the hallway, I placed a hand on the brass doorknob and turned it. Locked. No surprise. I regularly locked my church office and sacristy. I'd seen Marek lock his door too, but I'd anticipated this roadblock and had done my homework by going to the source of all knowledge — Google.

I had always thought that unlocking doors with a credit card was merely Hollywood make-believe or urban legend, but I'd found two different methods online, one with a video demonstration. I couldn't afford to damage my ATM or credit card, so I'd practiced with my library card, which was more flexible. The trick had worked so well at the rectory that I'd left a Post-it note on my desk as a reminder to call a locksmith and have more secure locks installed.

I slid my card between the door to Marek's office and the jamb. The small crucifix that I wear beneath my shirt felt as heavy as a ship's anchor. I tilted my end of the card until it touched the knob and pushed. It slid forward slightly. I leaned against the door, bent the card toward the doorjamb to help lever the slanted spring bolt, and pushed again.

Nothing. So much for *practice makes perfect.*

I heard two women in the foyer whispering and prayed that they wouldn't wander in my direction. A cold drop of sweat rolled down my spine, and my breathing sounded like a wind tunnel.

I repeated the technique, higher this time, along the upper edge of the spring bolt. Wiggling the card, I pushed and bent it away, then toward the doorframe. I'm not sure if the angel on my shoulder had a halo or a pitchfork, but the resistance ended with a loud pop. I turned the knob, entered, and softly closed the door behind me.

CHAPTER TWENTY-FIVE

Sunday, July 30, 11:00 a.m.

The beating of my heart seemed louder than the ticking of the small mantle clock on the bookcase. The emerald banner and its metal stand were nowhere in sight. I crossed the room and opened the closet. The folding chairs that Marek reserved for unwelcome guests were there, but no banner. I rummaged through the closet and discovered two fifths of Grey Goose hidden under blankets on an upper shelf. Vodka, the beverage of choice for covert drinkers. And apparently, the full collection basket allowed Marek to buy the very best.

I closed the closet door and inspected the bookcase. Religious tomes and history books rested on either side of the mantle clock. The upper shelf held a selection of mystery and true crime novels. Two sliding doors in the base of the bookcase concealed an old boom box and several photo albums.

The choir's joyous crescendo echoed from the nave, sending me into a panic. I removed a few random books from the shelves, found nothing, replaced them, and examined Marek's desk.

An old-fashioned, paper calendar on the desktop indicated that Marek had very few activities outside of church functions, except for the days that he volunteered at the Free Clinic. Three telephone number were scribbled along the top of the calendar. I recognized two of them. One was for Bishop Lucci's office, the other for the Sacred Heart rectory. Could Marek have made the threatening call that I'd found on my answering machine? The third number was unfamiliar and I jotted it on my hand with a pen.

Rifling through the desk drawers revealed office supplies, a dictionary, and a Bible. The top drawer was locked and when I yanked it, the bulky computer on the desk sensed my movement, awakened from its slumber, and requested a password.

Although unlikely to reveal anything relevant, I considered trying a few of the obvious computer passwords, but the organist launched into the Kyrie and Gloria with a great flourish. An army of voices from the church joined in, indicating that Mass was

205

progressing quickly, so I moved on.

If I couldn't locate the banner, maybe I could find Marek's peephole. Logic dictated that there had to be one somewhere, since the *miracle* only happened when someone was looking directly at Mary's statue. His office abutted the left side of the church, so I turned my attention to the shared wall where three paintings hung.

St. Wenceslaus's portrait was the largest and located between the other two. It was reminiscent of the famous statue in Prague, the bearded Duke of Bohemia wearing a suit of armor hours before his martyrdom.

I lifted the picture from a hook on the wall, found nothing, and replaced it. Wenceslaus was flanked by John Paul I, the Italian pope who died after just thirty three days in the Papal Palace, and John Paul II, the first Polish pontiff. Both of these portraits merely concealed small areas of water damage and chipped paint.

The Alleluia filled the church. Marek would begin his homily soon. Hopefully, he would be longwinded. If he opted for brevity, I had little time left.

The two large metal filing cabinets near the portraits were locked. I had no card trick for that problem. If Bishop Lucci wanted a cat burglar with lock picking skills, he'd sent the wrong guy. The cabinets were also too heavy to move. I pulled a small Maglite from my pocket and used its beam to peer behind each one, but saw only dust bunnies on the floor. No peepholes were visible in the wall.

An unlocked leather briefcase leaned against the wall. I thumbed through a half dozen church-related file folders, flyers for the Free Clinic, and a couple of magazines.

The Offertory Hymn rang out. Marek's sermon had been brief. Hopefully, the communion line would be long and slow. I rummaged through several wooden cupboards near his desk. One contained boxes of prayer candles, the rest the usual odds and ends. A small refrigerator hummed away beneath the cupboards. A cursory examination of its contents revealed snack food, a bottle of cranberry juice, and a few cans of Coke and Sprite, probably mixers for Marek's vodka.

Out of ideas and frantic, I began lifting couch cushions, unearthing loose change, cookie crumbs, and a paperclip. Feeling ridiculous, I made sure that everything in the room was as I had found it, stepped into the hallway, and locked the door as Marek recited the prayer after communion. Time was running out.

I refocused on what I'd seen in the church — a drop of blood materializing from nowhere. *A drop.* Maybe I'd find the emerald banner or something significant in the attic above the statue.

Doors were located on either side of the restrooms in the church foyer. The nearest was locked. It gave off the faint aroma of ammonia, suggesting a janitor's closet. I tried the card trick again. No matter how I jiggled it or how hard I pushed, the door wouldn't budge.

The organ erupted into the exit hymn, and my heart up-shifted.

Damn it!

As I turned toward the other door, worshippers surged from the nave like a raging river, streaming out of the main church entrance or into the restrooms. I tried crossing against the current to reach the second door, but parishioners hurrying to lunch or in need of a toilet can be an aggressive lot.

I was halfway through the crowd when I heard Emily's voice.

"Father Marek, would you help me, please?"

Emily stood in the doorway connecting the church to the foyer, wielding her red and white cane in a wide arc, parting the flow of humanity. Her voice was loud, a warning.

Marek froze. "Why are *you* here again, Miss? I don't want any more trouble from the two of you."

I squeezed between a fat man and elderly woman.

"Oh no, Father, I'm alone. A friend dropped me off for Mass."

"By a friend, I assume you mean Father Jake."

"Ah . . . no. A girlfriend. I came like everyone else," Emily said tapping her sunglasses, "hoping for a cure."

"*Girlfriend,* huh?"

"Please, Father." She reached out and took his arm. "Everyone's in such a hurry, I'm afraid I'll be knocked down."

"Okay, I'll walk you out."

I was in the thick of the crowd and my progress was slow. Marek and Emily were close enough that I could make out their conversation over the din, so I tried to keep my back to them.

I heard Emily say, "Oh, wait Father, I dropped my cane. Could you get it for me?"

I glanced over as Marek reached down and retrieved it for her. As he stood, Emily swayed unsteadily and grabbed his arm again. "Oh, I'm so dizzy. I should have eaten something before receiving communion.

May I sit down somewhere till my friend arrives?"

And the Oscar for most helpless heroine goes to . . . .

There were no chairs in the foyer. Marek looked back at the church, but the faithful were still pouring out. "Fine. In my office. This way."

I collided with a young man who was texting, then slipped through the last of the crowd to the second door. It was unlocked. I entered, closed it behind me, took out my Maglite, and followed its beam up a dark, narrow staircase to an unfinished attic. The hot, moist air smelled of mildew. Someone had written DANGER on the top step in red paint.

Without windows, there was no natural light. Plywood boards partially covered the rough-hewn rafters near the stairs. Numerous dusty cardboard boxes were stacked on one side. Some were labeled. Christmas lights. Ceramic Nativity. Hymnals. Pageant costumes. Easter decorations. Choir robes. If evidence was hidden in an unlabeled or intentionally mislabeled box, I had no chance of finding it.

The mobile stand holding the PRAISE HER banner was stored on the other side. Next to it, a metal chain hung from a bare ceiling bulb. I didn't turn it on, however, fearing that light might show around the door at the bottom of the stairs and give my presence away.

I inspected every inch of the banner and stand using my flashlight. The cloth banner contained no hidden compartment. Disassembling the stand's metal tubing revealed nothing.

Crap! I was so sure!

My legs felt rubbery. I leaned against an old wooden chair, noticed the telephone number I'd inked on my hand, and dialed it on my cell. A soft female voice responded.

"You've reached the office of The Very Reverend Father Stefano Demarco. The office is closed. Office hours are Monday through Friday from nine a.m. until five p.m. If this is an emergency, please call . . . ."

What? Why would Marek have the number of my Superior General? Did he have powerful allies in the Camillian order? Was he trying to undermine my ministry? Had he already made the call?

That did it! If Marek wanted to fight dirty, I'd give him a bare-knuckle brawl. The gloves were off.

I had to think. If the banner and stand weren't the source of the blood, then I needed to examine the area directly over Mary's statue approximately twenty feet away, beyond where the plywood flooring ended.

Rolled insulation covered the space between the support beams. My only option was to tight-rope along one of these ancient timbers. If I lost my balance and fell onto the insulation, I could end up crashing through the church ceiling.

The attic swelter was oppressive. Perspiration had soaked through my dress shirt, gluing it to my skin. I removed my tie and sport coat, and rolled up my sleeves.

The church ceiling beams were substantial and wide enough to walk on, but I couldn't tell exactly where the statue was located below me. Unable to decide which to choose, I guided my light down each timber. All were filthy — except for one. Its layer of dust had been disturbed.

As I stepped onto it, the beam creaked loudly. I hesitated for a moment, directed my flashlight into the gloom, and took two steps. My loafer clacked against the wood, the sound echoing throughout the attic. Worse, the leather soles were slick and provided no traction.

I stepped back onto the plywood floor and removed my shoes. With my arms extended to the sides for balance, I started again, carefully making my way in stocking feet to a point on the timber where the grime was undisturbed.

Crouching down, my light found a hand-print in the dust on the insulation. I lifted a sheet of pink fiberglass, then another. A thin, red-stained plastic tube lay beneath it, leading to a long needle, the kind used in hospitals for lumbar punctures. Marek had shoved it through the plaster ceiling. From the church far below, it would be nearly impossible to see or would resemble the tip of an errant carpenter's nail.

Got you, Marek! Miracle my ass.

But why had he left the evidence here? Why hadn't he removed it? Had he become cocky when Bishop Lucci's investigators found nothing? Or had he been boozing and simply forgot to remove it? Doubtful.

More likely, Marek intended to perform more *miracles* in the future. With a twenty foot distance to the statue below, any slight movement of the needle tip would dramatically alter where the drop of blood landed. That explained why the blood had appeared in Mary's left eye for Milan Cierny, above it for Maude Dvorak, and on the left cheek for me. It must have taken considerable trial and error to get the trajectory right. Once

213

he had, he undoubtedly was afraid to touch it.

One end of the plastic tube was still connected to the needle. The other end was capped, but designed to attach to a syringe. I removed the cap and a thick red drop trickled out. The blood must have contained an anticoagulant to keep it from clotting. I recapped the tube and took photos with my cellphone, then removed the tube and needle, placing them in a plastic bag I'd brought with me.

I hadn't found the peephole that Marek used to time his miracles so that they occurred when someone was looking at the statue. I was sure one existed somewhere in the attic, but its location no longer mattered. I had all the evidence I needed and couldn't wait to deliver the knockout punch in our bare-knuckle brawl.

Chapter Twenty-Six

Sunday, July 30, 12:45 p.m.

Making my way carefully back across the support beam, I put on my shoes, grabbed my sport coat and tie, and scrambled down the rickety attic stairs into an empty church foyer. Emily was nowhere in sight. I doubted that Father Marek was a threat to her, but Bishop Lucci had indicated that Marek had intimidated the priests he'd sent to investigate and may have damaged their car. Stir in a pint of booze and anything was possible. If Marek was the one who left the threat on my answering machine, then there was no telling what he might do. Unwilling to take any chances, I placed an ear against his office door, heard muffled voices, and charged into the room.

Emily sat on a folding chair across from Marek's desk, her legs crossed primly at the ankles. He was smiling at her, his head swaying side to side. Somehow she had

215

worked her magic and charmed the cobra.

Marek's eyes ping-ponged from Emily to me and back, then lit with rage.

"Well, well. What a surprise," he said. "This must be the *girlfriend* you spoke of, Emily." A crooked smile danced across his lips. "I would never have taken you for a cross-dresser, Father Jake." He ran a finger down the telephone numbers scribbled on his calendar, picked up his desk phone, and said, "I have a friend in the Camillian Order who will be very interested to hear about the way you climbed all over the Virgin Mary's statue and desecrated the altar the other day."

"Cut the crap, Marek, and put the phone down." I threw my sport coat on the couch. Protected by my helmet of Faith and shield of Righteousness, I raised the plastic bag containing the needle and blood-stained tube like a sword of Vengeance. "I found *this* in the attic."

Marek's mouth opened and closed like a fish stranded on the beach. He wilted into his chair and swiveled away from my glare, staring out the window as if he'd never seen the sky before.

I opened a second folding chair and sat next to Emily.

"What is it, Jake? What's happening?" she asked.

When I told her, her confusion dissolved into a painful sadness. Her shoulders slumped and she wiped moisture from her eyes.

With a few simple words, I'd extinguished her last hope of recovering her vision. I wondered if I'd done the right thing. Proving Marek a fraud had cost Emily dearly. Maybe I should have buried his secret under the insulation and walked away.

Marek spun his chair back toward us. His forehead had taken on a sheen and his eyes refused to meet mine.

"Guess I knew this day would come." His words were soft and measured. "I underestimated you two. Now what?"

"Now, I report your deception to His Excellency."

"So, Bishop Lucci wins after all. Game, set, match. That cold-hearted pencil-pusher can finally shut down this venerable old church." He laughed without a hint of humor. "And you can bask in his good graces and move up the ecclesiastical ladder. Bully for you, Father Jake."

Marek unlocked the top drawer of his desk, pulled out a ledger, and tossed it to me. "That's all I ever wanted, you know. To keep this church open. The bishop can have his accountants tear my records apart. Every dollar, every donation is accounted for. I transformed a huge deficit into a surplus. Everything went into renovation and repair. Look at the attendance this morning. I singlehandedly brought this church from the financial brink and complete obscurity back to her glory days." He spread his arms like Moses parting the Red Sea. "Behold the renaissance of St. Wenceslaus."

"Except your *renaissance* is built on lies and deceit." I watched him swallow hard, then gestured towards Emily, who had lowered her head and gone silent. "Behold the anguish you've caused the faithful."

His eyes danced around the room, landed on Emily, then returned to me. "I caused . . . or *you* caused?"

The question hung between us for a long time. Finally he said, "I did what I had to do. You saw the huge crowd, the joy in the church today." His voice didn't waiver. "Do what you must, Father Jake. I'll sleep fine no matter the outcome. How will you sleep tonight?"

In truth, Marek was right about Lucci. The bishop was a number cruncher of the first order with a history of blind adherence to rules, and no regard for the hurt his decisions caused.

I stood at the crossroad of duty and conscience. As wrong as Marek's actions had been, I understood his motivation — and the bishop and I were about to strip him of his vocation and end his career in disgrace. I wondered if I would sleep at all.

I remained mired in my thoughts until Emily uncrossed her ankles and gently kicked mine. She cleared her throat and softly recited:

For me, for you, for all, to close the day,
Pass now the evening's sponge across
    the slate;
And to that spirit of forgiveness keep
Which is the parent and the child of
    sleep.

Marek and I were both startled. He said, "I don't remember that psalm, my dear."

"That's not from a psalm. It's from a poem by Robert Louis Stevenson, but every bit as wise and timeless as any bible verse."

The poet in Emily often spoke in metaphors and similes, and I was usually one step behind this woman, struggling to understand. I placed my hand on her arm.

"What're you trying to tell me, Em?"

"That the reins of this runaway horse are

still in your hands — at least they are until you hand them over to Bishop Lucci."

"What? You think I should ignore what he's doing, Em, what he's done to the Church? Sweep another scandal under the Vatican rug?"

"The Church has survived for two thousand years without your protection, Jake. This isn't a sexual abuse scandal, and if parish funds are accounted for, there's been no theft. I think you should weigh the heartache and loss of faith for all those poor people he duped. Their only crime was praying for an end to their suffering, praying for a miracle. Maybe their prayers would never have been uttered without this . . . fraud. Who's to say that God didn't hear each and every one?"

Marek tapped the eraser of his pencil on the desk and nodded. "All I ever wanted was to give hope to those who'd lost it, keep them connected to God, and protect St. Wenceslaus."

"That's *our job* as priests — to provide hope and guidance." I waved the plastic bag containing the needle and tube. "Most of us do it without manufacturing miracles."

"I tried!" Marek threw the pencil on his desk; it bounced and clattered to the floor. "For decades I tried everything I could

220

think of. But I'd run out of time with the bishop and was desperate!"

Emily found my arm and squeezed it. "You saw the parishioners this morning, Jake. If that wasn't rapt devotion, I don't know what is. Who's to say the return of faith for all those people isn't a small miracle in itself?"

Marek's demeanor had shifted from resignation to sorrow. He slowly traced a finger along the wood grain of his desk while avoiding eye contact.

"A cover up? No way, Em. I can't ignore this."

"No, clearly you can't. Unfortunately, this is checkmate both for Father Marek *and* for his parishioners. He may deserve this, but they don't. Look at it a different way. If you gave a despondent patient a sugar pill instead of an antidepressant and he felt better, wouldn't that be the best of all outcomes?"

When I'd powered into Marek's office, I knew exactly what direction this conversation was headed and was sure of the outcome. Somehow, I'd lost my compass and become dead in the water. Thank God for Emily. In her youth, she had been one of the brightest bulbs in the high school chandelier. Now, as a woman, she was a beacon, guiding me home.

"I don't believe faith is a placebo . . . but I see your point, Em." I quickly charted a new course. "All right, Father Marek. Let's make a deal."

I expected a response. He remained mute, his eyes downcast like a convict awaiting his sentence.

"If you want to continue as pastor here, I have three conditions. First, the Bleeding Virgin miracles end today, and you will not encourage the myth in any way. I will assure Bishop Lucci that he need not fear any further . . . surprises from you."

"And St. Wenceslaus? Will it stay open?"

"That's entirely between you, His Excellency, and the Almighty. I suggest you pray about it regularly. If you maintain this large, active congregation by providing a supportive ministry, the bishop won't want to close St. Wenceslaus. And if for any reason he tried, the standing-room crowd I saw today would undoubtedly protest his decision loudly in front of every television camera in the state. That kind of negative press would put tremendous pressure on Lucci to keep the church open. I doubt His Excellency would risk shuttering your doors in the face of that kind of publicity."

Marek set his clasped hands on the desk

and leaned forward.

"And the other two conditions?"

I watched the subtle twitching of the muscles between his thumbs and index fingers.

"Take off your glasses, Father Marek."

"What?"

"Just do it, and follow my finger with your eyes."

When he did, I confirmed what I had suspected. He had nystagmus. His eyes rapidly twitched side to side in a pattern indicating weakness of the muscles along the outer edge of each eye. I had already noted his wide-based unsteady gait, ruddy complexion, and puffy eyelids.

"You have to stop drinking. Completely. Today."

"The hell I will! I'm no drunk, damn it." He slammed a fist on the desk. "How dare you? I only drink socially. That's all!"

I walked to the closet, removed the bottles of vodka, and set them on his desk.

"Social drinkers don't keep two fifths of booze hidden under blankets in their office closet." I sat down again. "I mean it. Not another drop. You have Wernicke's encephalopathy."

"What are you talking about? How the hell would you know anything about —"

"Father Marek," Emily interrupted, "Jake is also a physician."

Marek collapsed back into his chair and gazed at the ceiling.

"You're in the early stages, and Wernicke's is curable with vitamin B1 injections . . . *if* you stop drinking. If you don't, it will lead to permanent brain damage. Eventually, you'll develop double vision, memory loss, hallucinations, and you won't be able to walk or speak. This is a non-negotiable part of the deal."

Marek's eyes remained fixed on the crown molding.

"The third condition is that you see Dr. Marcus Taylor, a neurologist at St. Joseph's Hospital in Lorain for your treatment. I'll tell him you'll be calling for an appointment." Taylor could confirm my diagnosis and rule out less likely possibilities. "He will keep your diagnosis confidential from the Diocese, but *you will* allow him to notify me if you fall off the wagon. Do we have a deal?"

Marek shook his head. "I . . . I don't know."

"This road will be hard, but listen Father Marek, if you don't stop drinking, no one will be able to conjure up a miracle to save you. You're standing on the precipice, about to fall into the abyss. Do this for yourself. Please."

Marek's head continued to shake from side to side. After a while, he stood.

"And if I say no, what then Father Jake?"

"Then I'll tell the bishop everything. He'll immediately remove you as pastor of St. Wenceslaus, suspend your faculties, tell everyone what you did, and make sure you are not received at any diocesan parish or institution. Without assignment, you'll be a pariah, living in complete religious isolation. He'll also begin Canon Law procedures for your permanent suspension. You'll no longer be able to celebrate Mass and the Sacraments. And you'll suffer a slow, horrific death from your alcoholism."

Marek walked to the window and peered out as if in a trance, then returned to his desk.

"Okay, you win. I'll do my best. We have a deal." His words held the ring of sincerity. "Lemme ask you a question, Father Jake. Do you believe God really performs miracles?"

"Sure. Every day. Not necessarily what we ask for, but how else can you explain this amazing world? Maybe what just happened here is your own little miracle, Marek, if you seize the opportunity."

"So then, what happens if a *real miracle* occurs here at St. Wenceslaus?"

"Today is as close to one as you will ever get, Father, so count your blessings."

I unsealed the plastic bag that contained the needle and tube. "Put the syringe and the blood in here. Give me everything you used."

Marek walked to the small refrigerator in the back of his office, removed a margarine container, opened it, and produced a 10cc syringe and a purple top test tube half-filled with blood. He dropped them in the bag.

A wry smile creased his lips.

"Ah, so you're collecting my fingerprints too, Father Jake? How gumshoe of you. You won't need them. I'll hold up my end of the bargain."

"I hope so, but I'll keep all the evidence and photos from the attic as insurance." I resealed the bag. "Where'd you get the anti-coagulated test tube and the blood? The tests I ran proved it wasn't yours."

"I figured Lucci would test the blood against mine. I wasn't foolish enough to use my own. That's why I happily gave him my sample." He shrugged. "The nuns who run the free clinic know and trust me. If they're short-staffed, I help out by manning the front desk or running errands. Sometimes I bring them coffee and doughnuts and sit in the nursing station. It's a busy place, too busy to keep track of every blood sample and syringe."

Marek stood and pointed to the bottles of vodka.

"Take those with you. I don't need the temptation. Enjoy. It's great stuff." I must have given him a wary look because he added, "I love a stiff drink or three, but I love the Lord more. Don't worry. I'll be fine."

Emily and I left his office and walked in silence to my car. I put my new supply of top-shelf vodka on the floor in the back seat and opened the passenger door. I was feeling quite selfsatisfied about what we had accomplished until I saw Emily's expression of utter defeat. She clutched my arm with both hands, leaned against me, and sighed.

"Oh Jake, I . . . ." Her sobs were raw and primal. "All those prayers . . . I only wish . . . Stupid! I'm so naive."

She buried her face in my chest and I wrapped my arms around her, then her knees buckled and I held her tight. I had no words. What the hell had I been thinking? I should never have involved her in this fiasco, knowing how much she was hoping for a

miracle. I never meant to hurt her.
We held each other for a very long time.

CHAPTER TWENTY-SEVEN

Sunday, July 30, 4:00 p.m.

Emily said nothing for the first half of the drive back. She slouched down in the seat, shoulders hunched, facing the passenger window. Although I knew I'd done the right thing with Marek, I understood how my actions had devastated her and why she might not want to be anywhere near me.

Finally I asked, "Em? You okay?"

"Oh, I'll be all right. I've had my hopes dashed before. I could use a glass of that vodka, though."

She pulled a tissue from her purse and dabbed her eyes.

"I have a question," she said with a weak smile. The very sight of it lifted a weight from my chest. "Fingerprints? Getting Father Marek's prints on the syringe and test tube? Really, Jake? That's a little over the top, even for you, don't you think?"

I laughed. "Honestly, I never thought

about that till Marek suggested it."

She drew a deep breath and tilted her head to one side. "I am proud of what you did today. You showed the wisdom of Solomon."

"I don't know about that. I was pretty ticked off. Solomon? Heck, without your guidance, I would've sliced both Marek and his church into tiny pieces." I patted her hand. "Way to keep a level head, Em. You're good, very cool under pressure."

"You have no idea." She chuckled softly. "So, how will you deal with Bishop Lucci?"

"With extreme care, like you'd handle nitroglycerin. I'll figure something out. The seminary taught me how to dance around unpleasant realities."

"What if the bishop finds out that you covered for Father Marek?"

I had no answer, and no dance for that one. As I pondered her question, my cell rang.

As if reading my thoughts, Lucci said, "Jacob, my son. Any news about . . . our friend?"

"I searched every inch of St. Wenceslaus, but I'm afraid I can't give you proof that Father Marek's been concocting miracles." *If I did, you'd destroy him and close the church, and I can't let that happen.*

"Not exactly what I was hoping to hear, Jacob. I'm disappointed."

Disappointing His Excellency was not a judicious career move, nor wise for those of us dependent on his largess, so I added, "I am, however, almost certain that there'll be no further miracles at St. Wenceslaus."

"What does that mean? You'd better not be protecting that man. I won't tolerate disloyalty." I heard voices in the background and he said, "Hold on a minute."

When he returned to the phone, he asked, "How can you be sure Marek won't cause me further problems?"

"I put the fear of God and Mother Church in him, Excellency." And I was damn sure Marek was scared to death of me, the attic photos, and my plastic bag of evidence.

"Fire and brimstone, huh? That didn't work when I tried it." He exhaled loudly, more of a grunt. "I guess there's an upside. The media would jump all over me if Marek was exposed as a fraud. At least I won't have to deal with more bad press. All right. I guess that'll have to do. But consider him your personal responsibility from now on. Keep an eye on the old lush, and call me if you sense trouble. I'm depending on you."

And with a click, the bishop was gone.

Emily reached over and tapped my arm.

She was grinning like the proverbial Cheshire cat.

"*Can't* tell him? Or *won't*?"

"Semantics, Em."

She nibbled on the arm of her sunglasses for a moment. "If you told the bishop the truth, could he defrock or excommunicate Father Marek?"

I drum-rolled my fingers on the steering wheel.

"No, Marek's transgression doesn't merit excommunication, and only Rome can restore a priest to the lay state, or what you call *defrock*. At the very least, however, he'd suspend Marek's faculties, which means he could no longer celebrate Mass publically. That would be bad enough for any priest, but . . . who knows how far His Excellency might go? He can be very vindictive."

"Think he bought your story?"

"No, I'm sure he suspects I'm holding out on him. He turned a blind eye because I gave him what he really wanted — plausible deniability. If the poop ever hits the fan, it'll be my butt on the line. As Lucci said, Marek's my problem now, so I'll have to make sure he stays on the straight and narrow."

My stomach rumbled angrily. "Are you hungry, Em?"

"Starving."

I thought about stopping at a great restaurant I knew about in Westlake, but Colleen had already spent a long day babysitting and I couldn't ask her to stay late again. And with his mother in the hospital, RJ needed my attention and reassurance — and frankly, I missed being with the boy. I dialed the rectory.

"Sacred Heart, Colleen Brady speaking."

"It's me. How are things with RJ?"

"Excellent! Aren't we getting on famously? When he said that RJ stood for Randall James, I told him the story of St. James — but left out the gory bits. You'll have to tell him about St. Randall, Father. For the life of me, I know of no such saint. And don't you worry about your dinner. It'll be ready when you arrive."

"Thanks, Colleen. Is there enough for a guest?"

"And might I ask who that would be?"

"Emily Beale." I glanced at Em. She nodded. "She'd like to see RJ before his bedtime, and I was hoping she might join us."

"I made meatloaf and there's plenty," she answered, but not before hesitating. As a devout Catholic and confirmed busybody, Colleen had expressed her concern about my *relationship* with Emily. "Yes, I suppose —"

"Wonderful." I didn't wait for her approval or a lecture on propriety. "Please stay and have supper with us, Colleen."

"Oh, I couldn't do that, Father. The Legion of Mary is sponsoring a potluck dinner at the fellowship hall tomorrow and . . . ."

Her voice trailed off.

"Colleen, are you still there?"

"Yes, I am, Father." I could almost hear the wheels spinning in Colleen's mind. She was my self-appointed chaperone and protector of my virtue. "On second thought, I can make my dish for the potluck in the morning. Indeed, I'd love to join you for supper. See you soon."

I clicked on the radio. As Emily leaned back against the headrest and sang along with the oldies, I wondered for the thousandth time why our relationship had crumbled so many years ago. She was an incredible woman and the best friend I'd ever had.

Deep down, I knew the answer. Like many high school athletes, I'd been arrogant and self-centered in my youth, strutting through the halls in my letter sweater. A beautiful, intelligent girl like Emily on my arm seemed a well-deserved perk for my heroics on the

football field or a buzzer-beating basket —
until my stint in the army and the nightmare
of war slapped me back to reality. The
demise of our relationship was completely
my own doing.

Maybe in some bizarre way, it had all been
part of God's greater plan for my future in
the priesthood. Who could say? The cloud-
less heavens offered me no other explanation, so I let my past drift through the open
car window and added some harmony to
Emily's soprano — until the DJ spun an
oldie from the 70's by the band America.
Their words tore into me like shrapnel, the
repeated refrain *I need you* slicing healed
scars open.

I tried to sing along but couldn't. For
years, I'd needed no one. Now, I was no
longer sure I could ever be without Emily's
friendship in my life again.

The song lyrics slashed at me once more
and I punched a button on the radio,
switching stations. Emily turned to me with
a look of surprise.

"Just channel surfing, Em, searching for
some Beatles."

We resumed our stroll down memory lane,
singing our way through a series of moldy-
oldies by one-and-done rock groups until
we reached the rectory.

Colleen met us at the door, her expression dour.

"Your sister's doctor called." She handed me a Post-it note with a telephone number. "He wants you ring him at home, Father. Says it's urgent."

At home? On Sunday? Not a good sign. I called immediately.

"Doctor? This is Jake Austin, Justine's brother. You wanted to speak with me?"

"Ah, yes. Your sister's condition is deteriorating. We need to push up the schedule and perform her bone marrow transplant tomorrow. Not the way I'd like to go, but . . . . Please arrive at Desk R-20 in the Taussig Cancer Institute by 6:00 a.m. sharp."

"I'll be there. Thank you."

I was so surprised by the call that it never occurred to me to ask *where* in the massive Cleveland Clinic complex the building was located. It didn't matter. I would find it. Tomorrow couldn't come too soon as far as I was concerned. Justine had lost so much weight in the short time that she'd been staying with me that when I dropped her off at the hospital, she had looked like one of RJ's stick-figure drawings. Even he had noticed.

Before it got any later, I called Justine at the hospital and handed the telephone to

RJ. His face lit up as he told her about his day, recounting the story of his namesake, St. James. Colleen, his self-appointed spiritual guru, beamed at his enthusiasm.

Justine barely got a word in before he switched topics, going on and on about his *pet lightning bugs,* detailing how they twinkled in his bedroom all night long and how we released them in the morning. Apparently he'd named one of them "Tinker Bell," although I had no idea how he could differentiate one from another. Emily, Colleen, and I were all chuckling nearby when RJ suddenly stopped talking, said "I love you too, Mommy," and gave me the phone.

"Jake, they want me to hang up soon, but I need you to do something for me."

"Sure. What is it?"

"I been doing a lot of thinking, and I want you to become RJ's legal guardian and my power of attorney, in case things don't go well."

My breath lodged in my chest. I stepped away from my nephew and lowered my voice. "Don't you dare give up! You're going to get through this, Sis."

"It's not giving up. It's doing the right thing — for RJ. Jake, there's no one else. I'm begging you. I don't want RJ shipped off to some foster home. Do this for me, please! I called the Legal Aid Society and gave them the address of the rectory as my home but they're so short-staffed and backlogged, I'm afraid they won't get things done soon enough. I know you don't have much money, but can you hire a lawyer to do the paperwork? I'll rest a lot easier if RJ's future is secure."

Of course she was right. Her failing health and my nephew's tenuous future had worried me since they first arrived in town. I couldn't even begin to imagine what my life would look like if I lost her and assumed guardianship of her child. I also hesitated because I had no idea where I could get the money to pay a lawyer, but forced myself to set my concerns aside.

"Of course, Sis. I'll get it done."

"Thanks, Jake. Gotta go now. Take care."

I asked Colleen to please serve dinner, then stepped into my study and called Tree Macon.

"Please tell me you found my old man, and he's on an airplane headed to Cleveland as we speak."

"He may be on a plane, Jake, but I got no idea where to. Word is, he crossed Angie Giordano, took some drugs and money, and made a run for it. Giordano's thugs blew up your daddy's car before he made it out of

Louisiana. No crispy critters inside, so your father's probably alive and in the wind. We may never find him though . . . alive anyway. Sorry, buddy."

I hung up and wandered to the dinner table shaking my head. My old man never failed to disappoint — leaving my half-sister in desperate need of a miracle. I prayed that she and I had enough shared genes from the bastard to give her a fighting chance.

Colleen's meatloaf, spiced with sausage and onion, was one of my favorite meals, but I had no appetite and found it tasteless. I forced myself to eat, and cast my sister's impending bone marrow transplant in a positive light for my nephew's benefit, hoping my concerns didn't bleed through.

My performance did little to elevate RJ's mood. He was maudlin and a thousand miles away. Emily hardly spoke during the meal, most likely mentally replaying the loss of her own miracle at St. Wenceslaus. Colleen filled the frequent silences, blathering on about the upcoming potluck at the church. When we finished eating, Colleen volunteered to drive Emily home, promising to arrive at five in the morning to care for RJ.

After bathing him, I maneuvered my nephew into bed where the floodgates of his fear suddenly burst open in a deluge of tears. I cuddled him in my arms for a long time trying to comfort him.

After he finally fell asleep, I obtained coverage for Monday morning Mass from Father Vargas. He had already covered my Saturday Vigil Mass and Sunday morning Mass so that I could play detective at St. Wenceslaus, and I owed him bigtime.

Unwilling to break the third Commandment by failing to keep the Lord's day holy, I offered a private Mass in my room for Justine's recovery. Then I showered, set my alarm for 4:00 a.m., fell into bed, and let fatigue carry me away.

CHAPTER TWENTY-EIGHT

Monday, July 31, 5:45 a.m.
Light rain dappled my windshield as I raced toward Cleveland into the amber light of dawn well before the usual traffic snarl could materialize. Thanks to MapQuest, I had no trouble locating the Taussig Cancer Center building on Carnegie Avenue. Finding nearby parking, however, was more difficult, and I literally had to sprint to Desk R-20, arriving five minutes late. After completing the insurance information, consent forms, and other obligatory paperwork, I sat in the pre-op area for what felt like days.

I'd made Tree Macon promise to call if by some stroke of luck he located my old man. I checked my cellphone repeatedly for messages but found none.

Bottom line: I was Justine's last hope. *Thy will be done.*

At last given a hospital gown, I changed

in a dressing room and stored my belongings in a locker. A young, blond woman in her early twenties, cheery beyond all reason at that early hour, literally danced into the waiting room pushing a wheelchair. She had the faint stamp of a local nightclub on her hand and a fresh hickey peeking over her collar. Softly singing Beautiful Day by U2, she rolled me to a small operating room where a nurse plugged an IV line into one arm and slapped a blood pressure cuff on the other, then left me alone with my thoughts.

The air was cool and laced with disinfectant, the table cold and hard. Two men in surgical scrubs entered. Justine's oncologist was in his mid-fifties, short, stout, and balding. He introduced himself and said, "You understand, we don't have the luxury of five days to do a peripheral blood donation. We'll have to do this the old fashion way, directly from your pelvic bones." He gestured to the other man and added, "You'll be awake, but Dr. Gavacs here is a fine anesthesiologist, and he'll minimize your pain. Nothing to worry about. No sweat."

No sweat *for him,* maybe. And I could think of more than a few things to worry about.

I rolled onto my side and the anesthesiologist inserted a spinal needle into my back, injected the anesthetic, and laid me on my belly. My hips and legs tingled for a few moments, then went numb.

While the nurse draped my bottom and sterilized my skin with Betadine, the anesthesiologist infused a sedative through my IV, resulting in a pleasant buzz.

I couldn't see what the oncologist was doing, but he morphed into a Howard Cosell-like play-by-play description for the benefit of an intern who'd entered the room.

"An incision here. Come on, nurse, more suction so I can clamp that bleeder. That's better. Hand me the large-gauge needle with the cutting trocar. And we shove this through the muscle, twist, then use the jagged edge to penetrate the iliac bone . . . apply suction with the syringe, and harvest some marrow. Now, same thing on the other side."

He struggled more with the second aspiration, and I heard an unnerving grinding sound as he penetrated bone on the left, then he said, "And voila! We're done and out the door."

As the nurse carried the precious cells out of the room for my sister's infusion, the oncologist snapped off his latex gloves, apparently remembered that I was there, and said, "So how're you doing? Still with me? You didn't holler. That's a good sign." He patted my shoulder and added a hearty, "See, nothing to it. Don't even need stitches. You'll be sore for a few days. No big deal. I'll send you home with some painkillers just in case."

In truth, all I had felt was intermittent pressure during the procedure. Three cheers for anesthetics, and for anesthesiologists who understand that all patients are anxious human beings.

While an orderly wheeled me to the Recovery Room, I prayed silently for Justine. As a physician, I understood the risks and potential complications of her transplant. The next few weeks were critical for my sister's recovery. Her hold on life was tenuous and in the Lord's hands.

Slowly the anesthetic wore off and sensation returned to my legs. The soreness from the procedure felt minor, however, compared to the pain of knowing that I'd missed three decades of Justine's life and my nephew's early years. The holes in my pelvic bones couldn't compare with the void that she and RJ might have filled had I met them sooner.

When they released me from the recovery room, I was still slightly woozy and didn't want to drive home. I dressed, relocated to the hushed family consultation area, and spent my time mumbling prayers and fingering my rosary beads. Minutes stretched into hours, and the room grew smaller and smaller until it became a cage. Sitting was more painful than standing, so I clipped my phone to my belt and wandered the mammoth Cleveland Clinic complex.

The halls were almost as crowded as a busy downtown sidewalk. I meandered into the hospital gift store and shopped for something to take my nephew's mind off his mother's absence. A toy doctor's kit caught my attention and I snatched it up. On my way to the checkout counter, my cell startled me.

The update from the oncologist was brief. "So far, so good. Fingers crossed."

But that was exactly what I needed to hear. Hope is a powerful medicine. I felt a renewed spring in my step as I reentered the hallway.

Because Justine's immune system had been suppressed, she would remain in the Isolation Unit for now. I wasn't allowed to visit her, yet I couldn't force myself to leave the hospital. I found the chapel, knelt and prayed, then wandered the manicured grounds between Euclid Avenue and Carnegie. The sky had transformed to pig-iron and low clouds stretched westward into an endless mottled gray.

A silver Lincoln Town Car and two television trucks roared into the driveway and screeched up to the hospital entrance. Because the Clinic treated foreign dignitaries and celebrities, media presence was not uncommon. Normally, I ignored this kind of hoopla, but I needed a diversion and joined a crowd of gawkers.

The young couple that I'd seen on TV leaped from the car. She wore a black pantsuit, he a navy-blue suit. She was weeping uncontrollably, and he wrapped an arm around her as they pushed their way through reporters and photo journalists into the lobby. An elderly woman nearby asked me who they were.

"They were featured on the local news recently. Their baby has a bad heart and is dying. He needs a new one." I thought of Justine and the countless others who desperately needed organ donors and hoped it wasn't already too late for this family.

Wandering back inside, I meditated about dying children over a cup of coffee in the snack shop until the last of my sedation wore off and I could postpone leaving the hospital no longer. I made certain that

Justine's nurses in Isolation had my cell-phone number, then hurried off to spend time with RJ and to relieve Colleen of her babysitting duty. Since my sister's hospitalization, the poor woman had spent more time at the rectory than I had.

I was driving through Westlake, fighting off the urge to swallow a painkiller dry, when my phone chirped.

"Jake, it's Tree. Just checking in. How's your sister doing?"

"As well as can be expected."

"If you want to skip the tribe game tonight, it's okay by me."

I'd completely forgotten. Tree and I usually watched televised games together whenever the Indians played the dreaded Yankees. It didn't matter to us where Cleveland was in the standings, as long as they beat New York.

"No, that's fine. I could use the distraction." And I wanted him to hear the threatening message on my answering machine.

"Great. I'll get there early so I can see the little guy before his bedtime. He's the real reason I come over. And I'll bring some party provisions for the grownups, cop style — doughnuts and beer."

"Forget the doughnuts. But after getting poked in the butt by large gauge needles this morning, I could definitely use a beer. See you tonight."

On my way to the rectory, I stopped briefly at St. Joseph's Hospital, swiped two rolls of gauze and a surgical mask and cap from the Emergency Room, and slipped them into the toy doctor's kit.

I was anxious to get home but needed to visit one parishioner who was terminal. As I passed the hospital chapel, I noticed Jenifer Dublikar, the head nurse in PICU, kneeling in a back pew. She whispered "amen," stood, then noticed me.

"Oh! Hi Father. I didn't hear you come in."

"Sorry to disturb you. I was just passing by. It's nice to see you on my turf once in a while."

"Whenever I get off my shift early, I stop in and say a quick prayer for my patients." She smiled. "I'm very good at my job, but sometimes I need help from above." The smile faded. "Especially with Pablo. I think we're losing him."

"Any threatening behavior from his mother?"

"Nope. She and I have become *real close.* Literally. Whenever she walks into intensive care, I stay two steps away." She glanced at her watch. "Well, I have to get home. Take care."

Long shifts in the hospital, *and* prayers for her patients. When she left, I knelt and asked God to bless her and all the nurses and other hospital personnel who go above and well beyond the call of duty every day.

When I finished, I headed off to visit my dying parishioner. The elevator doors opened and a flock of Candy-Stripers spilled out like white-streaked flamingoes, giggling as they passed. I hurried inside, collided with Dr. Taylor, and dropped RJ's gift, spilling the stolen supplies and toy stethoscope from the plastic black bag.

Taylor laughed. "I realize you took a vow of poverty but *really,* Jake. Want some of my old equipment? I have some used tongue depressors you could have."

"Very funny. It's a present for my nephew." I collected my things and added, "I hear Pablo's not doing well."

A family carrying a bouquet of flowers boarded the elevator. Taylor took my arm and led me out into a quiet corridor.

"Got a few more tests to run, Jake, but Pablo's brain damage appears irreversible. I spoke with his parents about turning off the respirator, and I may need your help with them. Miguel has always been resistant to the idea, however Tina had been on-board . . . until today. Soon as I started explaining the organ harvesting procedure, she grew vehemently opposed. Now she wants nothing to do with autopsies and organ donation. Not only is she against pulling the plug, she's pushing Miguel for cremation if Pablo dies. I don't know how to deal with her anymore."

"Jumbled emotions aren't unusual, Marcus."

"Of course, but to do a complete flip-flop? One moment she wants to donate Pablo's organs, and the next she wants cremation? Hell, I'm worried she's having a psychotic break."

"I suggested grief counseling. Did they ever see anyone?"

"No, Tina refused. And she won't consent to a psych consult either. I'd appreciate any help you can give me."

"Their world is upside down. I doubt either one is thinking clearly. I left a message on their machine and hope to speak with them tomorrow."

"As a doctor or a priest?"

"Both."

"Well, see if you can convince them to donate Pablo's organs, Jake. The boy is never going home — but some other kids might, if they get his kidneys, lungs, heart, and liver."

"I'll do my best."

"Oh, by the way, I just saw a patient in my office that you referred to me. Father Marek. He definitely has Wernicke's encephalopathy, and it's a good thing you caught it when you did."

"Please keep me posted, especially if he falls off the wagon, so I can get him back onboard."

"Will do, Jake. He's already asked me to keep you in the loop. Interesting guy."

You have no idea.

CHAPTER TWENTY-NINE

Monday, July 31, 7:00 p.m.

That evening RJ was gloomy and nearly mute. Usually a chatterbox, he hardly spoke except for questions about what his mommy did for fun in the hospital and whether the doctors hurt her. To help allay his fears, I coaxed him into the surgical mask and cap that I'd filched from the hospital, presented the toy doctor's kit I'd purchased, and conferred a medical degree on him.

As he examined me, he became so inter- ested that I fetched my black bag and let him listen to my heart and lungs through my stethoscope. His fear quickly trans- formed into fascination. Like most four year olds, he embraced the role-playing, examin- ing my eyes and ears, and smacking my knees repeatedly with the reflex hammer. Then, having made his diagnosis, he wrapped me head to toe in gauze until I could barely walk.

By the time the doorbell rang and Tree entered, I looked like a mummy. The big man's howls of laughter were contagious and RJ joined in, rolling on the floor uncontrollably.

I unwrapped my bandages while RJ marshaled his plastic army. He led a fierce assault on the combined clothespin forces that Tree and I commanded. We fought valiantly, but the little general's determination and his indestructible troops pursued us relentlessly up the stairs and into his bedroom. We surrendered, pledging with our hands over our hearts to *never be bad and always be good,* sealing the peace accord with a pinky promise.

Tree retreated downstairs, and I dressed my nephew in his GI Joe pajamas and tucked him into bed. He began to fret again about his mother. I was forced to offer him assurances that I knew were at best wishful thinking, and at worst flat-out lies. After I read him two stories, he finally closed his eyes and slept.

Downstairs, Tree was pacing in the living room. He had opened one of the bottles of Guinness that he'd brought and had nearly finished it.

I pointed to his beer. "Long day, or bad day?"

"If I told you it was shitty, I'd be boasting. And, yeah, they're all long."

"I'm sorry to add to it, but there's something I want you to hear."

I motioned him into the kitchen and played the threatening message on the answering machine. His eyebrows knitted together in a scowl, then he popped the cassette tape out and slid it into his pocket.

"Not sure if that's a man or a woman, Jake. No doubt that was intentional, but the rectory's machine is ancient. That tape's probably recorded a million messages. And *mind your own damn business* and *you'll be sorry* are pretty vague as far as threats go." He downed the last of his beer. "I'll have my tech geek take a listen and see if she's got any tricks up her sleeve. Want me to have a black and white drive by the rectory every couple hours at night?"

"No, that's not necessary. Call me if you come up with anything." I opened the refrigerator, grabbed two bottles of Guinness, handed him a replacement, and said, "Let's go watch the game."

In the living room, Tree picked a few Lego blocks off the sofa, placed them on the coffee table, commented on my lack of housekeeping skills, and plopped down hard.

I found the sports channel, lowered the

volume so as not to wake RJ, and eased gingerly into my recliner. The painkiller I took after dinner was wearing off, and the surgical sites in my pelvic bones ached. I took a long draw of beer and tried unsuccessfully to find a comfortable position.

The Indian's leadoff batter walked, and the two-hole hitter drove a fastball into the bleachers. The Tribe was off to a terrific start and we enjoyed the game until our rookie pitcher panicked and the wheels started coming off the bullpen bus. Being a Cleveland fan is not for the faint-of-heart.

I spied a drop of blood on Tree's shirt collar and pointed to the jagged scar on his neck.

"Did you have a dermatologist examine that growth yet?"

"You're joking, right? I been *busy* lately, Jake. I'll get to it. And if you keep bugging me about it, I'll have you arrested for invasion of privacy and being a pain in the tush."

I raised both hands in surrender. "Sorry. You really *have had* a bad day."

"Yeah, partly because of you. The County Coroner gave me an ass-chewing this afternoon for not bringing in a child abuse expert on day one of the SIDS case. I told her you were my consultant and an expert in all things."

"Nice of you to defend my competence."

"Forgive me Father, for I have lied." He smiled. "Anyway, the Sheriff called too. I expected to catch more grief from him, but instead he told me he was retiring and asked me to run for his job in November. What do you think?"

"It gives me hope. If you can be the sheriff, then I have a shot at becoming the Pope." I chuckled and we clinked bottles. "Seriously, you'd make a great sheriff, since you're an expert in, well . . . a few things."

"I don't know, Jake. I'm not very political."

"Or tactful."

"Yeah, that too. I'm used to dealing with dumb-as-dirt criminals, but a bunch of dim-witted politicians? I might have to shoot one or two."

"Hey, Tree, this is America. Everyone has the right to be stupid. It's just that some politicians abuse the privilege."

"The job would mean a big pay raise, and there's never been a black sheriff in the county. My wife and preacher are pushing me hard to do it, but I'm not sure I want to put myself and my family though the usual media rectal examination of an election."

"If you run, I might even register here and vote for you. Drop off a six-pack of Guinness, and I'll try to convince the faithful to vote for a Baptist."

Tree's beeper screeched and he checked the number.

"Sorry, gotta make a call," he said and walked into the kitchen. When he returned, his expression was grim.

"What happened? Did some kid let the air out of the tires on your cruiser?"

He shrugged his massive shoulders like Atlas collapsing under the weight of the world and slumped onto the sofa. "One of my uniforms found out that the parents of the SIDS baby wrote a check to a life insurance company for a policy on him . . . for twenty-five grand."

"Found out? I thought you were having trouble getting a warrant."

"Ah . . . no warrant. I tried, but the judge said we didn't have sufficient probable cause."

"All right, so how'd you get the info?"

"Don't ask, buddy."

"I just did. Fess up. Confession time."

I waited him out.

"Shit. Okay. It was a trade. An officer, who will remain my unnamed source, is dating a bank employee and . . . and well, I guess she had something *he* wanted."

"Quid pro quo?"

"More like tit for tat. Or tit for that."

"What the hell, Tree? Please tell me she didn't do this on your orders."

"Don't give me that pious priest look. I had nothing to do with it. She's been working the case with me, knew what we needed, and did this on her own. Hell, she's a consenting adult and has been dating the guy for a while. She can do whatever she wants. But that's why I'm *not* jumping up and down for joy. It's not admissible as evidence — though it sure as hell sounds like motive to me and I can't ignore it."

In my mind I saw Pablo in the morgue, a twenty-five thousand dollar price tag hanging from a tiny, cold, blue-gray toe.

"Would anyone kill their child for a lousy twenty-five grand, Tree?"

"We're not talking big bucks, but Pablo's folks are in debt up to their eyeballs." He downed half of his beer. "I'm going to see if they had insurance on their first kid, the baby that died in Pennsylvania, then try again to get a warrant to examine their computer and finances."

I needed an excuse to get off my sore behind and walk around, so I fetched another bottle of Guinness.

"Another beer, Jake?"

"It's for the pain, Officer, and I'm not

driving anywhere."

"On top of pain meds, Doctor?"

I shrugged. "Do as I say, not as I do."

He raised his bottle in salute. "What a relief. When you came back to town as a priest, I was afraid you'd have no redeeming vices."

"Don't let it get around, okay?" I took a sip. "I'm not sure if this means anything, but Dr. Taylor told me that Tina stopped pressuring him to turn off the respirator and donate Pablo's organs. The moment he explained the procedure and mentioned the mandatory autopsy, she changed her tune. One moment she wants to donate Pablo's organs, the next she's pushing for cremation if he dies. Taylor's worried she's having a nervous breakdown."

"Huh, so Mommy did a one-eighty? That's interesting. If they tried to kill Pablo, would an autopsy prove it?"

"It's unlikely — but she may not know that. Babies can't fight back, so they have no defensive wounds. The CT scan showed no evidence of fracture or head trauma. If they suffocated Pablo with a pillow or other soft object, that's difficult to differentiate from SIDS, since death results from lack of oxygen in both cases."

"How'd Miguel react, Jake?"

"He's been hesitant about withdrawing life support and autopsies on religious grounds from the very beginning. I explained the Church's position on both, however, and he seemed to accept that. I'm more suspicious of Tina's sudden resistance."

"Problem is, *Miguel* signed the check for the insurance. If they're a Bonnie and Clyde duo, Miguel is definitely not the brains of the outfit. I doubt that he could count to twenty-one with both hands and both feet and his pants down. But a team effort isn't likely, since Tina's talking with a divorce lawyer — unless Miguel doesn't have a clue she's about to bail out on him." He drained his beer bottle. "Let's just watch the damn game."

The Indian's late-inning rally fell one run short as Mariano Rivera slammed the door closed for the Yankees in the ninth. Tree and I called it a night, both of us unsatisfied.

Two beers hadn't done much to relieve my pain. Although it's unwise to mix pills and booze, I reached for the bottle of painkillers the oncologist had prescribed, thought of my old man, then hesitated. Not dealing with life was *his* way. I refused to become my father, putting my needs above everyone else, disappearing into a haze of booze and pills. I was still on duty — for RJ, who needed me now more than ever. No way would I let him down by zoning out. My bone marrow had provided a chance to save Justine and what was left of my family, and I was more than willing to trade my discomfort and a crappy night's sleep for their well-being.

CHAPTER THIRTY

Tuesday, August 1, 9:30 a.m.

After morning Mass, I buttered a piece of toast and sat at the kitchen table as the coffee maker gurgled and belched on the counter. Now that Colleen was draining the rectory food budget to buy toys and books for my nephew, egg and bacon breakfasts were on hold.

Little feet pattered into the room and a small grumpy face peered up at me. RJ climbed onto my lap and demanded to visit his mother in the hospital. I reminded him that she was still in the Isolation Unit, and it would be a while before she could have visitors. Whiny mutated into cranky, and it was all I could do to keep him from a full-blown meltdown.

Failing logic, I tousled his hair and suggested that we play with the new Lincoln Log set that Colleen had purchased. The grin that I'd grown to love reappeared. I tossed back an OxyContin, dropped a sofa pillow on the living room floor, cautiously eased my sore behind onto it, and showed my nephew how to assemble the tiny notched timbers. He laser-focused on the task, and before you could say Paul Bunyan, he was building his second log cabin.

I snuck into the study to download my email, then checked on Justine's status. Still serious, no improvement. I asked to speak with her. The nurse suggested that I call back in thirty minutes.

With a moment of time for myself, I thought about Justine's request. Tree would probably loan me enough money to hire a lawyer, but I hated to impose on my friend. Flipping through the church directory, I called a parishioner who practiced law and asked what it would cost to become my sister's Power of Attorney and apply to become RJ's guardian if she became inca-pacitated or passed away. She replied that her firm required her to do one pro bono case a year, and that I had just won the freebie lottery. I gave her the pertinent information and thanked her, emphasizing that time was of the essence.

With one weight off my shoulders, I returned to the living room. Colleen stood in the doorway, arms crossed, shaking her head.

"Would you look at him, Father? I buy him games and toys to distract him from his soldiers, and *this* is what I find!"

RJ's plastic army was bivouacked in one log cabin. Clothespins peeked from the windows and doors of the other.

"Uncle Jake, Uncle Jake," he said, pointing proudly at his handiwork. "I made two forts!"

Paratroopers plummeted down from my recliner to the rat-tat-tat of machine gun fire. Three clothespins fell.

"What am I to do with the lad, Father? He won't even play a game of Snakes and Ladders with me."

"It's *Chutes* and Ladders in this country. The idea of serpents probably scares the boy. Besides, didn't St. Patrick drive all the snakes out of Ireland?"

Colleen gave me the icy glare that Sister Mary Nancy, better known as Sister Very Nasty, often trained on me in grade school when I'd transgressed.

"Nonetheless, Father, I'm at a total loss as to how to put an end to this behavior. Thank the good Lord I never had children!"

"Trust me, playing soldier is a phase most boys go through. He'll outgrow it." *Probably when he discovers girls.* "There's nothing to be done."

Colleen climbed the stairs, grumbling in Gaelic until the sound of the vacuum cleaner masked her displeasure.

I took command of the clothespins and let RJ rout my troops until it was time to call his mother. After RJ entertained her with a detailed description of his Lincoln Log adventures, he let me speak to her.

I told her that I hadn't forgotten her request and had contacted a lawyer, then asked how she was doing. Justine sounded exhausted but insisted that things were going well and she felt fine. When I pressed for specifics about her care, she dodged my questions, adding that RJ and I might be allowed to visit her in a few days. When she ended the call, her son was re-energized. I, on the other hand, could barely rise from the chair, the possibility of a failed procedure and its implications for RJ and me lingering in my mind.

Having delayed my task as long as possible, I asked Colleen to take over with RJ, called Miguel Hernandez, and requested to stop by. He said that he'd had a tough nightshift and was on his way to bed. I promised to keep my visit short and he relented.

When I arrived a few minutes later, he

took the sofa and offered me a chair. Their tiny apartment reeked of marijuana, an aroma I was familiar with from my checkered youth and time in the Army.

"Is Tina here?"

"Nah, she's working."

"How's Pablo?" Miguel looked out the window. When he didn't respond, I asked, "Is there anything I can do for you and Tina?"

"Pray for all of us, *por favor*! Pray hard. Pablo's . . . he's dying. I'm not stupid, Padre."

"Of course not. All three of you are in my prayers." I cleared my throat, thought about my conversation with Dr. Taylor, and searched for the right words. "Miguel, I want to assure you that the Church sees organ donation, if it ever comes to that, as an act of charity, not a sin."

His head snapped in my direction.

"Yeah? How's the Church feel about me pulling the plug on my child? Should I just let him die? I'm his *father*, for Christ-sake. I'm supposed to protect him! What the hell happened to *Thou shall not kill*? You think it's okay to slice up my boy and give his parts away? Ay . . . Madre de Diós!"

"The Church allows people to decide to discontinue extraordinary measures, like

266

ventilators, when there's no hope of recovery. Death doesn't have to be prolonged artificially."

"Who told you there was no hope? God, or those butchers at the hospital? And Pablo can't *decide* nothing. He's a baby!"

"That's why it falls to you and Tina to make the decisions." I stood and placed a hand on his shoulder. "I know the choice is —"

Miguel swatted my arm away. "You don't know shit. You got any kids, Padre?"

In my mind I saw RJ building forts in the living room and couldn't imagine what Miguel was going through. I closed my mouth and studied the filthy green carpet until he spoke.

"What they want us to do, ain't that the same as *mercy killing*? It's . . . what's the word? *Youth . . . in Asia?*"

I had dealt with this question many times.

"It's definitely not the same. What we're talking about here is *allowing* a dying patient to pass away naturally. The goal of euthanasia is to end someone's life early to stop their suffering. But pain, whether physical or psychological, can often be controlled with medicine and therapy. The Church encourages doctors and hospice to treat suffering patients aggressively, including narcotics, even if the treatment speeds up the arrival of death. There's a huge moral distinction. Life must always be held as *precious* until the Almighty chooses to call us home."

"Wish He'd call me home instead." Miguel ran his fingers through greasy, thinning hair. He grabbed a can of Bud off the coffee table and gulped the last of its contents.

"Is my niñito suffering, Padre?"

"Pablo's in a deep coma, so I doubt that he's in any pain. But the longer he's confined to a bed with breathing and feeding tubes keeping him alive, the greater the chance he'll get an infection or bed sores. That can be painful for the patient and hard on the family to watch."

Miguel went quiet for a while. Finally he said, "The doctors want an autopsy. Tina won't allow it, and I don't want some ghoul in a morgue cutting Pablo up."

I took a deep breath. "Sometimes the law mandates an autopsy and there's no choice, but it's done with the utmost respect. An autopsy is always required before organ donation."

"Part of me wants to help other kids if Pablo . . . ."

"No matter what you and Tina decide, no one will criticize or second-guess you. In my mind though, the decision to donate organs to help others is the height of Christian compassion." I thought about Justine. "There are more than a hundred thousand people in the country currently waiting for a life-saving transplant, and many die needlessly each year without one."

Miguel lit a cigarette, gazed at its angry red tip, took a deep drag, and blew smoke at the ceiling.

"We saw that baby on the news the other night, you know, the one dying in Cleveland with the bad heart. Tina and I talked about it a long time. Don't seem right not to help him. How can we let other kids die, if our hijo can . . . save them?"

"I can't think of a better way to honor Pablo's memory than to help save dying babies. Please talk to Tina and try to get her to understand, for the good of a lot of other sick children and scared parents. I'd be happy to speak with her anytime she wants. Here's my card; it has all my phone numbers."

"I never had a father when I was a boy." Miguel stared at the card, tossed it on the coffee table, and cradled his head in his hands. "I try to be a good one, try to take care of my family, my baby, but . . . mierda, I'm useless!"

"I'm sure you're a fine father, doing the best you can."

"Maybe if I didn't crap out in my recliner that night, I wouldda heard him hollering sooner, before . . . ."

Loud, ominous alarm bells clanged in my brain, and every muscle in my body tensed.

"Hold on. You heard Pablo crying?"

"Yeah, but not soon enough. He was throwing a real shit-fit. I saw Tina go in to quiet him and must have dozed off again." He looked up. "Tina had the day off and we were partying, you know? I was pretty wasted, and the baby monitor wasn't on." His face flushed. "I don't get it. How the hell's that possible? The damn thing's *always* on when he sleeps, hissing and squawking away. Even with the TV on, we can hear every peep he makes."

"After you fell back asleep, what happened?"

"Pablo musta gone off again 'cause he woke me. We don't really need the damn monitor in our tiny apartment when he's screamin' his head off."

"So, what'd you do when you heard Pablo the second time?"

Miguel eyed me as if that was the dumbest question he'd ever heard.

"Dragged my tired ass to the john, drained

270

all the beer I drank, splashed water on my face, and opened the door to his room . . . but by then, he'd stopped crying."

I doubted that he'd been in the bathroom for very long.

"Where was Tina when you came in?"

"In the rocking chair with her head down, kinda whimpering." The painful memory contorted Miguel's expression. "Pablo's color wasn't right, so I picked him up and he was limp, like a rag doll. I called 911 and tried the CPR stuff I seen on TV, but . . . ."

Was Miguel telling me that Tina had tried to kill Pablo, or was he diverting the investigation away from himself? Was he oblivious to the implication of what he'd said? I wasn't sure.

Miguel went silent, then said, "That's enough, Father. I'm done. I gotta live with this shit every day and see it all over again in my nightmares. I only got a few hours to sleep before I go back to work tonight." He stood and offered his hand. "I'll tell Tina what you said about autopsies and stuff, but don't get your hopes up. Tina's . . . well, you know, she's *Tina.*"

I thanked him and left. The short drive back to the rectory felt endless. No matter how many times I spoke to the families of dying patients, it never got any easier.

CHAPTER THIRTY-ONE

Wednesday, August 2, 7:00 a.m.

Wednesday was Colleen's usual day off. With Justine in the hospital and me tending to the parish, she was overworked caring for my nephew and definitely in need of a break. The boy ran continuously at full throttle like an Energizer Bunny on a sugar high, and since his mother's admission, he'd refused to take a nap. There was no rest for the weary at the rectory.

Although Colleen offered to give up her personal day and come in to work, I assured her that I could handle things on my own for one day and told her not to worry. I, however, was completely out of my league and terrified.

I dressed and fed RJ early and sat him on a pew with several picture books in the glass-enclosed, soundproof "quiet room" in the back of the church. Iris Wells, a regular at morning Mass, agreed to stay with him

273

during the service. She was in her seventies, a major donor to Sacred Heart Church, and a volunteer on bingo nights and at potluck suppers.

During the service, I could see RJ becoming more and more restless. He started to use his books as building blocks. During the Gospel, I heard a thud as his tower crashed to the floor. I watched Iris transform from placid grandmother, to overwhelmed helper, to panicked old lady.

Normally, offering Mass was a joyous experience and a highpoint of my day, but when RJ began using the pew as a balance beam, I got as nervous as a cat in the dog pound. I rushed through the prayer after communion, omitted the announcements, bid the faithful "go in peace," and scrambled to Iris's rescue.

When I thanked her, she gave me a weak smile, grabbed her cane, and hobbled from the church faster than I'd ever seen her move.

"RJ, what was that about?" I asked as I gathered his things. "You're supposed to sit quietly at church."

"I couldn't, Uncle Jake, I was hungry. It's not fair!"

"What's not?"

"I wanted some of those cookies you were

giving everybody," he said stamping a red sneaker, "and you didn't even give me *one*!"

How do you explain communion to a four year old? Clearly, the seminary had failed to teach me all that I needed to know. Back in the rectory, I gave him a glass of milk and a stack of Oreos despite Justine's prohibition of sugary snacks. RJ wolfed them down, then plunged back into a funk about his mother.

I was worried too and hated being out of the loop. If she'd been admitted to St. Joseph's Hospital, I would have had friends and colleagues who could have checked in on her regularly. At the Cleveland Clinic, I knew no one.

We spoke with Justine over the telephone, but RJ's behavior deteriorated again after we hung up. Out of desperation, I promised to take him to the Memphis Kiddie Park if he played quietly until lunch. The park had amusement rides designed for very young children. I described the carousel and miniature roller coaster. He nodded, said "deal," and marched into the living room, which now looked more like a rocket-propelled grenade had exploded in a toy store.

When a young couple arrived for their pre-marriage counseling appointment, I

275

guided them into my study and immersed myself in the welcome distraction of helping others. On the topic of love, I was merely a well-read consultant rather than a practitioner. I'd never been married, but had made enough relationship mistakes to write my own textbook on the subject. After they left, I returned a few phone calls from parishioners, paid a bill for the repair of the church roof, and signed a baptismal certificate.

I was feeling like a multitasking genius until I remembered that I still needed to replace the wax-stained altar cloths and spent candles, and insert new missalettes in all of the hymnals. As I considered taking RJ into the church with a box of Legos to finish my to-do list, he hollered, "Uncle Jake, I'm hungry."

With further church duties on hold, I made peanut butter and jelly sandwiches, lathered RJ with sunscreen after lunch, and strapped him into his car seat. My mother had taken me to the Memphis Kiddie Park when I was a boy and I wanted to share the experience with my nephew, but it was an hour-long drive.

To pass the time, I sang every children's song that I could think of, then tried playing the "I spy a color" game. RJ soon tired of my efforts and resumed his relentless refrain of "Are we there yet?" By the time we arrived, my temples were throbbing and I would have traded my medical degree for two Tylenol. Not only did I not possess the parental gene, apparently I was not cut out for this particular kind of "fatherhood."

We spent a couple hours and nearly all the cash in my wallet at the small amusement park. Although RJ was afraid to ride the child-sized roller coaster, he loved the merry-go-round and train, and rode the spinning teacups until I was sure he would throw up the cotton candy he'd devoured.

Standing at the exit gate of each ride watching my nephew's grin, my mind kept wandering back to Justine and all that her loss would mean to RJ and me. There was nothing I could do for her now except pray. Things were in God's hands and those of the Cleveland Clinic staff, so I fought off the impending gloom.

Idle time, the Devil's plaything.

And watching young couples revel in their children's excitement made me painfully aware of my isolation. Even though my own childhood had been rocky and the priesthood had brought me serenity in many ways, there was a part of me that would have loved to have had a family of my own and a more conventional life.

The final carousel ride seemed to last forever. I banished unwelcome thoughts from my mind and when RJ hopped to the ground and skipped back to me, I corralled him into his car seat and began negotiating rush hour traffic toward home, glad for the distraction.

My tiny human hurricane napped on the ride home, proving that there is a merciful God. By the time I finally got him bathed and into bed at night, I was certain that Colleen was sainted and couldn't wait for her to come back in the morning. I collapsed onto my recliner, mindless and exhausted, and dozed off while watching an episode of CSI.

The cellphone in my pocket vibrated like an angry rectangular insect, dragging me back to consciousness. I muted the ten o'clock news.

"Jake, it's Tree. You watching the Tribe?"

"No. I had RJ today and conked out."

"I wish the damn Yankees were in town. Tonight, the Indians would have kicked their butts big time."

I fought my eyelids downward drift. "So, what's up, Tree?"

"Got a little follow up for my ace consultant and part-time police snitch. My rookie cop's been pounding the pavement and geeking on her computer. She found another life insurance policy that Miguel bought on Pablo for fifty grand. That's a total of seventy-five big ones. Definitely sounds like motive to me. He may have tried to avoid detection by buying policies from two different companies."

My eyelids popped up. "Hold on a second, Tree. Aren't there laws or rules about buying insurance on babies, especially from multiple companies?"

"Yeah, I wondered about that too, so I checked with someone in the business. He said there's no problem as long as the parents have their own insurance. Miguel works at a union shop and gets a nice term policy as part of the job. And apparently it's okay to buy policies from different companies if the second policy provides an advantage or different benefit. The first one Miguel bought on Pablo was whole life, the second term insurance. But the agent also said that most companies would have hesitated to issue any policy for a baby with cerebral palsy who'd spent much time in intensive care."

"Well, Dr. Taylor said that although Pablo was premature and had a rough delivery, he wasn't in intensive care long. Because he seemed fine, gained weight normally, and didn't need any medication, they sent him home. It wasn't until several months ago that the pediatrician noted developmental delays suggesting brain damage. When did Miguel buy the insurance policies?"

"Lemme check. Here it is. He bought them a couple months after Pablo was born, most likely before the pediatrician diagnosed the brain damage. That's probably why no alarm bells went off. Heck, insurance agents get paid to *sell* stuff. And if Pablo had no symptoms or diagnosis, the policies were probably real cheap at that young age."

"You can't really blame the agent. If you or I applied for insurance with no known illness, there's no reason *not* to sell us a policy, even though we might be developing early cancer that only becomes apparent months later."

"Wait a minute. Pablo appeared okay for a while after he left the hospital? *That* makes me wonder if his brain damage is the result of abuse at home, not birth trauma. I'd love to speak with the agents who sold those policies, see what they knew, but I can't."

"Because of the shady way you got your information, Tree?"

"Yeah, yeah, not exactly textbook, except

the evidence all points to the parents. My finely-tuned detective senses are tingling, but the damn judge balked again at a search warrant. Guess I'll have to keep Nancy Drew pecking at her keyboard and see what else she turns up. Did you talk anymore with Mom and Dad? I could use more ammo to convince Her Honor to grant me a warrant."

"Mom was working. I did have a real interesting discussion yesterday with Dad. I'm still trying to make sense of it."

I recounted my conversation with Miguel.

"Drunk is no surprise with Daddy. And a crying baby? So what?"

"SIDS babies die *in their sleep,* Tree, not when they're awake and crying. Also, it's strange that the baby monitor wasn't on. And why was Tina already in his room if Miguel was the one who found Pablo unconscious? When I first met them, Tina told me she had been the one who'd discovered that Pablo wasn't breathing. None of this adds up."

"Conflicting stories, now we're getting somewhere. Damn, I need that search warrant soon, before they wipe their computer clean and rabbit out of town to some other state like they did after the first child died. Maybe I'll bring those two in for an interview, crank up the heat, and see if they boil over. Thanks for the info, Jake. I'll keep you posted."

I turned off the television, trudged to my bedroom, and plunged into a bottomless sleep, floppy babies whirling through my dreams.

CHAPTER THIRTY-TWO

Thursday, August 3, 7:00 a.m.

I slipped on a cassock, dressed RJ, and brought him downstairs for breakfast as Colleen entered the rectory and took command of the kitchen. I placed him in his booster seat and poured his glass of milk, offering her a cheery good morning.

"Be a better morning, mind you, if I didn't find the back door unlocked again. Oberlin's a small town, Father, but it still has its share of ne'er-do-wells. I'd prefer not to be the only adult in the rectory."

Lost in my worries last night, it hadn't crossed my mind to lock up. As I offered my mea culpa, she held up a hand and stopped me mid-sentence.

"And just so you know, Father, you look unseemly. Your cassock is covered with the fur of a beast. Have you been wrestling with a tiger, then?"

I glanced down and groaned. I'd found

my cassock on the floor in the sacristy closet yesterday. That darn tabby must have thought it was a climbing tree, pulled it off the hanger, then used it as his bed. Trudging up the stairs to my room, I decided to buy Martin Luther a cat tower for his basement home. Either that or I'd have to permanently excommunicate him from the church like his namesake.

After changing clothes, I crossed the hall to my study to fetch my homily and noticed a piece of folded paper on my desk. I opened it, assuming it was another crayon masterwork of a red-brick house, ringed in flowers, under a golden sun rendered by Justine's budding, junior Michelangelo.

It wasn't. The same short, not-so-sweet message I'd heard on my answering machine six days earlier was typed in capital letters: MIND YOUR OWN DAMN BUSINESS – OR YOU'LL BE SORRY!

What the note *implied,* however, was far more frightening than its message: I CAN GET TO YOU AND YOURS!

Whoever left the note had roamed the rectory while RJ and I slept.

I clenched my teeth and slammed my fist on the desk as ice-cold sweat rolled down the back of my neck. For years, I'd tried to exorcise the angry, violent young man I'd once been but knew he still lurked in the dark corners of my psyche. I felt him stir — and welcomed him back.

Forget lines in the sand; this line was chiseled in stone. I'd be damned if I would turn the other cheek when RJ's safety was at risk. God help you, whoever the hell you are, if you ever come in here again! No one threatens my family. No one!

The real question was who? I doubted that my recent sermon against abortion could drive anyone to this extreme, although I couldn't entirely discount the possibility. Lunatics and fanatics prowled the fringes of both camps. And in a liberal town like Oberlin, being Catholic and pro-life made me one step above a snake-handling fundamentalist, and about as popular as a conservative Republican.

With the St. Wenceslaus matter resolved, I had removed Father Marek from the disgruntled list — perhaps prematurely. Could he have fallen off the wagon so soon and decided in a drunken stupor that I had ruined his life? Even priests have anger issues and thoughts of revenge, especially if their brains are pickled in alcohol.

I had been on a leave of absence from the hospital and hadn't seen any new patients for weeks. Could I have somehow angered one of my prior patients, or was one of them striking out at me because of a disappointing outcome? Unlikely, but not unheard of in a world filled with workplace violence. No one came to mind except for the guy I'd ticked off because I wouldn't prescribe narcotics for him almost a month ago.

The only recent confrontation I'd had was with Miguel, when I approached him about withdrawing life support and performing an autopsy on his child. But he'd immediately calmed down and listened to reason. Tina hadn't been at their apartment that day, and I wondered how she'd reacted when told about my visit. Confirming Miguel's whereabouts last night probably wouldn't be hard. He worked the nightshift, so Tree could easily check with his supervisor and coworkers at the factory to see if he'd been on the job all night. If he had, then Tina had been home alone without an alibi.

Crap! I realized that my fingerprints were now all over the note. I set it on the desk, called Tree, got voicemail, and left a message about the intruder.

Enough fretting and analyzing! I wouldn't cower in the corner and become a victim. Nobody would put RJ in jeopardy on my watch.

I didn't own a weapon and hadn't touched

a gun since my time in the Army. I considered moving a kitchen knife to my bedroom nightstand, but didn't want RJ to find it and hurt himself. Then I remembered my autographed Louisville slugger. The prior pastor and I were longtime Indians fans, and he had bequeathed his baseball paraphernalia to me when he passed away. I pulled the bat from my closet and leaned it against the wall next to my bed, under his cherished 1948 Cleveland World Series pennant.

That would have to do in a confrontation. I'd been a pinch hitter in high school and had struck out a lot, but when I connected . . . .

I would ask the bishop to install an alarm system in the rectory. Until then, I could attach the smaller handbells from the church to strings and hang them as warning chimes over the doors and across the top of the stairs.

It was unlikely that the intruder would make a move in the light of day, but I couldn't be certain. I was heading downstairs to warn Colleen about the threat when the grandfather clock struck the hour, reminding me that I was already late for Mass. As I hurried from the rectory, my car's front tires appeared low on air. I walked over. All four tires were flat.

Damn it!

My time with the Lord was tainted by thoughts of home invasion, vandalism, and threats. Not my finest hour at the altar, I muddled through the Mass. After greeting the few faithful who had attended, I dressed in my street clothes and walked to my car to assess the damage.

The valve stem caps lay next to each flat tire, indicating that the air had been let out but the tires were undamaged. The next visit from this miscreant, however, might involve an icepick or razor. I re-inflated all four tires with a small electric pump that plugged into the cigarette lighter, wiped my grimy hands on my jeans, and walked into the rectory.

Colleen had already set the table for lunch. As my nephew and I were finishing, the telephone rang. It was Justine. I gave the phone to RJ and he regaled her with stories of his visit to the Memphis Kiddie Park. Then he gave me a wicked little smile and said, "And Mommy, Uncle Jake let me have a snow cone, and a hotdog, and a great big cotton candy."

I cringed. Et tu, RJ? I loved the boy, but he was a darn stool pigeon.

When he finally handed the phone to me, I expected to get an earful about my woeful child-rearing skills, so I took control of the conversation.

"How are you feeling, Sis?"

"Oh, I'm getting by." A long pause. "So, you're surviving RJ?"

"Barely. It's been . . . humbling. I'd be lost without Colleen's help."

Justine laughed and Colleen grinned.

"Sorry, Jake, I had no one else to turn to. I really appreciate your help . . . even though you're a soft touch, a pathetic rookie, and completely overmatched."

She sounded more upbeat than she had in days.

"Honestly, Sis, my time with RJ has been a joy and given me a whole new respect for motherhood."

It had also shined the spotlight on my regrets about never having a family of my own.

"Hello, Jake? Are you still there?"

"Yup. Sorry. I'm here."

"Listen, I have some good news. My doctors told me I can have visitors for a couple hours this afternoon. Can you and RJ come?"

"Hear that ringing sound? That's us coming with bells on. As soon as I get RJ's shoes on and take him to the bathroom, we're on our way."

"Ah, there is one problem . . . and I need

your help." She hesitated, then added, "My oncologist is the head-honcho of the transplant unit, and he said it's against policy to allow young children in my room. Begging got me nowhere, but when I told him you were a physician, he said he'd be willing to discuss it with you." She gave me his phone number. "Please Jake, try to convince him to let RJ visit. I been so depressed without him that I can barely make it through the day. I've just *got* to see my son."

"Sure, Sis. I'll see what I can do."

I called Justine's oncologist. When he came to the phone, he was in no mood for a debate.

"Look Dr. Austin, it's been our policy for years not to let children in the room. They are exposed to all kinds of illness at school, and they're behavior is just too unpredictable. Besides, as you know, we had to push up the timetable on your sister's chemotherapy, and with ongoing immunosuppression she's at high risk for infection."

I made an impassioned plea on Justine's behalf, pointing out that her deepening depression was also counterproductive and unhealthy. Noting that RJ was not yet in school, I explained that as a physician I could ensure that my nephew didn't break protocol or pose any risk to her. I also mentioned in passing that Dr. Taylor and I were close friends, allowing him to assume that I was referring to Taylor's brother, who was high up on the hospital totem pole and a major player in funding decisions, including for the transplant unit. Not exactly kosher, but it got his attention.

After a long pause and a deep sigh he said, "Well, we have been discussing the possibility of allowing children in the isolation rooms. I guess we can make you the test case. I'll let the nurses know. But I want to error on the side of caution. Even though we have positive pressure rooms, I want you and the child to both follow the old-fashioned gown and glove procedure until her white blood cell count is completely normal. No direct physical contact with your sister for the moment, and any toys the child brings must be sterilized with alcohol and Virex. Are we clear?"

"Very. You won't regret this." I hoped to God that I wouldn't either.

I thanked him, hung up, turned to Colleen, and told her that she'd just won the *childcare lottery* and could take the rest of the day off. As RJ galloped around the room on a pretend horse, I thought I heard Colleen sigh with relief.

CHAPTER THIRTY-THREE

Thursday, August 3, 1:00 p.m.

On the drive to the Cleveland Clinic, I shook off the fact that someone had snuck past our bedrooms last night into my study and began preparing RJ for his first hospital visit with his mother. I warned him that he might see some tubes and needles that the doctors use to make her feel better. In the rearview mirror, I watched his eyes grow large. He remained silent the entire trip, hugging his Pooh Bear.

The quiet produced a void and thoughts of Emily quickly filled it. I hadn't spoken with her since Sunday and decided to call her that evening. The sight of the enormous Cleveland Clinic complex, however, refocused my mind on my sister.

As we entered the hospital, my nephew became so excited that he bounced up and down like a tiny, human pogo stick. He'd brought a few toy cowboys and soldiers to play with, and we gave them to a nurse to be disinfected. Then I conjured up my sternest doctor persona as I lead RJ through the rigorous sterile procedure.

We washed his hands thoroughly with antibacterial soap, then did it again for good measure. After dressing him in a yellow paper gown, booties, and mask, I told him not to move until I finished scrubbing and gowning too.

When we walked into the small, sea-green room that would serve as my sister's entire world for the next few weeks, a ghostly-pale Justine welcomed us with a feeble smile. She'd been in the hospital six days, but it felt more like six weeks. She had lost more weight, and her lower lip was ulcerated and swollen. Her bruised arms were plugged into IVs and a large-bore central venous catheter protruded from her upper right chest like the hilt of a dagger. In stark contrast, her thinning rust-colored hair was now thick and bright red-orange.

My nephew's bounding enthusiasm vanished. He grabbed my gowned arm with a gloved hand and refused to move.

Justine said, "It's okay, RJ. I'm doing great! Come over here and let me get a look at my big man."

"Mommy?" He took a tentative step forward, gazed up at me, and whispered, "Can I hug her, Uncle Jake?"

"No, RJ, not today. Soon though."

My nephew's disappointment struck me like a kick in the gut. He climbed onto a chair next to Justine and sat quietly for a few moments, before reverting to the chatterbox I'd grown to love. He expounded on the kiddie rides at the park, complete with elaborate descriptions of each one, adding, "I didn't go on that rolling coaster, Mommy. It was too big and scary!"

Justine and I laughed, but RJ grew somber again. If the pint-sized roller coaster scared him, his mother's condition must have terrified the poor kid.

I answered a few of her medical questions, remaining as positive as I could without lying, then we shifted to life at the rectory and other more mundane topics. She had enough to worry about without telling her that an intruder had entered the rectory, so I said nothing. Protecting RJ was my job now, not hers.

As I summarized Colleen's relentless efforts to civilize RJ by purchasing story books and nonviolent children's games, a nurse entered and gave RJ his sterilized toys. He quickly converted his surroundings into a rumpus room and filled the air with the sound of gunfire. His troops donned Kleenex parachutes and leaped from a plastic-cup tower that he'd commandeered from the bedside tray table. With whispered orders and high-pitched explosions, he led his army across the rugged terrain of the armchair, taking command of the only thing in the room that he could control.

"Appears the score is RJ one, Colleen zero." Justine shrugged. "I appreciate her effort to civilize him, but my money is on my son."

Justine caught me staring at her hair.

"Oh, this. Like my new hairdo?" She chuckled, then the sparkle left her eyes and she leaned in, adding softly, "The Clinic gives free wigs, scarves, and ball caps to all cancer patients. I was just getting my hair back from my last round of chemo when we left Louisiana for Ohio in such a hurry that I forgot my wig. This has been hard enough on RJ without him having to watch me go bald again."

"Not that it's unattractive; it's just that I was surprised."

"I can't wait to take the darn thing off, though. I've had a killer headache ever since I got it yesterday."

A *killer* headache. Although it was possible that her pain was due to wearing the wig, I hoped to God that it didn't mean her leukemia was invading her brain. Every so often, too much medical knowledge scared the hell out of me. When Justine's nurse returned to tell us that visiting hours were over, I cornered her and quietly voiced my concern about my sister's headaches.

I told RJ that it was time to go and asked him to leave his toys on the table for our next visit. The fearless general erupted into tears and refused to leave his mother's side. I resorted to W.W.C.D. — What would Colleen do? Having sat as an acolyte at the feet of the master, Colleen the Wise and Devious, I bribed RJ with the promise of a hot fudge sundae today and another trip to see his mother tomorrow. It worked like magic.

Justine shook her head.

"Better get well soon, Sis, before Colleen and I spoil him rotten."

RJ was solemn and befuddled after our visit and said almost nothing on the car ride home. He did, however, temporarily emerge from his funk when I asked the ice cream store employee to add whipped cream and a cherry to his sundae. When we arrived at the rectory for dinner, Colleen noticed the stains on his shirt and gave me hell for spoiling his appetite.

With both of us in need of happy endings,

RJ and I read fairytales after dinner until he fell asleep in my arms. I tucked him into bed and checked the answering machine. The last message was from Tree, and I returned his call.

"Got your voicemail, Jake. Sorry I took so long. Been a busy day. So, nothing was stolen from the rectory or vandalized? Just a threatening note in your study and the air let out of your tires?"

"Just? That's not enough? Damn it Tree, somebody was in here while we were asleep! RJ could have been hurt or kidnapped."

"Easy buddy, I hear you. I checked on Miguel like you asked. He punched in at the factory at eleven p.m. and didn't clock out till seven this morning. No one saw him leaving during his shift, so he's probably not the doer."

That did not, however, exonerate Tina as our home invader.

"Anyway, bring the note to the station house tomorrow and we'll examine it." He paused. "I'll have a black and white prowl the neighborhood and drive past the rectory every couple hours. Lock up tight at night, and call my cell if you see anything hinkey."

"Thanks." I remembered the angry lesion on his neck, and against my better judgement asked, "Have you had a Dermatologist look at that growth yet?"

"Buzz off, Doc. I barely got time to pee. If you need drama in your life, go watch General Hospital." Changing the subject, he said, "Oh yeah, speaking of hospitals, I pulled the video from the intensive care security camera at St. Joseph's. I agree, Tina's behavior around her baby is . . . worrisome, but not enough to act. I hope to have a warrant to search their apartment tomorrow."

"Good luck."

"Yeah, I'll need it. Talk to you mañana, amigo."

I locked up the rectory including the windows and set out my handbell alarm system. With my baseball bat within easy reach, I left my bedroom door ajar so I could hear RJ, then slept poorly.

CHAPTER THIRTY-FOUR

Friday, August 4, 5:30 a.m.
I woke up well before dawn drenched in sweat, my covers on the floor. I'd had intermittent nightmares ever since the war, but my dream that night had nothing to do with the horrors of battle. In this one, RJ was locked in a cage, screaming for help.

Sleep was no longer a possibility, so I made coffee and spent the early morning hours buried in parish paperwork, although it was hard to concentrate with Justine's life and RJ's future hanging by a thread. Having completely forgotten about the handbell that I'd hung over the back door, I jumped when Colleen entered. She demanded an explanation and when I gave it to her, she calmly removed a rolling pin from a drawer. All she said was, "Best to be prepared." No one would get past Colleen without a fight.

After Mass, I was heading back to the rectory when Tree called.

"I got roadblocked by Her Honor, Jake. Judge *Ima Upfer Reelection* is afraid to alienate voters over right-to-privacy issues. She went ballistic that an unidentified source had scored information about Miguel and Tina's finances and insurance, and gave me some legal mumbo-jumbo about tainted fruit and poison trees. Not only did she refuse to issue a search warrant, she called my request a blatant affront to grieving parents everywhere. Worst of all, it's personal for her. I found out the judge lost a baby to SIDS several years ago. Without more concrete evidence of foul play, I'm dead in the water. There's no way I can give up my source."

"Can't you ask for another judge?"

"Judge shopping? That's frowned upon. There are just a handful to choose from and they're all friends. Judges hate to overrule their colleagues, and I don't want to get on Her Honor's bad side. Any attempt at an end-run would piss her off big-time, and I'll have to work with her again in the future."

"Sorry, Tree. It sounds like you're out of options."

"Problem is, with what we know about Miguel and Tina, I can't walk away. I invited them to the cop shop for a chat this afternoon around three. Miguel sounded real spooked over the phone and asked if you could be there. Besides, I could use your help, buddy. You in?"

"I'm free, but I'm not sure what I can do."

"You can be an extra pair of ears and eyes. Use your x-ray vision, Doctor, to see through any medical crap. I'll play the bad cop and try to crack their story or turn one against the other. You, Father, will be a friendly face in the room. Wear your priest duds. You're good at reading people. Check out their reactions and give me a nod if your BS meter goes off."

"All right, Tree, I'll be there."

I gave Colleen the morning off and asked her to come back at two-thirty to babysit, then RJ and I hustled over to the Cleveland Clinic. Eager to see his mother, he mastered the scrub-gown-and-glove ritual faster than most adults.

When we entered Justine's small room, we found a team of physicians surrounding her bed. They professed to be pleased with her progress but postponed her scheduled discharge from the isolation unit. She attempted a weak smile through her cracked and swollen lips, then looked away. The weight of her disappointment and of my concern could have sunk a Lake Erie freighter.

After the doctors left, RJ shared an in-depth summary of Elmo's latest exploits on Sesame Street. Somehow his four-year-old mind managed to segue into a story about Jesus walking on the water and feeding the multitudes — without a doubt, Colleen's handiwork. Satisfied with his biblical rendition, he located his sterilized plastic horse and cowboy, and galloped them across the table by the window.

Justine sighed and gestured toward her television.

"I've been stuck here watching so much TV that bible stories are starting to sound exciting. The only things on the news now-a-days are drunken pop stars and political bickering." She lowered her voice. "Maybe God needs to pass out some leukemia to these folks . . . to give them something important to focus on." Her speech was reedy and labored. She pointed heavenward. "Have a word with your boss, will ya? There's nothing like a little cancer to get a person's priorities straight."

She leaned forward and whispered, "Any progress on RJ's guardianship papers?"

"I'm working on it, Sis. I should have them for you soon."

We exchanged small talk for a while until Justine tired. Promising RJ to return in the morning, I left the hospital enveloped in a gathering cloud of worries, the Cleveland skyline fading to a gray backdrop through my rearview mirror.

My nephew was unnervingly quiet and didn't speak until we were almost back to Oberlin.

"Is Mommy gonna be okay?"

"Of course," I said, praying that I hadn't lied to him.

He fell back into silence for the remainder of the trip, leaving me to ponder a world that made no sense to adults, let alone to a kid. At the rectory, Colleen recognized RJ's sullen mood, suggested a visit to the park, and they left me alone.

I called the parishioner who practiced law and asked where things stood with Justine's Power of Attorney and her guardianship request. She said she'd get the paperwork to me in the next few days.

Having done all that I could on the legal front, I put on my clerical shirt and Roman collar as Tree had asked and refocused my thoughts on baby Pablo, trying to comprehend why anyone would intentionally hurt or kill a child.

CHAPTER THIRTY-FIVE

Friday, August 4, 2:45 p.m.

Sleep deprived from tossing all night and emotionally drained from my hospital visit with Justine, I felt as limp as a wet dishrag and in desperate need of a medicinal jolt of caffeine. Because the thick black sludge at the police station was undrinkable and borderline toxic, I made a quick stop in town for coffee. When I arrived with two iced mochas and handed one to Tree, a smile almost slipped past his game face. Almost.

He ushered me into a faded beige interview room. The walls were scarred by deep scratches and chipped paint. The scuffed floor had all the elegance of a neglected bus station restroom. A large mirror covered one wall, probably a one-way concealing observers. Bright fluorescent bulbs hummed above. High on the far wall, a pale shaft of sunlight filtered into the room through a smoked-glass window protected by a cross-hatch of thick metal bars. The decor was designed to intimidate and demoralize suspects, and coerce them into cooperating or confessing. The one item out of place in a police interview room was a tripod easel holding a large white paper tablet located just below the barred window.

The heavy metal door slammed behind us with deafening finality, and Miguel and Tina abandoned their whispered conversation.

They sat at a slate-gray metal table, their backs to the window and the easel. He'd worn a dress shirt, but it spread apart between the buttons where it rode over his beer belly, revealing a gray-stained under-shirt. In contrast, Tina's makeup was flaw-less and her trim waitress uniform empha-sized her wasp-waist figure.

Definitely the odd couple.

Miguel appeared pleased to see me. Tina was clearly miffed. She no longer reminded me of the beautiful actress who had played Ginger on Gilligan's Island. With anger in her eyes and an intense scowl, she more closely resembled her namesake, Martina, the warrior goddess.

Tree sat across from them, pointed to the chair next to him, and I sat. The initials of prior inhabitants of the room were gouged into the battered tabletop along with several four-letter expressions of displeasure. Tree set a small, old-fashioned tape recorder on the table, which surprised me given the modern equipment I'd seen in the station house.

He switched on the recorder and gave the date and names of the participants, thanked Tina and Miguel for coming, and asked them to restate the events leading up to Pablo's hospital admission. Miguel wrapped an arm around Tina's shoulder and let her do most of the talking in her sweet-cream voice.

As Tree interjected a few non-threatening questions to flesh out their story, he slowly removed the curves from a paperclip until it was straight as a pin. I almost laughed. Whenever Tree had been nervous or unable to answer a question back in high school, that's what he would do — unfold a paperclip. As far as I knew, it was the only outward sign that Mr. Calm-Cool-and-Collected ever felt edgy. This behavior was also strangely appropriate. As a policeman, he spent his life removing the kinks from society.

Without warning, Tree flipped the reformed paperclip onto the table, stood, walked to the large mirror on the wall, and asked, "Why was the baby's monitor off?"

Miguel removed his arm from around Tina and said, "Beats me. The things always on, screechin' and squawkin' away. Maybe the battery died."

Tina put a hand on his. "It wasn't off. I turned the volume down 'cause Miguel was asleep in his chair."

"No, I'm pretty sure it was off."

They had a brief staring contest, then Miguel reclaimed his hand and said, "Maybe you're right."

"Was Pablo normally a good sleeper?" I asked.

"Nah, Padre. Pablo was tough from day one. Real colicky."

"But he was so quiet that morning, I went in his room to check on him," Tina added. "Like Miguel said, he was usually a real cranky baby. I was worried."

"Quiet? What quiet? His screaming woke me up from my nap. He was raisin' hell from the moment I got home from work."

Her head snapped in his direction.

"How would you know? You were passed out in the recliner the way you always are!"

Tree paced the room for a minute allowing the uncomfortable silence to linger, then returned to his seat, pulled the pin on the next question, and lobbed it like a grenade.

"Tina, who discovered that Pablo wasn't breathing?"

"I already told the cops this at the hospital. I did."

Tree nodded at me, a signal to join the fray.

I cleared my throat. "I don't understand, Tina. Miguel told me that *he* discovered that Pablo was unconscious. He said you were whimpering in the rocking chair when he came in."

Tina's eyes pinballed around the room and landed on me.

"I picked Pablo up and he was floppy and . . . I guess I panicked. The whole thing's hazy, Father, like a bad dream." She hesitated. "I remember crying in the rocking chair. I think I set Pablo back in the crib and screamed for Miguel. That's probably what woke him . . . from his nap."

Miguel had said Pablo was lying prone and motionless in his crib when he entered the room. Had the baby's cerebral palsy made him so weak that he couldn't roll back over, causing him to suffocate accidentally? Or had Tina shoved his face against the Big Bird pillow or his fluffy teddy bear until his little legs finally stopped flailing? Or were they in this together?

"Hold on, Tina," I pressed on, my voice

308

rising. "Pablo wasn't breathing and you put him back down . . . *on his belly*?"

"Course not! At least, I don't think so. The whole thing's a blur."

"Well, that's the way I found him." Miguel wiped moisture from his eyes. "I rolled him over, shook him, and called 911, then tried to . . . ." He choked on the last few words.

Tina's pupils grew large, her cheeks reddened, and a large vein throbbed in her neck. "What're you suggesting? That we hurt our own child? This is a god-damn nightmare." Tina dropped her head into her hands and sobbed. "Don't you get it? I screwed up . . . failed as a mother . . . failed my baby!"

"Leave her alone! This ain't her fault." Miguel jumped to his feet and his chair crashed into the wall. "You saying we tried to kill Pablo? Bullshit! We *love* him. Why the hell would anyone do that to their own kid?"

"Good question." Tree rose and stepped around the table, his six-foot six-inch frame towering over Miguel. His voice dropped an octave and he said, "Sit down, sir. We're not done here."

After Miguel complied, Tree returned to his chair and laid his right hand next to the tape recorder.

"I only have a few more questions. Let's talk about what we do know." Tree looked at me and said, "Father, please go to the easel under the window."

I had no idea what Tree was up to, but I rose to my feet. All eyes followed me around the table to the easel. When I glanced back, I saw Tree turn off the tape recorder, then quickly place his hands in his lap and lean back in his chair.

What in the hell? Damn it, he was wandering out onto thin legal ice — and taking me with him.

"Tree?" I began.

He raised a hand and said, "Thank you. Father. Now, please flip the first page of chart paper over."

When I did, the second page revealed five words in large capital letters printed in black marker. The first line read BABY MONITOR, the second WHO FOUND PABLO?

"Good. Bear with me, Father, and stay there for a moment please."

I did as instructed. Tree stared at Miguel like a bug collector deciding where to stick the pin, then he picked up a manila folder.

"You bought two life insurance policies on Pablo from two different companies. Why?"

Tree took a sip of his iced mocha, as cool as the coffee. He let the question hang in the air.

Miguel slumped down in his chair and studied Tina, then Tree. "What the hell you talkin' about?"

"One policy for twenty-five grand and another for fifty. That's a lot of money — and a lot of motive."

Tree opened the folder and played his trump card. He slid a sheet of paper across the table to Miguel.

"Got your signature on both checks."

Miguel gazed at the photocopy, motionless as an oil portrait.

Tree snatched up the paper, showed it briefly to Tina, and set it on top of his folder.

"Still don't remember, Miguel?"

Tina was on her feet with the darting eyes of a cornered animal.

"What the hell's going on here? How'd you get those?"

No denial about the purchase. It sounded like a tacit admission to me.

Tree maintained his poker face. "Not important. What's important is *why* you wanted all that insurance on a baby. Just explain that to me and we all can call it a day." Tree looked over at me. "Now, Father, flip to the third page."

I hesitated.

"Please, Father, the next page."

Tina and Miguel swiveled back in my direction. When I complied, Tree turn the tape recorder back on.

Page three read EXPENDITURES.

"Thank you, Father, have a seat. You too, Tina. Now, both of you already said money was tight, so let's talk about your expenditures. How about we start with insurance. Miguel, do you and Tina have life insurance policies?"

He didn't answer.

Tree said, "Miguel? Nothing? Okay, maybe you can answer that, Tina."

"Miguel gets insurance from the company he works for, and I bought a term policy on me. What's this got to do with anything?"

"And life insurance on baby Pablo?" He waved the photocopy of the insurance checks. They remained mute. "It's a simple question. Please answer it."

Tina sat down and took a deep breath.

"We want to have more kids, officer, but we both have to work to make ends meet, and daycare is expensive. We planned on getting some insurance on each child. If something happened to one, we'd have some money to care for the others. Insurance is cheap when kids are young."

As I walked back to my seat, Miguel's jaw dropped open and he stared at Tina.

"When'd we talk about this?" He grabbed the copy of the two checks from Tree. "I didn't write no checks to insurance companies!"

Tina chewed the inside of her cheek. "Sure you did." She focused on Tree. "We work opposite shifts and don't see each other much. We do that kind of stuff in the morning, before I go to the diner to work the lunch shift."

On the two times that I'd seen Miguel in the mornings, he was nearly falling-down drunk.

Tree took the photocopy back from Miguel. I leaned over and examined it. The Date, Pay To, Dollars, and Memo lines were written in a strong, clean hand that slanted to the right on both checks. The signature was jagged and slanted left.

Tree took a moment to straighten another paperclip, then asked, "So, if something . . . unfortunate happened to Pablo, you'd have money to help raise future children? Is that right, Tina?"

"Yes."

"Did you write the checks for Pablo's insurance policies?"

"I, ah . . . I'm not sure. That was probably

Miguel. It was a long time ago."

Tree inclined his head to one side. "Who writes the checks?"

"Usually Miguel."

"But not always?"

"No, sometimes I write them."

Tree reached over and switched off the tape recorder. No distraction from me this time. He pulled another photocopy from his folder and slowly slid it across the table.

"You mean checks like the one *you wrote* for three hundred dollars to a divorce lawyer, Tina? I thought you were planning on having more children together."

Miguel tried to grab the photocopy, but Tina got there first and crumpled it into a ball. Tree turned the tape recorder back on.

"Are you playing games with us?" she shouted, jumping to her feet. "Or are you charging us with something?"

"I'm trying to understand, that's all. Please sit down and we'll —"

"The hell I will! We're done here."

Tina grabbed her purse and disappeared out the door.

Miguel's eyes bounced from her to Tree and then to me, as if he was the only kid in the lunch room not in on the joke. He kicked his chair back, stood, and shoved a finger in my face.

"Cabrón! What kind of fucking priest are you?" he yelled, and stormed from the room.

I smiled at Tree. "Gee, officer, that went well."

He raised a hand to quiet me, leaned forward, and said, "At this point, the couple became agitated and suddenly left the interview room." He turned the recorder off, tapped it, and added, "That went better than you might think, Jake. This tape gives me more ammo to get a warrant from the judge. And I got their fingerprints on both soft drink cans, which I can run through the system."

"A *tape* recorder? Really, Tree?" I shook my head. "Didn't tape go out with buggy whips and carbon paper? I realize you're an old guy, but we're in the twenty-first century now."

"Don't be a smartass." He lowered his voice. "Our digital voice recorders automatically stamp the date and time when turned on and off. Tapes don't."

"The problem with that, Tree, is that when you produced copies of the checks, the witnesses behind the one-way mirror saw you. You can't expect them to lie in court."

"They won't have to. My staff was . . . busy during the interview." He pointed at the black plastic ball near the ceiling in the corner of the room. "And our surveillance camera was out of service today."

"Well, *I saw you* switch the machine off when you showed them the photocopies! If their attorney calls me to testify, you know I can't lie about what happened here. I'm sure as hell not going to commit perjury for you."

"Easy, Jake, I get it. Without a warrant, these two were gonna walk. I did what I needed to do — and you'll have to do whatever you need to do. I'm pretty damn sure they killed their first kid before they moved to town, then tried to kill their second. And I got no doubt they'd do it again. My duty is to the victims." He threw the manila folder on the table. "Sure, I rolled the dice and if they come up snake eyes and this blows up, it's on me. I'm the one who'll have to live with the fallout. The tape may be illegal, but the judge will assume that any telltale noise or clicks she hears is you walking to the easel and back. What's on this tape should be enough for Her Honor to issue a search warrant."

"I don't like it, Tree. What about Tina and Miguel?"

"They can tell their version of this interview in court, but when the prosecutor lays

316

out all the evidence against them — the conflicting stories about the baby monitor and who found Pablo, the suspicious death of their first kid in Pennsylvania, Miguel's drunkenness, Tina's plan to bail on their marriage, and especially the insurance — I doubt any jury will believe a word they say."

"Let me be clear, Tree. I won't lie under oath in court!"

"I don't expect you to. Just do your best to avoid the truth. That's why I didn't tell you what I'd planned to do." He put a meaty hand on my shoulder. "Okay consultant, time to consult. What was your impression of our little staged soap opera?"

"Miguel was genuinely surprised and confused by everything. He was convincing. I bought everything he said. Tina's eye contact and body language screamed sheer panic to me."

"Yeah, she looked like a meth addict coming off a high. Nice timing, by the way, when you told Tina that Miguel said *he* found Pablo unconscious. Worked like a charm. You rattled her cage real good. I'm pretty sure she's the doer, but Miguel signed the life insurance checks. Maybe they are a tag team.

"With a divorce lawyer in play? I doubt it. And the handwriting on those checks was written by two different people."

"I know, a righty and a lefty. Miguel picked up the photocopy and his soda with his left hand. Tina used her right. Soon as I get ahold of the checks legally, I'll have a handwriting expert analyze them."

"His signatures could be forgeries, Tree, but I'll wager he signed those checks when he was dead drunk."

"That's a good bet. And there's no doubt in my mind which one of those two actually tried to kill their baby. Damn, I want that warrant! When I get it, I'm gonna pounce all over them and watch them squirm — and I want you here again when that happens."

"Are you kidding me? After you used me for your stunt today? I'm not sure I can trust you anymore."

"Come on, buddy! We make a great team and I could use your smarts. Think about it. If these two walk, there'll be another kid in ICU or on an autopsy table in a year or two."

I mulled over the haunting image of Pablo's tiny body pierced by multiple tubes and catheters, tethered to this world by a ventilator and heart monitor.

"Only if the game is on the up and up, Tree. No more dealing from the bottom of the deck."

"I promise." He held up his right hand with his thumb holding the little finger down, and grinned. "Scout's honor."

"Now who's the smartass? Okay, Tree, I'll be there, but no more shenanigans. I mean it. I swear, friend or not, I will personally blow the whistle on you."

"Deal."

CHAPTER THIRTY-SIX

Saturday, August 5, 10:00 a.m.

RJ and I were building Lego towers in the living room when Emily called.

"Jake, I can't attend church in the hospital chapel this Sunday, and I was hoping you could drive me to the Mass tonight at Sacred Heart instead."

"Be happy to. The bishop directed me to use my initiative to increase attendance — like I have nothing else on my plate at the moment. I'll tell him I started a free shuttle service. How's *that* for initiative? I could stop by at four."

"Perfect. How's your sister?"

"Not good. It's a rocky road, and she has a long way to go."

"I'd love to see her the next time you visit."

"Well, RJ and I were just about to leave. We could pick you up on the way."

"Meet you out front in thirty minutes, and then I can join you for Mass afterward."

The drive to the Clinic was more fun with Emily along. I slipped a tape of children's music into my ancient Toyota's player, and we sang classics like "Itsy Bitsy Spider" and "Old McDonald" all the way to Cleveland. Not exactly Mozart, but at least it put an end to the "Are we there yet?" questions.

RJ guided Emily through the sterile scrub and gown procedure, taking pleasure in telling an adult what to do for a change.

A nurse was removing an emesis basin filled with vomit from Justine's room when we entered. Justine was slumped on the edge of the bed, her head in her hands. The phlebotomist vampires had signed their work with angry yellow-green bruises extending from her right elbow to her wrist. She appeared so weak that if the air conditioner had kicked on, the draft might have knocked her over. She rubbed her eyes, then noticed us.

"Sorry, Sis. If you're not up to company, we can —"

"No, no. Company is exactly what I need. Hi Emily. Nice of you to visit. Please, come in." She wiped her face with a damp washcloth. "How's my big boy?"

Justine reached out to tousle RJ's red curls, remembered her restriction, and dropped her hand into her lap. Her wig rested on the dresser. What was left of her own hair had lost its fire and was damp with sweat, clinging to her forehead like rivulets of rusty water.

As usual, RJ dominated the early conversation. His stories slowly revived Justine the way the sun and rain renew a wilted flower. I couldn't help but notice how Emily also focused on the boy, smiling and hanging on his every word. He had the same effect on me, filling a void yet constantly reminding me that I would never quench that longing for my own child. I wondered if Emily felt the same inner turmoil.

When my nephew finally tired of us, he scampered off to play on a table by the window.

Emily said, "I wish I could see RJ. Who does he resemble?"

"He has Justine's freckles and red hair," I replied. My sister winced and combed back the remaining strands with her fingers. Removing my foot from my mouth, I added, "And he has my father's silver-blue eyes, like mine, Em."

She nodded, then told Justine about the first time that she and I met in grade school, adding that as a young boy, I'd had long girly eyelashes.

Justine chuckled. "Emily, you made my

brother blush. Tell me more, please!"

Emily shared a couple of humorous tales from our childhood together, and I retaliated with one about her from our dating years. Because our philandering father had sired Justine in Louisiana, she didn't know much about my childhood and encouraged us to continue. A story duel ensued. Just when I thought I had the best of her, Emily produced a yellowed sheet of paper from her purse, mischief dancing in her eyes.

"Jake only wrote one poem for me in high school, trying to get back in my good graces as I remember." She giggled like a schoolgirl. "I found it in the back of my old yearbook. God knows why I saved it."

I groaned. "Oh Em, don't! Please."

"I'm sure your sister will enjoy learning what a devious brother she has." Emily handed the paper to Justine, who read aloud:

At our picnic, I
listen to your hair
singing in the wind
grateful to be there,

and as your lips part
I can only stare,
my longing for your love
my one and only prayer.

"My God, Jake, that's awful!" Justine clapped her hands. "What a conniving little Romeo you were."

"How embarrassing! And that's why I leave the poetry to Emily."

The three of us roared with laughter. With my past and present together in the same room, I felt light-hearted for the first time since Justine's hospital admission. We'd thrown the pall of her illness aside and were truly enjoying each other's company. I hoped that there would be many more times like this in the future.

I caught my breath and added, "I'd swiped some of my mom's wine for a picnic that day, and we were both a bit tipsy. I guess being smitten and liquored up doesn't make you a better poet."

It wasn't long before my sister's chortling became a coughing fit, deep and moist. When she couldn't stop, RJ put his toys down and took a step in our direction. A nurse peeked in and scolded us for sapping Justine's strength and disturbing the other patients on the floor.

Justine sipped some water and calmed her cough, and we regained our composure. Emily leaned over and said, "I've been dying to show that to Justine. No hard feelings, Jake?"

Her perfume stirred long buried memories of the taste and touch of her lips. What a pathetic fool I was! We had no future together, and yet she seemed to radiate her own gravitational force. I struggled mightily to resist the pull.

"You're lucky I'm in the forgiveness business, Em."

She smiled at my sister and said, "Next time we visit, I'll bring cheesecake, plastic forks, and throw a cloth over your tray table for a picnic."

"Just don't forget the wine, Jake, okay?" Justine replied.

"For you, Sis, I'll see what I can do."

We stayed much too long, completely exhausting Justine. Fearing I'd be late for Mass, I did my best imitation of Mario Andretti at the Indy 500, weaving through traffic back to Oberlin. I settled Emily and RJ in the soundproof "quiet room" in the back of the church with barely enough time to dress in my vestments.

For a change, the pews were nearly filled, and the singing loud and vibrant. It had been a good day all around, and I thanked the Lord for His blessings and prayed for Justine's recovery.

After dropping Emily at her apartment and wrangling RJ into bed, I settled into my recliner and let a Michael Connelly novel transport me to the unseemly underbelly of Los Angeles corruption. I was finishing the third chapter when Tree called.

"That charade with Miguel and Tina worked, Jake. I got a warrant! My tech guru is working on their computer, and a bean-counter is examining their finances as we speak. I'm gonna grill their asses tomorrow afternoon. One o'clock, sharp. You're invited to the barbeque."

"I don't know." I thought of Pablo hooked up to machines in intensive care and wanted to be there when Tree roasted them on the spit. But considering how he had used me to carry out his stunt with the tape recorder, I felt conflicted. "Okay, I'll be there. But no more *sleight of hand* or illegal hanky-panky."

"No need now. Their necks are on the chopping block, and that warrant is my ax. See you tomorrow, buddy."

Returning to Connelly's dark world of L.A. crime, I realized that sadly, the City of Angels hadn't cornered the market on treachery and violence.

CHAPTER THIRTY-SEVEN

Sunday, August 6, 11:15 a.m.

The organist gave the exit hymn a bluesy edge as my parishioners filed out, which reminded me of Andrew Carnegie, the wealthy industrialist. In addition to funding public libraries across the country, he had also purchased thousands of organs for churches because, as he said, he hoped to lessen the pain of sermons. I kept that in mind every time I wrote one.

As I greeted the faithful after Mass, the parishioner I'd consulted about guardianship papers and Power of Attorney approached, handed me a thick envelope, and whispered, "Have these signed and witnessed, put them in a safe place, and hope you never need them." I thanked her and was still smiling as I entered the sacristy.

The century-old rhythms and rituals of Mass had once again served as my daily meditation, calming my anxiety and adding

327

perspective. I had even come to love the trappings of my faith — the heavy silk vestments in their stained-glass hues of emerald, violet, and blue, the intoxicating aroma of fresh flowers and incense, and the miraculous weight of holding the body and blood of Jesus Christ in my hands. This was where I was most at peace, where I surely belonged.

The last place I wanted to be on the Lord's Day was in a police interrogation room, but I'd promised Tree. After lunch, we spoke with Justine on the phone, then Colleen took RJ to the school playground to wear out the little cyclone in hopes that he would nap. I put on a dress shirt and a pair of trousers, then headed for my car in the rectory garage.

When I swung the driver's door open, a foul smell assaulted me. I stepped back. My mind refused to accept what my eyes saw. An icy cold slid slowly down my spine. I held my breath and inched forward.

Martin Luther lay motionless on the passenger's seat, his head twisted at a grotesque angle. Blood oozed from the cat's mouth and nose, matting his fur and staining the car seat.

I stared at the cat's lifeless body, which had begun to bloat in the summer heat. RJ would be devastated. When Justine was admitted to the hospital, I'd employed Martin Luther to cheer up my nephew. His face lit with excitement whenever I took him to the church basement and he fed the cat a saucer of cream and stroked the contented, purring beast. On some days, it was the only way I could take his mind off of his mother's illness. Now this!

The bitter taste of bile rose in my throat. I swallowed hard as it came to me who had killed him.

I had reached detente with Father Marek a week ago and violence wasn't in his nature. No irate pro-choice advocate would go to this extreme over one anti-abortion sermon by a Catholic priest. That left Tina and Miguel. The hands-on brutality of strangulation suggested a man had done this — although all the evidence Tree had presented so far, and Miguel's apparent confusion at each revelation, pointed to Tina as the one who'd tried to murder her own child. If she could suffocate her own children, killing a cat wouldn't even show up on her moral radar, if she had any. The person who had entered the rectory in the middle of the night had undoubtedly been the one who'd killed the cat last evening — and Miguel had a solid alibi at work the night the threatening note was left in my study. Martin's cold-blooded execution *had to be* Tina's handiwork.

Tree's ruthless grilling at the police station probably had inflamed her, but threatening the Chief of Police was out of the question. This was either a message to him through me, or payback for my participation. It didn't matter which.

A lunatic reckless enough to strangle an innocent animal and enter the rectory in the dead of night with a threatening note probably *had killed* her first child and attempted to suffocate her second. There was no reason to believe that the people I loved would be spared. RJ and Emily were both as defenseless and trusting as Martin Luther had been. This had to stop today.

Enough blood had saturated the beige fabric of the car seat that I was sure I could never completely remove the stain. The scent of death and decay resurrected images of carnage from the war, the screams of comrades, and the lust for revenge that I had buried years ago. The young soldier that I'd once been rose from his grave. I wanted to wring Tina's miserable neck, and Miguel's if he'd been involved.

Vengeance is mine saith the Lord — but for me, there would be no turning the other

330

cheek today. Any hesitation I'd had about participating in Tree's interrogation vanished. I was mad as hell and all in.

Already late, I didn't have time to bury the poor cat, yet didn't want Colleen or RJ to accidentally find him, so I slipped on a pair of work gloves and unceremoniously dumped poor Martin Luther's body into the trash can. I quickly wiped down the passenger's seat with rags, covered the stain with an old towel, and rolled down the car windows to clear the odor, then jammed the stick shift into gear. I was on a mission.

My boiling fury had cooled to a slow simmer by the time I parked at the police station. I thought of Pablo, motionless in his hospital crib, drew a deep breath, and said a short prayer, asking the Almighty to guide Lady Justice today. Although I firmly believed in a merciful, forgiving God, the notion of a vengeful one worked well for me in that moment. I wouldn't lay my hands on Pablo's vile parents, but I'd do everything in my power to help the system punish the hell out of them.

Tree was about to enter the interview room when I walked into the building. He waved me over, and I noticed a small bandage on his neck where the worrisome growth had been.

Before I could remark, Tree said, "Yeah, yeah. I saw a dermatologist, just to get you off my back." He opened the door. "Come on, we got a couple of slimy fish to fry."

CHAPTER THIRTY-EIGHT

Sunday, August 6, 1:00 p.m.

In the interview room, I sat next to Tree. Across the table, Tina and Miguel stared at me with enough rage to nearly set my hair on fire. To my surprise, they hadn't hired a lawyer. For a second, I wondered if Tree and I could be completely wrong, and they didn't think they needed representation because they were innocent. More likely it was a money issue. Defense attorneys usually required a retainer.

Tree activated a digital voice recorder on the table and it hummed softly. No tape recorder this time, no subterfuge. Tree was playing this interview straight, as I had asked. He finished the preliminaries, peeked into his manila folder, closed it, but remained silent.

Tension crackled in the air like an electrical storm and lightning flashed in Miguel's eyes. He pounded his fist on the table.

"Why the fuck are we here again? We already answered all your questions. What gives you the right to trash our apartment and take our computer and stuff?"

"A judge," Tree answered.

"Yeah, that's what you cops always say when you kick in somebody's door, beat up a black guy, or gun down an unarmed kid," Tina said, her expression hardening. "Not my fault. The law is the law. Just following orders. Bunch of goddamn Nazis!"

"No door kicking needed, and *it is* the law. You saw my warrant."

Tree was enjoying himself, playing with them like a cat with two mice, which was fitting after what had happened to poor Martin Luther.

Tina redirected her motionless gaze to me. "Come on. I was supposed to be at work two hours ago. Weekends at the diner are busy, and we got bills to pay, hospital bills."

Tree slid his chair back. "You can go to work after you answer a few more questions. For the last time, who found Pablo unconscious?"

Miguel glanced at Tina, then down at his lap. Solidarity? Intimidation? Or blind love?

"I did," she said, "but I panicked and

screamed for Miguel. He came in and dialed 911."

Tree ran his hand through what would have been his hair, if he hadn't shaved off the remaining fringe.

"How much did you have to drink that morning, Miguel?"

"Don't know. We both had a few. I'd finished my shift, and Tina had the day off. And with the heat and all, Pablo was in a mood. He just wouldn't stop hollerin'."

"I only had one beer," Tina corrected, glaring at him. "You had a damn six-pack."

His head snapped in her direction.

"That's cause you kept bringing 'em to me! Like you was still at the restaurant, hustling for tips. Madre mía! Come to think of it, what the fuck was that about?"

"I wait on you because you're too damn lazy to get off your ass. You were singing your usual tune." Tina lowered the pitch of her voice an octave and added a Hispanic accent. "*Mujer,* I been bustin' my tail all night. Get me a beer, would ya?" She dropped the accent. "Admit it, Miguel, you're a drunk! No wonder you can't remember shit about what happened to Pablo."

Tree let them bludgeon each other for a while and then continued.

"Why'd you ask the doctors to shut off Pablo's respirator and donate his organs?"

Anger lit Miguel's face like a bonfire. "Because our baby was *brain-dead,* asshole! What kind of fuckin' question is —"

Tina placed her hand on his forearm. "When they told us Pablo would never wake up, Miguel and I decided we didn't want other folks to suffer the way we were. Like that poor child we saw on TV, the one who needs a new heart. We figured we could help some other kids, make something good come out of this. Part of Pablo would go on living."

Tree nodded. "So, it was an act of compassion?"

"Exactly."

Saint Tina the Compassionate. Not a feast day I intended to celebrate.

Tree drummed his fingers on the table. "Then why did you change your minds about organ donation when Dr. Taylor told you that there would have to be an autopsy first?"

Tina patted her husband's arm again, back in control. "It's a religious thing. We're Catholic."

The first amendment defense. *Don't you dare challenge our faith, officer!*

I'd seen Miguel at Mass a couple times,

but I was sure Tina had never attended services at Sacred Heart.

I cleared my throat. "Tina, as I told Miguel, the Church sees organ donation as an act of Christian charity when death is inevitable. It's not a sin. Neither is permitting an autopsy."

Tina's dark onyx eyes became cold, her words measured and frost tinged.

"There's a big difference between donating my baby's organs to another child and some ghoul in a morgue cutting him up to see what's inside, like some damn frog in a science lab. That's disgusting!"

Before my eyes she'd transformed into Saint Tina the Righteous, defender of the helpless and all that is decent.

She retrieved her hand from Miguel's arm and pointed at me. "No *loving God* would ask a parent to slice up their baby."

In my mind, I saw Abraham from the Old Testament at the altar with a knife at Isaac's throat, about to sacrifice his own son as God demanded.

I began to respond, but Tree cleared his throat, indicating that he wanted his turn. The interview was becoming a tag team wrestling match, two on two, so I retreated to my corner and let Tree take over. He slid a blank sheet of paper across the table.

"How much have you had to drink today, Miguel?"

"None of your business!"

"How much?"

"A couple beers. That's all."

"Good. Sign your name."

Tree tossed him a pen, and Miguel caught it with his left hand and scribbled. His signature slanted to the left but was not as jagged as on the photocopy of the checks that I'd seen on Friday.

Tree handed the paper to Tina. "You sign too, please. And include your current address and telephone number."

The color drained from her cheeks. She took the pen in her right hand and complied.

Tree opened his manila folder and compared the writing.

"It appears that Tina filled out the checks for the life insurance on Pablo, and you signed them, Miguel."

Miguel opened his mouth, then closed it without saying a word.

Tree leveled his gaze at Tina. "With a joint account, why would you go through all that trouble? Why not just sign them yourself?"

She squirmed in the chair and looked down, suddenly finding something on the floor that attracted her attention.

"Because the insurance was *his idea,* and I'm tired of having to do everything myself. I wanted him to do *something* once in a while."

"What? That's mierda! I never said nothing about no insurance." Miguel stared at her. "And I *try* to help out. I'm working my ass off, doing the best I can, damn it!"

I was going to jump back into the fray but Tree was on a roll, so I sat back and watched a master at work.

He said, "Must be tough, Tina, working your job and caring for Pablo and Miguel. You have to feel a bit . . . isolated and lonely."

"Yeah, sometimes."

"Do you use the telephone and computer to keep in touch with friends?"

"Sure. Doesn't everybody?"

Tree motioned to the one-way mirror and a young, darkskinned policewoman entered the room. In addition to her uniform, she wore a deadly serious expression and a small red bindi mark on her forehead, indicative of her Hindu heritage. Tina's eyes, however, were hypnotized by the handcuffs swinging from the officer's belt.

"This is Shirley Kadu." Tree pulled out the chair next to him and the young woman placed a notebook on the table and sat.

"She's our I.T. expert."

So *this* was the computer guru that Tree had nicknamed "Sure Can-do," the one who could even recover data from a computer with bullet holes through it.

Tree continued. "I've been reading Officer Kadu's initial report. She's been examining your computer use, Tina, among other things. You did a lot of research on SIDS."

Tina was clearly startled, and I thought I saw a slight tremor in her hands.

Kadu said, "Oh, you probably think you deleted all that from the computer's history, but nothing is ever completely gone, Tina — if you're trained to know how to find it. Once you type it in, it's with you forever. So, tell us about researching Sudden Infant Deaths."

"Of course I googled it. My boy was in the hospital."

"That would make sense if your research hadn't begun two months *before* Pablo was admitted to the hospital," Kadu replied. "And who is this *Ted* fellow you keep in contact with?" She tapped her notebook. "Yeah, I found those deleted emails too."

Tina's complexion chameleoned to a deathly-white color.

"He's a friend'a ours. We've known him a long time." She looked at Miguel. "You remember Ted, right honey?"

Miguel gawked at her.

"*Teddy Bear* is a pretty affectionate name for a friend," Tree said. "That's what you call him in your emails, right?" He slid a copy of a check to Miguel, this one written and signed by Tina. "Is Teddy the reason you hired a divorce lawyer in town?"

Miguel snatched up the paper before Tina's hand got there. He studied it as if it were written in Sanskrit.

"Tina, qué pasa? What's he talkin' about?"

The hint of a twisted smile slowly creased Tree's lips. "Great question, Miguel. Maybe we can help with that." He turned toward Officer Kadu. "Find out anything else interesting, Shirley?"

"You mean like the dozen phone calls Tina made to her good friend Teddy over the past month, Chief? And here's one of the emails Teddy Bear sent to Tina about starting a new life together." She laid the printout in the center of the table where everyone could read it. It began: *My dearest Sugar Bear. It's been too long since I held you —*

Tina grabbed it before Miguel could react and balled up the paper.

"That's a copy," Kadu said, "and just the tip of the iceberg. Then there's the correspondence with *three companies* that you

341

bought insurance from on Pablo, for a total of a hundred and fifty grand. Smart of you to purchase those before your son was diagnosed with cerebral palsy — or maybe there's a reason his deterioration began *after* he got home. And it's funny, Miguel signed all three checks, but you, Tina, are the sole beneficiary on all of them."

Officer Kadu flipped to a new page in her notebook.

"Then, of course, there's the policy on your first child, the baby girl who died in Pennsylvania. And interestingly, that check for seventy-five grand was deposited in a separate savings account in *Tina's name only,* not in your joint one. Which brings our grand total to nearly a quarter million dollars. It's a pity the cops in that rural town in PA didn't pick up on that at the time." Kadu grunted. "Do you think we're all a bunch of country bumpkins? Is that why you moved to another small town? I've been chatting with those Pennsylvania bumpkins on the phone, Tina, and they are very interested now."

Kadu glanced at Tree.

"Ohio and Pennsylvania both have the death penalty for first degree murder, don't they Chief?"

Tina pushed back from the table, but Tree

was already on his feet.

"Don't get up, Tina. We're not done." His face hardened to black granite. "That was very slick, waiting till Miguel was drunk to have him sign all the checks, so blame would fall on him if your scheme went south. *Premeditated,* I'd say. And damn cold. That's motive, means, and opportunity." Tree was more relaxed than I'd seen in weeks. He cracked his knuckles; it sounded like giant oak limbs snapping. "If you're planning on that new life with good old Teddy Bear, don't get your hopes up. He's just been brought in for questioning. I'm dying to hear what he has to say."

Miguel wilted in his chair and glared at his wife. "You fucking puta! How could you do that to our babies?"

Tina leaped up, sprinted across the interview room, and grabbed the doorknob, but Tree got there first and blocked the door with his size 13 boot.

"I want my lawyer!" she said, hissing the words like a coiled snake. "Get out of my way! Now! I have rights!"

"Get a good lawyer, Tina. You're definitely gonna need one. If Pablo dies, attempted murder becomes murder one. With seventy-five grand in your separate bank account, at least you won't have to depend on some rookie public defender fresh out of law school. I'd pick one with experience at death penalty defenses." Tree shook his head in disgust. "Spitting out babies like a damn ATM machine, killing 'em, and cashing in on their life insurance? I've met some real scumbags in this job, lady, but you're at the top of the list."

Tree smirked. "As far as your rights go, Tina," he said producing a card from his pocket, "you have the right to remain silent. Anything you say can and will be used against you in a court of law. You have the right . . . ."

As Tree delivered his Miranda warning, Officer Kadu came up from behind and slapped a pair of handcuffs on Tina. I could almost hear the ghost of poor Martin Luther purr his approval, but the penalty for animal cruelty paled compared to the charges that Tina faced.

Miguel gazed across the table at me, tears streaming down his cheeks.

"Diós mío, Padre, what have I done? What a dumb fuckin' drunk I am! She was killing mis bebés . . . for money! And I did nothing!" His chin dropped to his chest. "Sweet Jesus, have mercy on my soul."

Miguel stood, wobbled, and sank to his knees.

As I slowly helped him back into his chair, I wondered what I could possibly say to this man who had lost everything.

CHAPTER THIRTY-NINE

Sunday, August 6, 3:00 p.m.

I don't remember driving from the police station to the rectory or entering the living room, but when I saw RJ, I hugged him so tight and for so long that he squirmed away, stomped a red sneaker, and screamed, "Stop it, Uncle Jake!"

Without taking his eyes off me, he scampered to the sofa and nuzzled his blue security blanket, looking scared and forlorn. During his mother's illness in Louisiana, he had been shuttled between a series of foster parents, some less than ideal, shattering his four year old world. Now, hundreds of miles away in a strange home, the poor kid had to deal with me, the eccentric uncle almost every family had.

Colleen abandoned her dust rag and scurried over.

"Saints protect and preserve us, Father! What is going on with you? Are you all right then?"

I couldn't tell the Queen of Gossip what had happened at the station house, so I said, "I'm just grateful to have RJ in my life. And Justine. And you too, Colleen. I've been blessed."

Colleen was speechless, a rare occurrence.

Tina's betrayal of her babies, her husband, and her humanity had left me ice-cold inside and in need of physical contact. If Justine had been there, I might have hugged the life out of her frail body. I spread my arms and stepped forward to embrace Colleen instead. She stepped back.

"There'll be none of that, if you please, Father."

RJ was rocking back and forth, rubbing his blanket against his cheek. My sister had given me strict instructions that he could cuddle with it only for naps and at bedtime, now that he was "a big boy." He gave me those sad, puppy dog eyes and I absolved him of this minor infraction. With Justine in the hospital, I had already broken the *no sweets before dinner* and *bedtime by eight o'clock* rules, so what was one more.

I walked over and tousled his hair. Although it was late, I said, "Let's go visit your Mom, RJ. Would you like that?"

The scowl slid from his face, and he nodded vigorously.

"All right, then. Make a pit stop in the bathroom and we'll leave."

I thanked Colleen for caring for RJ, sent her home, and grabbed the legal papers for Justine. As my nephew and I walked to my car, lightening flashed in the western sky. Thunder roared and dark, roiled clouds galloped toward us like the four horsemen of the apocalypse. I sent him inside for his raincoat, sprinted to the garage through the opening barrage of rain, and sprayed the interior of the Toyota with air freshioner. The scent of death from the passenger seat, however, still faintly lingered.

I parked near the rectory door. When RJ came out, I whisked him into his car seat in the back and we headed east. With visiting hours dwindling, I pushed well past the speed limit through the wind-driven torrent and gathering darkness.

At the Cleveland Clinic, RJ and I hurried through the scrub and gown procedure and entered Justine's room. My smile was short-lived. RJ sensed trouble, screeching to a halt just inside the doorway.

Justine's oncologist stood at her bedside, accompanied by a nurse and an intern who appeared young enough to be a boy scout. Their expressions were solemn as they again postponed her planned discharge from the isolation unit, citing the need to bolster her immune system.

I asked them if I could review my sister's hospital record. When Justine said that she wanted my "second opinion" and volunteered to sign a release form to keep the hospital lawyers happy, the oncologist relented but added that RJ couldn't be left in the room unsupervised.

The nurse spoke up. "I have a child about his age and know it's a chore to get him scrubbed and gowned. I'm going off my shift now and can stay with him for little while, but make it as quick as you can."

I thanked her, left the room, and trudged to the nurses' station. Justine's chart weighed almost as much as she did. I worked my way through it, searching for a missed opportunity, an overlooked clue, or a path not taken.

What I found made my heart hurt. Saving her life would take more than a skilled team of doctors and nurses and the latest medicines; it would take a miracle. As a physician, I recognized how dire the situation was, and even as a man of faith I knew it was a long way from Cleveland to Galilee. I contemplated Jesus's abbreviated thirty-three years on this earth, and whispered a prayer.

Merciful Lord, you made the lame walk, the blind see, and raised the dead. Please allow my sister to attend RJ's next birthday, his First Communion, his high school graduation. Sweet Jesus, have mercy on us.

When I returned to Justine's room, the nurse was making a quarter vanish from her hand and reappear in RJ's ear. My nephew was dazzled and bouncing for joy, and my sister was clearly enjoying the show.

As the nurse began to leave the room, I asked her to witness our signatures on the Power of Attorney documents and the form nominating me as RJ's legal guardian in case Justine became incapacitated. She helped Justine sign everything without violating sterile precautions, then went home to her own child.

When she was gone, Justine sent her son to play at the table by the window.

"Find anything in my chart? Give it to me straight, Jake. Is there a ray of hope?"

"There's always hope, Sis." I hesitated. "And prayer."

She looked away as if she'd read my thoughts.

"Then pray for me . . . and my boy, Jake."

Agnostic no more, or simply frightened

and desperate? I didn't know and didn't care. I held her hand and prayed aloud. RJ left his toys on the windowsill, came over, and took my other hand.

When we had finished, the remainder of our stay was bittersweet and filled with long silences. I was relieved when visiting hours ended.

CHAPTER FORTY

Wednesday, August 23, 2:00 p.m.

Days blurred into weeks with Justine barely hanging on. Another x-ray. Another blood test. Another disappointment.

With Justine in medical Limbo, her tiny hospital room soon became my earthly Purgatory. I suffered with her there daily. Unable to sleep at night, I sometimes dozed off in a chair by her bed when I visited. At the church, I became a stick-figure priest, merely going through the motions. I prayed for my sister so much and so often that my knees ached. The Almighty, however, apparently was too busy keeping the Big Bang rolling to respond.

My faith had been tested before, but not like this. Watching Justine slowly slip away was a form of Chinese water torture, eroding my convictions drop by drop, hour by hour, day by day, the endless trickle of despair carving a deep valley through the center of my faith. Faced with dashed hopes and unanswered prayers, even priests have dark days of the soul.

Every afternoon was spent with Justine. Somehow, she kept her spirits up. Despite painful mouth ulcers, unrelenting fatigue, and leg cramps, she managed to smile whenever RJ told her about his day.

Her continued deterioration was not lost on my four year old nephew. He began asking me about her hair loss, the mottled purple patches on her arms, and why she was so skinny. I tiptoed through the minefield of his questions as best I could, trying not to detonate what was left of his innocence and naïve optimism.

When we arrived back at the rectory, I no longer had Martin Luther to help distract him from the harsh reality of his collapsing world. I couldn't burden him with any more pain, so I lied about the cat's disappearance. The truth be damned! Sometimes there is righteousness in a good lie.

One evening after visiting his mother, my nephew fell into such a deep depression that it terrified me. When I offered to play soldier with him, he just shook his head, stared off into the distance, and resumed his repetitive, rocking-horse movement. Feeling helpless and desperate, I went up to my bedroom, and in my small collection of souvenirs and memories I found the Combat Medical Badge from my army uniform. The faded patch showed a caduceus mounted on a stretcher, surrounded by an elliptical wreath. It wasn't red, but a badge of courage nonetheless to those of us who had served. It represented the small amount of decency and compassion that I'd managed to bring to that shadowed valley of death.

I showed the badge to RJ, and he brightened and returned from the land of lost children. When I promised to sew it on the sleeve of his favorite shirt, he rallied his plastic troops and I fetched my clothespin army. For a few hours, he left the frightening, murky world of worry and stayed with me in the present moment. When he balked at bedtime, I reminded him that I was his commanding officer until his mother got well. To my surprise, he saluted, hopped into his GI Joe pajamas, and crawled under the covers.

My successes as a surrogate parent, however, were hard-fought and short-lived, and I fell into bed every night frustrated and depressed. Our shared adversity, however, drew RJ and me closer. We hugged often, clinging to each other for courage and hope, waiting to see what each new morning would bring.

CHAPTER FORTY-ONE

Thursday, August 31, 1:00 p.m.
With my life focused on RJ and Justine, I had virtually forgotten about the bleeding statue at St. Wenceslaus. As the days inched by, Tina's arrest became a distant footnote in my past. Tree Macon and the District Attorney, however, had prioritized her prosecution and were progressing at breakneck speed. They had sufficient probable cause and quickly brought a long list of charges, including aggravated child abuse, reckless endangerment, and attempted murder. The state of Pennsylvania was grumbling about extradition for the death of her first child.

At her initial appearance in Superior Court, the District Attorney made the case that Tina was a flight risk and the judge ordered her held without bail. He directed that all potential insurance money be held in escrow until a verdict was reached. He also froze her access to the insurance money she'd received after the death of her first child. Although the wheels of justice were grinding slower than Tree would have liked, Tina was about to be ground up.

A grand jury quickly indicted her. Unable and unwilling to turn the other cheek on what she had done, I quietly thanked God for raining down fire and brimstone on this vile woman, and prayed that Tina would go to prison . . . forever and ever, amen. On some days, even a life sentence seemed too lenient to me.

Rumors of my involvement swirled through town. When my parishioners asked about the case, I kept my bias against Tina to myself and used my seminary training to deliver noncommittal answers that deftly evaded the truth. I didn't even reveal my role to Emily or Justine.

Shortly after Tina's arraignment was scheduled, Dr. Taylor repeated Pablo's EEG and scans, conceding that the child showed no evidence of improvement and little likelihood of recovery. Somehow the vultures in the press sniffed out the test results and splashed them across the headlines of local newspapers.

Tina's defense lawyer immediately filed a motion for a gag order, claiming that information disseminated by the press would prejudice the proceedings and lead to a circus atmosphere. He also claimed that the initial publicity had tainted the jury pool and asked for a change of venue. The judge denied both motions.

Having heard Tina's version of Tree Macon's tactics in the interview, her attorney then filed a motion to suppress the search warrant, the evidence obtained with it, and all her admissions based on the tainted-fruit-of-the-tree doctrine.

This meant that as a witness to Tina's police interrogation, I needed to appear at the hearing. I couldn't sleep at all the night before the District Attorney prepared us for the big day. He had announced his intention to run for the Senate and the conviction of a woman who killed her children for money would virtually guarantee him a landslide victory, so he was anxious to go to trial. Consequently, he grilled Tree Macon extensively but didn't spend much time on me. No matter how he asked the key question about the tape recorder, Tree calmly repeated the *big lie* without flinching.

At the hearing, the District Attorney was relaxed and in high spirits. When Tree asked him what was going on, he told us that Tina's lawyer had been called away for a family emergency, and he'd sent a junior partner in his place. His exact words were, "Counselor Dumb has sent Counselor Dumber" — and Dumber proceeded to focus primarily on Tree's testimony, paying little attention to mine. As expected, Tree was a stone wall, and the judge refused to grant the motion to suppress Tina's recorded interrogation or the subsequent information obtained.

With the recorded police interview admitted as the primary evidence against Tina for the criminal trial, Counselor Dumber panicked. He petitioned the court for permission to depose all witnesses to the police interview prior to the trial — meaning me — citing a litany of legal gobbledygook. After hearing arguments pro and con, the judge finally consented.

When I asked about this, the District Attorney explained that the defense didn't want to put a priest on the witness stand who could corroborate Chief Macon's story in front of a jury, so he was hoping to break my version or get me to contradict Tree at the deposition, when no jury was present and he could be more ruthless. Not very reassuring.

Then Tina's attorney attempted to plead the case down to a lesser charge. The District Attorney refused and as he left the courtroom, he reiterated his hang-em-high philosophy on child abusers in front of every reporter and TV camera in the county.

After the hearing, I stopped at the church to discuss minor repairs with the janitor. A nun dropped in with suggestions to improve attendance on Bingo night. When I arrived back at the rectory, I received a letter informing me of my scheduled deposition by Tina's attorney.

I panicked, called Tree, and gave him hell. "When you asked for my help, I thought I was your consultant, not your stooge! Your shenanigans have painted me into an ethical, legal, and moral corner, damn it!"

"Get a grip, Jake, this isn't about you. You're not a shrink, but let me give you a peek inside my head. I don't give a crap about playing fair with Tina, and I won't apologize. She killed her babies! I'm sure of it. Period. As the father of three daughters, I don't ever want her to see the light of day."

"Tina's lawyer will try to force me to admit that you turned off the tape recorder during the interview — making your *evidence* and the search warrant inadmissible, and making me an accomplice." I was shouting and lowered my voice. "You *know* I can't and won't lie under oath."

"I get it, buddy. Do what you have to do,

but . . . do what you can for me." Tree drew a long, deep breath, then added, "You're an ingenious guy, and you understand the stakes."

I did, indeed. If the fancy footwork that I'd learned in seminary wasn't nimble enough to dance around the truth, I might end Tree's career, open Tina's cell door, and take her place behind bars for obstruction of justice or perjury. And given Justine's condition, if I went to jail, RJ would end up back in foster care.

No pressure there.

CHAPTER FORTY-TWO

Friday, September 1, 10:00 a.m.

As I walked into the rectory after morning Mass, Dr. Taylor called with the follow up report I'd requested on Father Marek. I was heartened to hear that Marek continued to see Taylor for vitamin B1 injections and was attending Alcoholics Anonymous meetings regularly. His physical symptoms of Wernicke's disease were slowly resolving. The Virgin Mary statue may not have wept blood, but maybe a small miracle had occurred at St Wenceslaus Church after all.

With my impending deposition hanging over me, I broke with my routine, gave Colleen the day off, and drove RJ to the Cleveland Clinic so that we could spend more time with Justine.

After her son gave her an in-depth update on his world, my sister and I spoke for a while on mundane topics, avoiding any mention of leukemia. When she asked about life with RJ, I confessed that even with his beloved blue blankie, I was having a hellish time getting him to sleep at night.

"There's a trick that usually works when he's cranky." She leaned forward and whispered. "You know the hankie embroidered with lavender flowers that I often carry?" When I nodded, she continued. "That was my mother's, his grandmother's. It's in my top dresser drawer. Add a drop of my perfume, give it to RJ, and tell him that Nana is waiting to see him in his dreams."

It was a simple and elegant solution that undoubtedly would come in handy. We had begun discussing preschool when Justine's oncologist and his entourage entered her room. Their bedside manner was decidedly more businesslike than it had been previously, their demeanor less warm. I'd seen these subtle signs before. They were distancing themselves emotionally.

Justine also seemed to sense this. After her doctors left, she said, "Come here RJ. I have something to tell to you." He walked over, and she held his gloved hands and said, "Because I'm sick, your Uncle Jake is going to take care of you. So listen to what he says and be a good boy, okay? He's my best friend and . . . your special friend. He needs your love too. This is very important

363

to me. Do you understand, RJ?"

"Yes, Mama."

He gave me a quick hug before returning to his toys. Justine signaled me closer.

"Jake, don't let Children's Services take RJ. The poor kid's life has been hell since I got sick. Please don't let that happen!"

"No one's going to take him away. I'll care for him till your better, Sis. Not to worry."

"One other thing, Jake. You know I'm not . . . a believer. RJ and I never were baptized or anything. Never went to church." She gazed at the ceiling tiles for a long time. "But maybe . . . you could baptize me and R.J?"

"Now?"

"Yeah. I think now would be a good time. Can you?"

Given Justine's critical condition, I was permitted to forgo the usual Rite of Christian Initiation for Adults. The Church allowed priests considerable leeway in death bed cases.

Death bed. I choked up and my eyes moistened. I wiped them and cleared my throat. "Of course, Sis."

Justine lowered her voice. "Do I need to confess my sins to you first, Jake? I don't think I could do that."

"That's not necessary. Baptism washes

away all sins."

She called RJ over again and explained that I was going to do something to help them, and that he would get a little wet but shouldn't be afraid. RJ stiffened and took a step away from me.

With my sister's compromised immune system, I feared infection, so I flagged down a passing nurse, asked for a bottle of sterile water, and began.

"Justine, I ask that you turn your life and your fate over to Jesus today. In St. Paul's Letter to the Romans he promised that if we die with Christ, we shall live with Him." I blessed the water and poured a small amount on their foreheads saying, "I baptize you, Justine and Randall James, in the name of the Father, and of the Son, and of the Holy Spirit."

My nephew startled at the first drop, jerked away, and bumped my hand. I spilled several ounces of water in his hair and on his forehead. He shook like a dog who'd run through a sprinkler, then put his hands on his hips and gave me a petulant four year old glare.

"Stop it, Uncle Jake! Stop!"

"Sorry, RJ. I didn't mean to frighten you."

Justine chuckled. "If I'd known you were gonna try to drown him, I'd have had RJ build an ark with his Legos."

With our emotions jumbled, we ran out of things to say. My nephew's confusion, however, was short-lived. After a few minutes, General RJ waved me over to his plastic army and awarded me a field promotion, placing me in command of a machine gun squadron. We parachuted from the windowsill and went on the offensive, recapturing the high ground of a Kleenex box.

My sister glanced back and forth between us, her two soldier boys. She closed her eyes, moaned, and sobbed softly. I prayed that she hadn't somehow glimpsed the future.

As visiting hours ended, Justine's doctors entered and informed us that she would soon be transferred to the Intensive Care Unit.

I told her Oncologist that I was a priest and asked if there was time to perform the Sacrament of Anointing of the Sick.

"The what?"

I leaned in and whispered, "Last Rites."

"Oh, sure, but make it quick. Okay?"

Since the day Justine had first asked me to pray with her, I'd brought my ritual book and Holy Oil to the hospital in my pockets. I took them out, read the prayers, and anointed her forehead. The Sacrament seemed to provide her with some comfort and courage. Then I opened my small gold-plated pyx containing the Blessed Eucharist, placed the Host on her tongue, and offered First Holy Communion to my sister. Other than my love, I had nothing more to give her. I held her hand until the transporter arrived to wheel her to ICU.

As we left the hospital, RJ was confused and upset. I couldn't delay telling him how serious things were. Fearing that this day would come, I'd read several books on bereavement and spent two hours with the hospital grief counselor learning how to approach a child with devastating news.

But nothing could have adequately prepared me for that conversation. When we arrived at the rectory, I began cautiously explaining to RJ how dire the situation was, treading like a man walking across red-hot coals — and it was every bit as painful. When I'd finished, we cried together for a long time, and the only way that I could get him into bed was to move my twin mattress onto the floor in his room and promise to spend the night there.

The day had been one of the hardest of my life, yet as tired as I was, I couldn't imagine sleeping. I found a mindless sitcom on the TV, but the media wouldn't allow me to forget about Tina. Between shows, the station aired a promo for the evening news promising a "breaking update" on her impending trial.

I had no doubt that Tina was a textbook psychopath. She showed poor impulse control and a willingness to take risks, no fear of the authorities, complete disregard for the welfare of her husband and children, and no evidence of remorse for what she had done.

Legal and medical insanity, however, were not synonymous. Although an insanity defense rarely succeeded for psychopaths, her lawyers entered a plea of diminished capacity anyway in an attempt to avoid or reduce prison time.

I was relieved when the news anchor reported that two independent psychiatrists had declared Tina competent to stand trial. In the short video clip that followed, the District Attorney promised a death penalty verdict, no doubt building a law-and-order platform that he hoped would elevate him to higher office.

Politics, money, and justice — a highly volatile combination that unsettled my stomach.

I clicked off the TV and stared at the black

screen, suddenly exhausted. Knowing that I would need all my wits tomorrow for my deposition, I collapsed onto my mattress in RJ's room and let a restless oblivion swallow me.

CHAPTER FORTY-THREE

Saturday, September 2, 6:00 a.m.
RJ woke me at daybreak. I wanted to visit Justine before my afternoon deposition, but when I called the hospital, they said her condition had deteriorated overnight. She was now listed as *critical.* I asked an ICU nurse if RJ and I could stop in sometime today.

No, maybe tomorrow.
Could we speak with her on the phone?
Not at the moment. Things . . . aren't going well. The doctors are working on her.

The news sent RJ into a tantrum and he refused to eat breakfast. Rather than argue and cajole, I retrieved a box of his favorite cereal that I'd stashed on an upper shelf in the cupboard, the sugary one devoid of nutritional value that Justine had expressly forbidden — and the one I kept for mornings like this.

The cereal worked better than a mood-enhancing drug, and RJ and I played with Lincoln Logs on the living room carpet after breakfast. His disposition cratered again a few hours later, and I was grateful when Colleen finally arrived to relieve me.

As I climbed the stairs to change clothes, I regretted not borrowing money from Emily to hire a lawyer for the deposition. I couldn't afford one and the diocese wouldn't pay unless the Church itself was in legal jeopardy. And if Tree paid for my attorney, he would appear to be tampering with a witness, and it would be the same as tattooing *police snitch* and *willing accomplice* on my forehead.

Tina's best chance of avoiding prison depended on proving that the police had broken the law and entrapped her — and I was the get-out-of-jail-free card that her attorneys intended to play in court. Had I known Tree's plan, I never would have agreed to participate. God, how I wished that he hadn't turned off the tape recorder during her interview and introduced those illegally obtained checks.

But it was all a moot point now. I was in the crosshairs and no matter what any lawyer might have advised, I had no intention of lying under oath. At some point in the trial, I would have to confront the hard questions.

Looking like a priest, however, was a prudent plan when headed to an Inquisition, so I dressed for the part before leaving the rectory.

Given Tina's shabby apartment and the fact that the judge had frozen her insurance money in escrow, I expected her to be represented by a young, acne-ravaged public defender fresh out of law school. I couldn't have been more wrong.

The law offices of Kirkwood and Steen were a study in opulence. An elegant Persian carpet adorned a polished marble floor, and oil paintings of portly attorneys wearing pinstriped suits and arrogant expressions lined the walls. And unlike the police station, their conference room had no one-way mirror. Instead, large picture windows overlooked the lush green lawn and red brick walkways of the town square.

Although I didn't know Sterling Kirkwood Esquire by name, when he entered the room I recognized him, and his involvement in Tina's case suddenly made perfect sense. I had seen him several times on late-night television commercials in which he wore his signature blood-red cravat. He would touch the crimson cloth and smile with no hint of humor, step toward the camera, and growl,

"Call me, I'll make them bleed!" I had always thought he should have added, "I'm not *just* a sleazy scumbag . . . I'm *your* sleazy scumbag."

Vengeance and half of your financial settlement are mine, saith the shyster.

Kirkwood was the definition of an ambulance chaser. His manicured beard, chipmunk cheeks, and slicked-back silver hair were plastered across the side of numerous busses, and his office telephone number painted on every bench. He must have taken Tina's case pro bono because of the publicity. Nothing grabbed the public's attention more than a baby killer. No doubt, he planned to milk the media for free advertising for the foreseeable future. He was the perfect attorney for a client as vile as Tina.

He eased his great bulk into a leather chair on the other side of a polished mahogany conference table. Instead of the crimson cravat that he featured in his commercials, he wore a red necktie, but the message was the same.

A digital voice recorder and video camera were set up to capture my every response. Two well-groomed junior associates flanked him, both displaying poker faces. Kirkwood, however, offered his patented plastic smile and began by lobbing a few preliminary softball questions as if we were colleagues having cocktails at an exclusive men's club.

When the game became hardball, his smile morphed into the attack-dog snarl that I'd seen on TV, as he tried to tear the flesh from my bones and the truth from my lips. The two pitbull puppies seated on either side of him said nothing as they scribbled furiously on their legal pads.

"You've sworn an oath to tell the truth here today, Father Austin, so please recount exactly what happened at the interview of my client on the afternoon of Friday, August 4th, and don't skip even the most minute detail."

I was relieved. An open-ended question gave me room to maneuver. I delivered a lengthy, sanitized version of the interview.

As I studied Kirkwood from across the table, his tiny darting ebony eyes, beard, and his skittery mannerisms reminded me of something my old man had said. He hadn't stayed in my life very long, but when he was arrested for a drunk-and-disorderly, he kept referring to his public defender as a furry-faced rat-bastard. It appeared that the hairy rodents were breeding.

"That's all very interesting, Father, but are you aware that police department policy prohibits civilians from attending confidential police interviews?"

"No, I was not aware."

"So, why were you there? Did Chief Macon invite you because you're a close friend, and he needed your help with the biggest case of his career?"

"That's not what happened. He permitted me to attend as a courtesy. Tina's husband asked me to come, for moral support." Which was true, although only half of the reason I had attended.

Lead us not into jail, but deliver us from lawyers. Amen.

"Did you meet with Chief Macon before the interview to discuss a strategy?"

"No, we didn't meet." True again, although we had spoken on the phone.

I folded my hands in front of me so that Kirkwood wouldn't see them tremble, and danced around his questions for twenty minutes like Muhammad Ali. I was, however, clearly outmatched and scared to death. He'd had me on the ropes several times, yet I'd managed to float like a butterfly away from the knockout punch.

"All I want is the truth, Father Austin, the facts about what actually occurred during the interrogation of my client. I hold no ill will toward you or Chief Macon, and simply require your candor and honesty."

375

I wondered if *lawyer* and *liar* were derived from the same Latin root word.

"As I'm sure you're aware, Father, in addition to sins of commission, there are sins of *omission*. Are you holding back anything that happened during Tina's interview to protect your buddy?"

"I've already told you everything I can, Counselor."

"But not all you know. Don't play word games with me, Father. Perjury and obstruction of justice are serious crimes, punishable by imprisonment."

The tone of Kirkwood's voice indicated that his patience had run out. He stood, took off his elegant silk suit coat, and carefully hung it on the back of a chair. The label read: Savile Row, London.

Then he took off the gloves. "Enough! That dog and pony show you and Chief Macon put on would fill any courtroom to the ceiling with manure!" He paced the room, touched his blood-red necktie, and sneered. "Priest or not, lie to me again and you *will* ble —" He stopped before completing his usual punch-line, glanced at the video camera, reconsidered his word choice, and said, "You will be . . . in need of a confessional."

Kirkwood looked down at his legal pad as

if he had forgotten the question he'd already asked me three different ways. "So, you admit that you and Chief Macon have been close personal friends for most of your lives, correct?"

"We went to high school together and played on the same football team, but I hadn't seen him in years. When I came back to Oberlin two months ago, we renewed our friendship. I haven't been in town long enough to describe our relationship as *close* and *personal.*"

"Answer yes or no."

"It's not that simple."

"Yes or no!"

Come on, Kirkwood, I thought, *if you're going to crucify me, at least hang your two crooks-in-training on either side of me — the way they crucified thieves next to Our Lord.*

"Yes, we are friends."

"And as a good and loyal friend, would you lie to protect Chief Macon?"

"Lying is a sin, Mr. Kirkwood." I straightened my clerical collar and leaned toward the video camera. "And as I've already told you . . . I don't lie."

"Oh, I too am versed in the Bible, in addition to jurisprudence. Remember, Father, 'Nothing is hidden that will not be made known, no secret that will not come to light.' Gospel of Luke, I believe. Only three of the Ten Commandments are punishable in a court of law — murder, theft, and the one that you're about to commit . . . perjury. Thou shalt not bear *false witness*. You're familiar with that one, aren't you Father?"

"I've done nothing of the sort here today, Counselor. Everything I've said about Tina and Miguel is the God's honest truth."

"But not concerning your good buddy, the police chief. Falsus in uno, falsus in omnibus. How is your Latin, Father?" When I didn't answer, he continued. "It's a legal dictum meaning, *False in one thing, false in all.*"

Kirkwood lowered his chin and glared down at me over the top of his eyeglasses.

"I know exactly what happened in that interrogation room. Chief Macon turned off his tape recorder illegally during my client's first interview, and you're covering for him. A young woman's life hangs in the balance, so I'll ask you one last time, Father. The truth, please. Did Tremont Macon switch off his recording device during the interrogation of my client on Friday, August 4th of this year?"

"And I'll tell you again for the last time, Officer Macon asked me to walk to the easel behind your client and flip several pages of chart paper. How could I possibly see what happened at the table? I don't have eyes in the back of my head. You'll have to ask Chief Macon."

"Oh, I'll ask him . . . under oath, on the witness stand." One of his junior associates handed Kirkwood a note. He read it and asked, "Did Officer Macon produce a check for $300 written to a divorce lawyer in town, signed by my client, and two checks to insurance companies signed by her husband?"

And there it was, the question that I had feared most, the one that could destroy Tree's career, set Tina free to kill more babies, and send me to prison.

I slipped on the mask of a righteous man who had been badgered for over an hour and peered directly at the video camera, feigning a confidence that I did not feel.

"I saw no checks."

I *don't* lie — but I am *a stickler* for the details. I had seen *photocopies,* not checks. It was a very fine line, like the blade of a scalpel — and the finer the line, the sharper the knife-edge, and the deeper and more dangerous the cut.

I continued to stare at the camera, the very embodiment of virtue and conviction, praying that Kirkwood had had enough for one day or would move on to a new line of questioning.

He loosened his tie and listened as one of his junior partners whispered in his ear.

"Fine, Father Austin. Have it your way. I know the video camera in the interview room was out of order, but I'll find other witnesses from the police station. Someone watching through that one-way mirror will corroborate my client's story. And then your lie will be revealed, and you'll need your own attorney."

He was about to be very disappointed. Either Kirkwood hadn't yet interviewed the police station personnel, or he hadn't figured out that Tree had intentionally kept the room unoccupied and his staff out of the loop.

Kirkwood gazed at his notes and plunked back down onto his leather chair. It groaned loudly.

"I'll see you in court, and we'll see who breaks first, Father. We're done here!" He nodded to an associate who shut down all of the recording devices, then he slammed his fist down hard enough to splash cappuccino from his china cup. "And believe me, Padre, if you lie to me on the stand, you'll need a blood transfusion when I'm done with you!"

I walked out of the richly appointed office on wobbly legs, took the wood-paneled elevator down to the first floor, and stepped into glorious sunshine like a man released from solitary confinement. I waited until I'd arrived at the rectory before calling Tree on a landline.

"How'd it go, Jake?"

He made it sound like a casual question. It wasn't.

"Well Tree, now I understand what my old man meant when he told me as a boy to never wrestle with a pig — you get filthy and the pig enjoys himself."

"That good, huh?"

"Kirkwood threatened me with perjury!"

"Did you lie to him?"

"No, I didn't flat-out lie. I answered the specific questions that he asked me, but I definitely misled him. If he had inquired about the insurance checks differently, you might be in handcuffs right now. And if he asks me again in court, you and I might end up sharing a prison cell."

"In some states, what you did is enough to be found guilty of a felony. The good news is that Ohio requires a *false* statement to be convicted of perjury. So don't lie to Kirkwood, on or off the witness stand. Ever."

I delivered a detailed summary of the deposition, adding, "Kirkwood's relentless and scares the hell out of me."

"Relax, Jake." Tree chuckled. "Tina made a really bad choice of lawyers. Kirkwood is all show and no go. He barely made it through a really crappy law school, and his plush office is leased. The guy's an empty suit and a complete doofus. He couldn't find his own butt with both hands and a map. He took Tina's case purely for the publicity."

"Damn it! You should have told me that, Tree. I've been shaking in my boots for two days."

"I didn't want you to get cocky and let down your guard. Even a brain-damaged squirrel like Kirkwood sometimes gets lucky and finds a nut."

"Dumb or not, I can't dodge his questions forever, and you know I won't lie under oath."

"You'll be fine. Just wear your collar and try to look saintly in court." Tree paused. "I knew the risks when I ran the game. This whole thing's on me. I never expected you to commit perjury, and I sure as hell don't want you to go to jail. Do what you have to do, buddy. I'll be okay."

I heard muffled voices in the background.

Someone called Tree's name.

"Sorry, gotta run. Talk to you soon," he said and hung up.

I thanked Colleen for her help and sent her home, then called the ICU at the Cleveland Clinic. They again refused to allow RJ and me to visit or speak with Justine by phone, citing *continued difficulties* and *ongoing intervention.*

I distracted my nephew for as long as I could that afternoon at the school playground, took him out for pizza, and then to a Disney movie at the Apollo theater.

After he finally fell asleep, I wandered downstairs, read a Dennis Lehane novel for a while, then put on the ten o'clock news. A young reporter appeared on the screen, standing in front of the hospital. Although she wore a solemn and professional expression, she was nearly vibrating with excitement as she reported that Pablo had passed away despite the heroics of Dr. Taylor and the pediatric ICU staff.

The TV image shifted to a photograph of Miguel, who had immediately offered Pablo's organs for transplantation. Tina soon acquiesced, probably on the advice of her lawyer, in hopes of garnering sympathy from prospective jurors.

A short video clip then showed the District

Attorney entering the courthouse to file first degree murder charges against the baby's mother. He stopped, faced the cameras, and again promised a death penalty verdict.

That ended any hope I had of falling asleep, so I clicked off the television and opened the novel. As the clock ticked toward midnight, I considered taking my last sleeping pill, but with a child in my care, I opted to continue reading instead.

CHAPTER FORTY-FOUR

Sunday, September 3, 6:00 a.m.

A hand grabbed my arm and tugged, then tugged again. I sat bolt upright in my living room recliner, the Lehane novel tumbling to the floor. The first crimson slash of dawn leaked through the picture window. I stared into RJ's silver-blue eyes. He scrunched up his face.

"Come on, Uncle Jake, get up! I'm hungry."

I shook cobwebs from my head, wiped drool from my cheek, and coaxed my stiff body into the kitchen. RJ made a play for the sugary cereal that he so loved; I countered with pancakes and honey.

He wolfed down his breakfast and half of mine, then we played a game of Candy Land. RJ promised to behave at church if we visited his mother after Mass. I let him take his Lego blocks into the quiet room, and remarkably, he kept his promise.

After the service, I phoned the hospital but was told that Justine was with her doctors. The ICU nurse suggested that I try again in the afternoon.

When we finished lunch, RJ and I walked to a nearby park. Against my better judgment, I allowed him to climb on the jungle gym. I scurried after him, head angled up and arms outstretched like an outfielder who'd lost the ball in the sun, hoping not to have to make a diving catch if my nephew lost his grip. Fortunately, the boy was part chimpanzee. When he tired of that, he tried out every slide in the park, and then I pushed him on the swings until my arms ached.

Between pushes, I called the hospital again and asked to visit Justine. The answer was *not today, but she appears to be doing better, so call in the morning.* RJ and I were disappointed but grabbed onto the word "better" like a lifeline.

As we were entering the front door of the rectory, a police cruiser rolled up the driveway. Tree Macon hopped out wearing jeans and a polo shirt. He read my surprise and said, "Sorry to pop in, but I thought you'd want to hear it from me. Want the bad or the good news first?"

"Don't play with me, Tree. My sister's in

the hospital, and I just spent all day with a four year old. I'm stressed and crankier than he is. What's up?"

He leaned in and whispered so RJ wouldn't hear, "You know that Pablo died, right?"

"Yes, I saw it last night on TV." I sighed. As optimistic as I was about life in general, both Tree's job and mine were often stark reminders of the darkness of the human heart. "Poor Pablo. It's so sad I can almost hear God weeping."

"No, Jake, that's me — crying about the bad news. Our friend Tina won't be getting the death penalty. Her sleazebag lawyer plea-bargained her sentence down to life without parole this morning. Whatever you said in Kirkwood's office yesterday must have shaken him, but when Tina heard that both Miguel and her boyfriend, *Teddy Bear,* couldn't wait to testify against her, she folded her cards and pleaded guilty. Sterling Kirkwood and the prosecutor finished the paperwork and signed off on the agreement an hour ago. The good news is that she'll never hurt another child."

"No, the *good news* is that I won't have to risk perjury trying to cover your devious behind, officer."

"Yeah, that too." Tree laughed. "I think a

celebration is in order. Indians game and Guinness tomorrow night?"

"Sure, at my place. We'll tip a few after RJ's asleep."

"All righty then. I'll bring the beer as a thank-you gift."

"That's not necessary, Tree. I *enjoyed* jerking around Tina's pompous attorney. Watching his frustration gave me a warm, fuzzy feeling inside."

"Oh, the beer's not for that. It's for being your usual irritating, buttinsky self."

"Huh?"

"Don't give me that innocent look. You nag me more than my wife does." RJ was playing on the foyer floor behind me, and one of his matchbox cars careened off my shoe. Tree lowered his voice again. "On the pain-in-the-ass scale, you are at least a 9½, Jake. You're like a dog with a bone who refuses to let go."

"What the heck are you babbling about?"

"I got the biopsy results yesterday." Tree lowered the collar of his shirt, revealing a small surgical dressing. "That growth on my neck that you've been riding me about? It was skin cancer. The doc says you found it early, and she got it all." He slapped my shoulder with a big paw. "I owe you, buddy. Beer's gonna be on me for a long time. See you tomorrow around game time."

"That's great news, Tree, but forget the beer. What I really need is a babysitter. Why don't you come in and amuse RJ for a while? Now *that would be* a thank-you gift. The boy is wearing me out."

"Tempting as that sounds, hell no! I raised three kids and I'm off duty till I get grand-children." He opened the cruiser door, reached in, and handed me The Cleveland Plain Dealer. "I almost forgot. Check out page three of the first section," he added and drove off.

I hefted the Sunday newspaper onto the dining room table, opened section A to the third page, and gazed in wonder. Pablo's organs had been transplanted to eight different sick children overnight.

What was shocking, however, was that the article revealed that the baby dying of heart disease who'd been featured on TV had received Pablo's heart. Hospitals and transplant teams insist on complete anonymity, refusing to reveal the names of organ donors and recipients. I didn't know who the "unnamed source" was, but reading the story helped ease the loss of Pablo a little for me.

The media feeding frenzy immediately began in earnest. "Baby Saves Baby" and "Killer Mom Gives Life" stories immediately dominated the headlines and evening news. The heart transplant had gone well, Miguel was heralded as a selfless hero, and everyone was happy — everyone except Miguel. He was last seen loading his battered station wagon with his meager possessions and heading west out of town. Only Tree Macon knew his destination.

CHAPTER FORTY-FIVE

Monday, September 4, 7:00 a.m.

The next morning, I was still feeling giddy because I didn't have to testify in court and would never have to see Sterling Kirkwood's nasty sneer again, except on his late-night, ambulance-chasing commercials.

After Mass, I called the hospital. Justine's condition remained critical and we were not permitted to visit her. I asked if we could speak with her on the telephone. The answer was *sorry, no.* I played the *I'm a doctor card,* hoping for professional courtesy, but I was rebuffed and told to try later today.

Frustrated, RJ and I passed the time by practicing his letters with a set of wooden alphabet blocks as we built skyscrapers in the living room. His matchbox cars would inevitably appear, however, and crash into each tower just before completion. Boys!

When RJ tired of demolishing block buildings, we switched to a game of Chutes and

Ladders. It didn't matter what number my nephew spun, he always moved his playing piece to a ladder and climbed ahead of mine. The boy cheated like the devil, but fortunately I was empowered to absolve him.

As RJ did his little happy dance after winning for the second time, I thought of Tina and wondered how anyone could hurt a child.

We were putting the game away when an ICU nurse called.

"Dr. Austin, your sister has taken a turn for the worse, and her condition's grave. I'm sorry. Her physician asked me to phone you. Please come to the hospital as soon as possible."

"Can I bring her four year old son?"

"No. That wouldn't be wise."

I whisked RJ to Colleen's house, explained the situation, and drove like a maniac under an ashen sky to the Cleveland Clinic. Patches of dense fog and an ominous gloom swirled around me the entire way, headlights coming at me like the white-hot eyes of demons. By the time I parked the car, crossed Euclid Avenue against the light, and scrambled up to the ICU, I was too late. Justine was gone.

When I broke the terrible news to RJ that

night, I got a glimpse of a very real fiery Hell.

That autumn, all hope tumbled to the ground with the frost-encrusted leaves. I'd had a family for the first time in my adult life and had begun to build my future around my sister and nephew. Justine's death crushed me, and my inability to comfort RJ left me drowning in a sea of helplessness. Although my friends rallied around me for support, I felt entirely alone.

Tree Macon loaned me money for Justine's casket and funeral expenses, knowing full well that it would be nearly impossible for me to repay him. Holy Trinity Cemetery, where my mother was buried, offered a section for the free internment of the poor, but I didn't want my sister laid to rest in the least desirable area. Before I was born, my parents had purchased two plots in the shade of a large oak tree. After my father deserted us, my mother assigned the second gravesite to me, which I allocated for Justine's burial. I wanted the two women I loved to spend eternity together.

I arranged for my sister's funeral but was certain that I'd break down during her service. Bishop Lucci volunteered to offer her memorial Mass in my place. I was honored and grateful.

My closest friend in the Camillian Order, Father Tom Winkel, arrived from Wisconsin for support. Justine's elderly aunt flew in from Florida, and she befriended Emily, serving as her eyes during that long, difficult day. Much to my surprise and Bishop Lucci's chagrin, Father Marek also joined us at the church. After what had transpired at St. Wenceslaus, however, Marek maintained a safe distance from His Excellency so as not to further endanger the survival of his parish. Lucci kept glancing warily at the Virgin Mary statue, no doubt fearing that a *miracle* would occur in his presence.

As we drove to the cemetery after Mass, black clouds gathered and the heavens shed icy tears. The only sounds in the car were the tires spitting slush and RJ's pitiful sobs. The ride was agonizing, and the infinite supply of orange construction barrels and detour signs made it feel endless.

RJ and I took our place beneath a green canvas tarp at the cemetery, both of us shivering in a bitter-cold autumn breeze that whispered plaintively through the trees like the voices of the dead. Colleen wrapped her shawl around my nephew. He didn't object, or even react.

Bone-weary, my grief raw and deep, I

gazed at Tree Macon. He returned to my side where he'd been most of the day and squeezed my shoulder, unable to speak.

The burial site felt other-worldly and the blackness of the grave looked like a bottomless wound in the earth. I seemed to hover above the gathering, lost and alone, gazing at the gaping hole in the ground. The grip of RJ's hand brought me back to reality. Emily took my arm and leaned against me as Bishop Lucci read prayers that I knew by heart. That day, however, all the words of hope and salvation that I'd been taught rang hollow. I searched the pewter skies for answers, for meaning, but the only ray of hope I found was when I looked down and saw the future in RJ's face.

After we had recited the final prayer, everyone stepped forward and placed a rose on Justine's casket. RJ balked, rooted to the wet sod. I held back with him until all the others were finished, then we walked up together and laid our flowers down. His lower lip trembled as he gazed up at me and we stood there, the third member of our trinity lying in a mahogany box inches, and yet an eternity, away. I scooped him into my arms, kissed his red curls — and the warmth of his embrace on that cold, cold day somehow began to restore my faith in God and His greater plan. With the service concluded, I took him home and began rebuilding our world.

CHAPTER FORTY-SIX

Monday, September 25, 7:00 a.m.
Winter came early and hard for RJ and me. In the dreary days that followed, the trees near the rectory dropped their colorful foliage, withering to charcoal sketches, and the world faded to gray as I muddled through an unfamiliar landscape.

Bishop Lucci placed me on a leave of absence until the "problem with my nephew," as he called it, could be resolved. Sacred Heart Church was still financially in the red and couldn't afford to subsidize me. My credit cards were maxed out and my savings account as empty as a church on Friday night. I had an extra mouth to feed who outgrew his clothes faster than I could buy them, but I could no longer borrow from St. Peter to pay St. Paul. I'd recently read about two financially troubled priests who had dipped into parish funds, one through an elaborate Ponzi scheme, and the other via a fraudulent renovation project. I rejected that dark and slippery path.

Since my ordination, all of my medical income had gone to the Church. I pleaded with my Camillian Order for additional funds, explaining the dire circumstances, but my request became tangled in red tape. Bishop Lucci lobbied hard on my behalf until my Superior General agreed to redirect part of my hospital salary to me during my family crisis.

My nephew and I vacated the rectory and moved into a small, furnished two-bedroom apartment near St. Joseph's Hospital. I didn't want to immediately resume my long hours, so I asked the administrator to postpone my night call and allow me to work in the mornings, freeing my afternoons and evenings for RJ. He agreed, and I enrolled my nephew in morning preschool. RJ and I missed Colleen's presence and support, but at least I was able to cover living expenses and begin repaying some of Tree's loan and my crippled credit cards.

Child Protective Services soon inquired about my nephew. When I told them that I was his uncle and recounted my sister's story, they contacted RJ's biological father, a womanizer in an already rocky marriage who wanted nothing to do with the boy. He gladly signed away his parental rights. Justine's frail, seventy year old aunt, the only other family member, supported my efforts to raise my nephew and keep him out of foster care. With the legal paperwork Justine had signed nominating me as RJ's guardian, and Tree Macon and Bishop Lucci as my references, CPS granted me custody in record time.

Returning to work at the hospital helped financially but as my hours increased, it complicated child care. Justine's death had upended RJ's world and I didn't want to add to his turmoil by placing him in after-school daycare or hiring a stranger. When I heard that Bishop Lucci hadn't found my replacement at Sacred Heart Church and had severely restricted Colleen's hours at the rectory to save money, I phoned and pleaded for her assistance.

"Please, Colleen. RJ and I miss you. Will you help us?"

"Certainly, Father. That would be fierce grand, it would! How could I not love the little goster? Sure, haven't I pined for RJ terribly since you moved?" She paused, and the decade-long queen of the rectory resumed her rightful position of dominance. "Mind you, Father, I'll be needing a raise."

"Of course. We'll work it out. We're a team again."

Colleen was the God-sent answer to my prayers. I hung up the phone and smiled. If I'd had the power, I would have canonized her as the patron saint of blended families.

It didn't take long for Colleen to whip our household into shape, and for RJ to become the child she'd never had. Her tart Irish tongue kept both "her lads" on the straight and narrow, and her love and attention soon transformed our tiny apartment into a home.

My job description changed from physician/priest to part-time doctor and acting "Father" to a flock of one. I still didn't have a clue how to raise a tiny tornado in red tennis shoes. The trial and error method proved painful at times for both of us, and I quickly acquired a profound respect for single, working parents.

When I hired Colleen and didn't place RJ up for adoption, Bishop Lucci called me to his office and expressed his displeasure in no uncertain terms. He had envisioned a childless Catholic couple raising my nephew. But RJ was all the family I had, and my vision of the future involved a childless priest caring for him as I had promised my sister.

This was one promise that I intended to keep.

I'd done my homework in preparation for Lucci's objections. In my defense, I reminded the bishop that RJ was my blood-relative and that there was logic and precedence in favor of my argument.

"Your Excellency, there is no Canon Law in the Church that forbids a priest from adopting children."

"And there is none that permits it."

I thought, *and there is no Canon Law that permits priests to drive a car, read murder mysteries, or write a blog either — but there is no reason that they shouldn't.* I decided, however, not to antagonize him and let him continue.

"The Church has always favored adoption by two parent families. It's best for the child. As you know, serving the faithful is very demanding and labor-intensive, leaving no time for parenting."

"But Excellency, several priests have been granted permission to adopt by the Church and have been exemplary parents. Father George Clements in Chicago adopted four African-American orphans in the 1980's. He also established the 'One Church, One Child' program funded by the Clinton administration to encourage people of all faiths to adopt at-risk children from the welfare system, particularly children of color and older kids who otherwise would never have found homes."

Lucci volleyed with, "First of all, your nephew is young and white, and there are plenty of Catholic families who'd be willing to adopt him. Second, Pope John Paul II himself approved Father Clement's adoptions, and *you* have no such permission."

"Your Excellency, even Pope Pius IX adopted a child. Wasn't he leading us by his example?"

"That was over a hundred and fifty years ago. Times were different then. And you, Father, are certainly not a Pope, and definitely not infallible."

We were at a stalemate. I didn't want to leave the priesthood, and he was already short-handed and didn't want to lose another worker bee from his diocese.

A long silence ensued. "All right, Father. I will discuss your request with the Cardinal and take the matter under advisement. For the time being, I will look the other way, but be aware that the clock is ticking. I strongly recommend that you rethink your plan during your leave of absence."

When you are outgunned and overmatched, sometimes a stalemate is almost as good as a win. Being RJ's guardian would have to do for now. I thanked Lucci and left his office before he could change his mind.

Slowly, my new life settled into a comfortable routine. Emily visited often. When I couldn't chauffeur her, she walked or came by cab. She memorized the layout of my apartment and the corresponding step counts, and babysat when Colleen was unavailable.

During my leave of absence, I was not allowed to celebrate Mass publically. So after RJ was asleep, I offered it privately every day in my apartment for my own spiritual well-being. I missed the communal fellowship of a church service, however, so every Sunday, Emily, RJ, and I attended Mass at various nearby parishes. When available, we sat in a soundproof quiet room, or what Emily referred to as RJ's "fidget room." I always dressed in street clothes on Sundays because a priest regularly seen in the company of a woman and child was bound to draw unwanted and erroneous conclusions.

When we attended Mass at St. Wenceslaus, Father Marek noticed and invited us to lunch at a local restaurant. I was relieved to see that his eye and hand tremors were gone, and that he was sober, motivated, and still on the wagon.

The weeks that followed Justine's death were a healing time for me. I cherished every hour with RJ. Whether building Lincoln Log and Lego villages or running wild at the park, it was always a learning experience for me and a refresher course in the limitless delights of a childhood imagination. More importantly, I learned a great deal about love and contentment from my little professor.

The highlight of my day came just before bedtime when he would select a book and crawl into my lap. RJ often picked *Where the Sidewalk Ends.* He loved the metered rhythm and silly rhymes. I would start a poem, and he'd finish it from memory. I decided to begin teaching him to read on my next day off.

"All right big guy, that's enough for tonight. Time for bed."

"Ah, please Uncle Jake. One more? Can we do Emily's book? Pleeease!"

I watched his freckled face fill with anticipation, pictured my sister, and caved.

"Okay," I said, puzzled by his request. "Only for a short while."

He jumped down, ran to the bookcase, and selected a children's story I had never seen before. RJ plopped back onto my lap and opened a book of braille. Fortunately, this one also had printed words and pictures.

I started to read it, but RJ said, "No, Uncle Jake. You're doing it wrong!" Then he began to teach me how to "finger read."

As always, Emily was one step ahead of me. I turned to share the joke with Justine and realized for the thousandth time that she was gone.

I let RJ manipulate me for another ten minutes, then kissed him goodnight and tucked him into bed.

The next day, I had to work late due to a colleague's illness. I hurried home from the hospital to find that Emily had relieved Colleen and was preparing dinner.

Who would have thought? Smart, beautiful, witty, and here she was, caring for my makeshift family. I'd definitely been an idiot in my youth to let her go.

Emily set a steaming platter of beef stroganoff on the table, but RJ complained that the noodles were too squishy, pitched a tantrum, and refused to eat. When her attempts at reason failed, I lost my temper and sent him to a timeout in the corner. His face scrunched up like a carved pumpkin two weeks after Halloween as he whimpered pitifully, his tiny body shaking.

I hated tough love.

"You know what, Jake?" Emily asked. "It's beginning to feel like a family around here." She leaned back and laughed. "You even sound like a *real father* now."

After supper, RJ and I drove Emily home, then we began our usual bedtime routine. I dressed him in his Sesame Street pajamas, tucked him under the covers, and started to read him a bedtime story. Halfway through, however, it became obvious that he was too restless and cranky to sleep. I remembered Justine's trick, fetched her embroidered handkerchief, added a touch of her perfume, and showed it to RJ.

Unsure how he would react, I drew a deep breath and said, "Your mommy wanted you to have this. She's waiting with Nana to see you in your dreams."

RJ snatched the hankie from me, rolled away, and rubbed it against his cheek, no doubt lost in her scent and her memory. I stood quietly in the doorway until he drifted off to sleep with a look of serenity that lifted my spirits.

Back downstairs, I opened a living room window to let in the crisp night air and switched on the CD player. Melissa Manchester's "Don't Cry Out Loud" floated into the living room. It had been one of my sister's favorites. But the lyrics were another reminder that I'd once had it all with both Justine and Emily, then had lost everything, so I took Manchester's advice and hid my feelings deep inside.

I punched the button for the next song, slipped into my recliner, and closed my eyes, pondering the strange relationship between miracles and science, fact and faith, and the mystifying way the disastrous events of the past two months had produced completely unexpected miracles. God and His mysterious ways!

My philandering old man had destroyed my childhood, yet he'd inadvertently provided me with a sister and nephew when he fathered Justine in Louisiana. My sister's illness and rare blood type had driven her to track me down, resurrecting a family that I'd never known existed. Science had failed her, crushing me, but her loss had placed RJ at the very center of my universe, a miracle greater than I'd ever prayed for.

Science and the pursuit of truth had exposed the bleeding statue fraud, dashing Emily's hopes for a miraculous cure for her blindness, but our time together had rekindled our friendship. And with Emily's deft guidance, managing the deception had not only allowed many believers to preserve their rejuvenated faith, but also had set

Father Marek on the road to recovery from his alcoholism.

Tina's betrayal of her baby and husband had been an act of sheer wickedness, yet eight dying children had received Pablo's transplanted organs and a second chance at life, which undoubtedly was both a marvel of scientific achievement and a genuine miracle for the families whose children survived.

This bizarre, inexplicable production of good from evil, however, convinced me that we mortals are blind. We think we have found the forest when we've only seen the first row of trees. With all of the chaos in the world today, I've come to believe at my very core that the Almighty has always had a much greater plan than any of us could even imagine — and that, I guess, is the definition of faith.

Content for the first time in weeks, I listened to the CD and was humming along with "Midnight Blue" as the mantle clock struck twelve. When I opened my eyes again at two a.m., the music had been replaced by a chorus of crickets. I lingered a while longer, listening to God's song.

ABOUT THE AUTHOR

Born and raised in the Cleveland, Ohio, area, **John Vanek** received his bachelor's degree from Case Western Reserve University, where his passion for creative writing took root. He received his medical degree from the University of Rochester, did his internship at University Hospitals of Cleveland, and completed his residency at the Cleveland Clinic.

He is a physician by training, but a writer by passion. During the quarter century he practiced medicine, his interest in writing never waned. Medicine was his wife, but writing became his mistress and mysteries his drug of choice. He began honing his craft by attending creative writing workshops and college courses. At first pursuing his passion solely for himself and his family, he was surprised and gratified when his work won contests and was published in a variety of literary journals, anthologies, and magazines.

John lives happily as an ink-stained-wretch in Florida, where he teaches a poetry workshop for seniors and enjoys swimming, hiking, sunshine, good friends, and red wine.

For more information, go to www.John VanekAuthor.com.

The employees of Thorndike Press hope you have enjoyed this Large Print book. All our Thorndike, Wheeler, and Kennebec Large Print titles are designed for easy reading, and all our books are made to last. Other Thorndike Press Large Print books are available at your library, through selected bookstores, or directly from us.

For information about titles, please call:
  (800) 223-1244

or visit our website at:
  gale.com/thorndike

To share your comments, please write:
  Publisher
  Thorndike Press
  10 Water St., Suite 310
  Waterville, ME 04901